T0209265

A Choice of Secrets

Barb Hendee is the author of:

The Dark Glass novels:
Through a Dark Glass
A Choice of Crowns
A Girl of White Winter
A Choice of Secrets

A Choice of Secrets

Barb Hendee

REBEL BASE BOOKS
Kensington Publishing Corp.
www.kensingtonbooks.com

The Mirror

Long ago, a vain lord enslaved a young witch so that he might force her to use her powers to keep him handsome and young. His most valued possession was an ornate three-paneled mirror in which he could see himself from several angles. Looking into its panels, he loved to admire his own beauty.

Seeking revenge on him, the young witch began secretly imbuing the mirror with power, planning to trap him in the reflection of the three panels where he might view different outcomes of his useless life over and over, and he'd suffer to see himself growing old and unwanted. But unknown to her, as she continued to cast power into the mirror, it came to gain a will and awareness of its own.

One night, the lord caught her as she worked her magic, and he realized she was attempting to enchant his beloved mirror. In a rage, he drew a dagger and killed her. But her spirit fled into the mirror. Though she had been seeking escape, she was once again enslaved...this time by the mirror itself. It whispered to her that it would protect her and use the power she'd given it for tasks more important than punishing a vain lord. Together, they would seek out those facing difficult decisions and show them outcomes to their choices.

"Wait!" she cried, inside the mirror. "What does that mean?"

The mirror vanished from the lord's room, taking her with it.

And no one knew where it might appear again.

Chapter 1

At the age of seventeen, I had no real understanding of the danger of secrets...of keeping them, of sharing them, of telling the wrong person for the right reasons.

But I was soon to learn the depths of my own ignorance.

One afternoon, in mid-summer, I was in the vast kitchen of my family home, with six other women, rolling dough for both peach and strawberry tarts. One of our housemaids, Jenny, stuck her head in the back door.

"Lady Nicole," she said to me. "Lord Erik and Lord Christophe have arrived. They're in the hunting hall."

This news made me smile. "Does Lady Chloe know? Or my mother and father?"

"Not yet. I'll go and find them."

"Thank you."

Not bothering to even take off my apron or shake the flour from my hair, I hurried out the door and into the open-air center of what was known as White Deer Lodge. All around me, ten large log buildings had been constructed in a circle. Small paths connected each building to the next. Two of the constructions functioned as our family's residence. Others housed guests or servants or our guards. One was designated for storage. The largest construction was called the gathering hall for communal events. On the outside of this circle, a village thrived, with dwellings, shops, stables, and a smithy.

A stone wall surrounded the village, and heavy forests surrounded three sides of the wall, but not far beyond the west side, the ocean stretched down the coast of the nation of Samourè. This lodge was my home and my father, Gideon Montagna, was lord of these lands.

In that moment, though, I gave little thought to my home or my father, and instead, I continued in my quick pace to the smallest of the log buildings—known as the hunting hall. I'd never cared much for this hall, as it was decorated with spears, longbows, and the heads of animals. But nonetheless, once inside the front door, I looked toward the unlit great hearth with a flood of happiness rising inside me.

My elder brother, Erik, and Lord Christophe de Fiore stood in conversation. Both men wore chain armor and swords. Several servants bustled about, pouring mugs of ale.

As I came through the door, Erik's face broke into a smile and he called out, "Nicole!"

I ran to him. Well over a head taller, he swept me up in both arms, lifting my feet off the ground. Our father was a tall man with solid bones, straight red-blond hair, pale skin, and blue eyes. Our mother was tiny, like a bird, with light brown eyes and a mass of wavy brown hair. Erik looked like my father. I looked like my mother. We had a sister between us in age, Chloe, who resembled a mix of both our parents.

I let Erik hold me for a while.

Then I struggled. "Put me down." Once he'd set me back on my feet, I grasped both his hands, inspecting his fingers and wrists. "You are all right, not injured?"

He and Christophe had been on patrol for nearly three weeks.

"No, I'm fine," Erik answered, "but look at you. What *have* you been doing? You're covered in flour."

"Making tarts, strawberry for you and peach for Christophe."

With that, I turned to Christophe, grasping his hands in turn for inspection. "And you? You're not injured? You're well."

He did not embrace me, but his eyes moved over my face. "I am well."

Though both men were tall, Christophe de Fiore was a sharp contrast to my brother. While Erik's nature overflowed with laughter and affection, Christophe was stoic and kept his thoughts to himself. He wore his dark hair cut short. His eyes were gray and his skin was tan. I'd heard once that he had to shave twice a day to keep his jawline from becoming stubbled. He and Erik were the same age, both having turned twenty-six the previous winter, but I'd known Christophe my whole life. The de Fiore lands bordered ours on the north. They were our closest noble neighbors and good friends to my family.

Turning back to Erik, I said, "We received your message that you'd be back today. Mother and I are planning a buffet banquet tonight, with dancing. While you were away, she made you a new tunic of red silk with gold thread, and I made Christophe a blue one, with silver thread. Do either of you want a bath ordered?"

"I do," Erik answered. "And something stronger to drink than ale. We rode hard to get home today."

"For goodness sake," I said. "Don't start drinking spirits until after dinner. You know Mother doesn't approve."

Flashing a grin, he was about to answer when the door opened again, held by one of our guards, and our sister, Chloe, walked in with the regal grace of a princess. I smiled at her, but she merely nodded in return—which is what I expected.

Chloe was the loveliest young woman I'd ever seen. She'd inherited our father's height and coloring, but our mother's small features and slender bone structure. Her long, blond hair hung down her back, and she tended to dress in narrow silk gowns of green or amber.

Erik did not call out to her, and she did not run to him.

Instead, she walked slowly, with her head high, to join us, nodding first to Erik, "Brother," and to Christophe, "My lord."

"My lady," Christophe answered, but his voice held no warmth and I wanted to sigh.

Though he and Chloe had been betrothed for several months, they hardly behaved like two people on the verge of marriage.

When she looked down at me, Chloe's features shifted to an expression of affection. "Look at the state of you. Have you been baking? You realize we do employ perfectly capable kitchen maids? You'll need to wash your hair before dressing for the banquet."

I drew in a quick breath and gripped her hand. "The banquet? Has Father—?"

She nodded. "Yes. I've spoken to him, and he's agreed to let you attend. I'll help you choose a gown."

At this news, Christophe's eyes moved over my face again, and a flicker of relief crossed his features. Was he glad for me? How kind of him.

"You're certain?" Erik asked in surprise. "Father agreed?"

"Yes," Chloe answered. "But it did take a little convincing. The way he treats her is absurd. Nicole is hardly a child."

"I'm well aware of that," Erik said.

Both happiness and nervousness rose up in my chest. This would be my first buffet banquet with dancing. As I was the youngest of my father's children, and I looked like a copy of my mother, my father had not bothered to hide his favor of me. Unfortunately, this favor had also caused him to perpetually view me as a little girl—and to treat me as one. I was included at formal sit-down dinners, but he'd never allowed me to attend more potentially raucous events.

Looking up at Chloe in gratitude, I said, "Thank you. But I do need to finish the tarts. You know Cook always makes too many of the strawberry this time of year, and Christophe prefers peach. Afterwards, I'll come to our rooms to dress. Please see what you can find for me to wear."

She and I had slept in adjoining rooms all our lives, and as a result, we had little sense of privacy when it came to each other.

After nodding regally to both Erik and Christophe, she said, "I am glad to see you both returned to us safely. Now, if you will excuse me, I must go and choose my own gown for this evening."

With that, she turned and walked toward the door. The same guard who had opened it for her still stood inside. Once she passed through, he followed after her and closed it from the outside. Chloe rarely had to touch a door.

When Erik glanced at Christophe, I couldn't help noting a flash of concern…as Christophe seemed to hardly even notice Chloe had left the room. However would those two navigate a marriage?

"How long will you be staying with us?" I asked Christophe.

"Only until tomorrow." His voice was low and quiet. "Then I need to get home to Whale's Keep. My sister, Lady Mildreth, has been managing in my absence."

"All right, then." I headed for the door. "I'll see you this evening. Mother has you in your usual guest room, and you'll find the new tunic on your bed. I'll order baths for you both."

"You'd best order one for yourself," Erik called after me. "And don't forget to wash all that flour from your hair." He was always teasing me, but I liked it.

Stepping out into the warm afternoon air, I looked around at the great circle of log buildings. Along with connecting paths, the grounds between each construction sported a mix of rose, herb, and kitchen gardens. Though I could not see the ocean, over the west side of the wall, I could hear waves crashing into the shore. We were safe here, protected. This place was a haven, and I wondered how Chloe could bear the thought of leaving it and going to live with Christophe. Was this the reason for her coolness to him? Perhaps I could ask her? In this regard, I wasn't sure. Even between sisters as close as us, some things were private.

But her betrothal was of great importance to our family, and she knew it.

Our property spread inland and down the coast for miles, and the people in the villages under my father's protection, who lived outside our wall, had come under a new threat over the past few years—one of which none of us could have foreseen.

The nation of Samourè was bordered on the south by the kingdom of Partheney, named for its capital city. The western coastline of the continent ran all along both nations. Under the rule of Queen Ashton de Blaise, Partheney enjoyed a strong border patrol. Few who were unwelcome would dare attempt a landing on their coastline.

My father's lands, Montagna lands, were at the southwestern point of Samourè, reaching the border between nations. King Amandine, who ruled Samourè, lived in the northwest, but our standing army was small and soldiers could not be spared to patrol the Montagna coastline.

Until recently, this had never been an issue. My grandfather, followed by my father, had no argument with the few smugglers who landed now and then, so long as they went about their business and troubled none of our own people.

For the most part, our shores were safe.

My family retained only enough trained guards to protect White Deer Lodge and to accompany my father or Erik when they went to check on harvests or collect taxes. We had never needed more. My father invested our money back into our lands, into improving our crops, the upkeep of villages, and the replanting of trees for future timber.

Christophe's family, the de Fiores, lived on their estate on an island called Whale's Keep, just off the coast. But their lands spread inland a good distance and along the coast to the north. Partly because of the geographical separation of the estate and partly because of his nature, Christophe's father had long invested in a good-sized, well-trained retinue of guards…soldiers. This was where a good deal of the family money went—for the payment, housing, and training of a standing private military. Christophe's mother had long been dead, and his father had died three years ago, leaving him in charge of the family.

Then, two years ago, the first wave of savage raiders landed upon de Fiore shores. We still had no idea from where they came, but they were large men, dressed in furs and plate armor. They would land in groups of about forty men and then raid villages; burning, looting, killing, and taking people as slaves. After one or two raids, they would return to their boats and leave as suddenly as they'd arrived.

Christophe responded swiftly and with force, ordering his men along the de Fiore coastline, where they were able to kill or send back any of these raiders before they ever reached the tree line.

All too soon, the raiders began landing on the unprotected Montagna shoreline, burning our villages, killing and taking our people. My family was safe inside our stone wall, but our people were suffering. We did not employ anything like the de Fiores' well-trained private military, and to create one of our own would take years and far more wealth than was available. My father had good connections at court and he was respected among the nobles, so he appealed to the king, but not enough soldiers could be spared to indefinitely guard our coastline.

Christophe sent help during the worst of the raids, but only after the fact, to try to chase down escaping raiders and recover any stolen people. Even so, due to distance, the soldiers rarely made it in time, and sending these men was clearly a favor on his part. My father did not care to be indebted, even to Christophe.

Over the previous spring, a solution occurred to my father, and he approached Christophe with a proposal to join our families in marriage. My father offered a thousand acres of prime timberland as dowry for Chloe, along with a yearly stipend. In exchange, right after the wedding, Christophe would send two hundred men to permanently reside near White Deer Lodge. These soldiers would patrol our shoreline and expel any raiders attempting to land.

The de Fiores needed good timber.

Even more, Father knew that Christophe cared a great deal for bloodlines, and he would accept a bride only from an ancient noble family. Ours was such a bloodline. The deal was struck.

Over the past weeks, Erik and Christophe had been riding from one Montagna village to the next, with a de Fiore contingent, assessing any damage, hunting for raiders, and promising our people they would soon be safe.

Soon, Chloe and Christophe would be wed, and our lands would be protected. This seemed a perfect solution but for the fact that the impending bride and groom barely seemed to notice the other's existence.

I hoped that perhaps at tonight's banquet, they might have the chance to dance with each other. This thought filled me with both hope and excitement…as I would be there to witness such an event.

A part of me still couldn't believe Father had agreed to let me attend. What gown would Chloe choose for me? She knew best in such matters. But first, I hurried back to the kitchen, as I needed to finish making Christophe's peach tarts.

He had never cared for strawberries.

* * * *

That night, the banquet started off well enough.

I was somewhat late in arriving, as it took longer than expected for my hair to dry, and I sent Chloe on ahead, not wishing to make her wait. There was nothing she loved more than a party with dancing. She loved to be admired and who could blame her? She was so graceful and beautiful.

Still, as I hurried down the path toward the gathering hall, I felt rather pretty tonight myself. Chloe had gifted me with a gown of lavender muslin. All her talk of "choosing a gown" had been a ruse. This gown had once been hers and she'd had it hemmed as a surprise. The color brought out my light brown eyes and set off my darker brown hair. Jenny, our maid, had used her hands to scrunch my hair as it dried, so that it fell all around my shoulders in even more waves than usual. I wore silver earrings and a small diamond pendant.

Tonight, my father would see that I was a woman now—and not a child. I knew for a fact that some noblewomen my age were married and running their own households—not that I had any desire to marry. I loved my home and my family and never wished to leave White Deer Lodge. But I did wish to be seen as a grown woman.

Though darkness had fallen, I knew these paths by heart.

Finally, I arrived at the door of the gathering hall and slipped inside… where the sights and sounds almost overwhelmed me. A loud mix of voices and music filled the crowded hall. Guests had been arriving all afternoon, mainly merchants and their wives who lived close enough to make the journey. But there were also a few military officers in Christophe's employ and a few nobles who were currently in residence at the lodge.

The walls of the hall had been strung with garlands, and the sconces above them glowed with light provided by fat candles. The tables were laden with food, and musicians played a lively tune.

My eyes scanned the room until I spotted my parents, and my mother smiled while holding out one hand toward me. I hurried over to her. She wore a red velvet gown that accented her small waist. In her late forties, her face was nearly unlined and her hair still a shade of rich brown.

"How lovely you are," she said to me.

My father stood beside her, staring down at me with a frown. "Where did you get that dress?"

"Chloe had it hemmed for me. Do you like it?" I asked, worried. The square neckline was a bit low, and I hoped he would not tell me to go and change. I had nothing so pretty in my own closet.

My mother glanced up at him with a challenging gaze.

"Of course I like it," he answered quickly. "It's fine…for tonight."

With that, I turned my attention to the festivities. Erik was out dancing with a merchant's daughter. I hoped to see Chloe dancing with Christophe, but she was not. When I saw her partner, mild distaste rose in my mouth.

She was dancing with Julian Belledini, a man to whom she paid far too much attention in my opinion. Julian was handsome and he knew it, with dark blue eyes and blond hair that curled down around his ears to the top of his collar. He was both slender and well built at the same time, and I had to admit he cut a dashing figure in a black, sleeveless tunic. But he was also the third son of a minor baron. He had no real prospects and yet never failed to mention the old bloodlines of his family. Not knowing what else to do with him, his own father had sent him to mine.

Julian had lived with us since the spring. The idea was that my father and Erik would teach Julian both archery and skill with a sword, and then my father—who had solid connections—would help him arrange for a commission in the royal military as an officer. Julian's father had no qualms about paying for the commission. He simply required assistance with Julian's training and introductions.

My father was always glad to help someone to help himself.

I had my doubts, however. From what I could see, Julian had little interest in either archery or the military. He preferred playing cards with our house guards and drinking wine from our stores and talking to my sister.

I didn't care for him and as a result, he didn't care for me. Julian was a man who liked to be admired.

And now, at Erik and Christophe's welcome party, he was once again monopolizing Chloe's time…and she was letting him. Wearing a gown of emerald green silk, she clung to his shoulder and hand, allowing him to spin her around the dance floor as if there was no place she would rather be.

No wonder my father was frowning.

"Nicole," someone said.

Turning, I saw Christophe coming toward us, looking fine in his new blue tunic. The silver thread had been a good choice, if I did say so myself. His eyes were on me as he crossed the room, taking in my lavender dress and the waves in my hair.

After greeting my parents politely, he said to my mother, "I thank you for this fine banquet."

As the evening meal was buffet, a number of people were already dished up and eating while watching the dancing. The food did look enticing, and I hoped to sample the roasted pheasant with plum sauce soon.

"Your safe return was a good excuse for a gathering," she answered.

"I've heard you encountered no raiders," my father said. "But were you and Erik able to reassure most of the villages?"

"Yes," Christophe answered. "They understand my soldiers will soon be patrolling your coast."

This seemed to please my father, and his tight body relaxed slightly.

But then Christophe held one hand out to me. "Would you dance?"

I knew a number of dances—as Chloe and Erik had taught me—but I'd never danced in public before, and although I'd been allowed to *attend* this event, I wasn't sure how far Father was willing to let me participate. Still, he could have little objection to me dancing with Christophe, who would soon be part of our family—and my brother-in-law.

Looking up at my father, I asked, "May I go and dance with Christophe?"

Father's expression tightened again. He glanced over at Chloe dancing with Julian Belledini. But he answered, "Yes. Of course."

Though he hardly sounded enthusiastic, I wasn't about to waste this chance and grasped Christophe's hand.

Without hesitation, he led me onto the dance floor.

"Do you often dance?" I asked him.

"No. Almost never."

A new song had begun. This dance was somewhat challenging, called the Evalada. The tempo was quick and the turns were fast, and after every ten steps, the man gripped the woman by the waist and lifted her above his head.

Still, as Christophe and I quick-stepped with the other dancers, I was not daunted. Erik had taught me the Evalada, and in his typical playful moods, he'd often lifted me higher than necessary. Because of this, I was accustomed to the strength in a man's arms and hands, so now I simply clung to Christophe and let him lead. As we rounded a turn, he gripped my waist and lifted me above his head as if I weighed nothing. With my hands on his shoulders, I laughed. I trusted him completely and knew he'd never drop me.

Once my feet touched the floor, we were off again. He was a skilled dancer and I needed to do little more than follow his steps as fast as I could. It was exhilarating. On the tenth step, he lifted me again, and I could see that he was having fun. It was good to see him smile. Christophe seldom smiled.

When the last note ended, we both laughed and clapped.

Chloe had been dancing with Julian and although she was smiling, she looked a bit pale and breathless to me. I wondered why. Normally, Chloe could dance all night. But my worries for her vanished when I saw Erik staring at Christophe and me. His usual jovial expression was gone, and as he approached us through the crowd, he seemed almost displeased.

"Did you see me?" I asked him. "I didn't miss a step."

He tried to smile. "Yes, you did well. But perhaps Christophe might dance with Chloe next?"

"Of course," I answered and then turned to Christophe. "You should ask her before the next song begins."

"Ask me what?" Chloe said, suddenly upon us.

"To dance," I answered.

"Perhaps later," Christophe said. "I was hoping to continue dancing with Nicole for a while."

"Please do," Chloe answered. "Julian is asking the musician to play the 'Ruodlieb' and I'm promised to him for the song." She still seemed pale to me, and I wondered if she'd eaten yet.

Erik frowned, but Christophe ignored him and took my hand again. I could see that Erik thought it might be best for Christophe to dance with Chloe, but if neither of them was inclined to dance with the other, what could be done? And in truth, at least Christophe wasn't dancing with some flirty merchant's daughter.

He was only dancing with me. What harm could there be?

Chloe joined Julian as the first note struck.

This dance was not quite so fast and more couples joined us on the floor. Once again, I just held Christophe's strong hand and let him sweep me around. It was great fun, and I loved the flowing movements and the joy of dancing in unison with others all around us. One song soon blended into the next…and the next.

After the fifth song, he asked me, "Are you thirsty?"

I nodded. "Yes, and perhaps hungry too. Have you eaten?"

"Not much."

He offered me his arm, and I took it with both hands so he could lead me through the crowded room for a table laden with food. With his free hand, he reached down and pinched off a bite of roasted pheasant.

"Here," he said, feeding it to me.

He took a bite for himself and then fed me part of a peach tart. After this, he poured a goblet of wine.

When he held it to my mouth, though, I hesitated. Normally, I did not drink wine and I wasn't sure what Father would think, so I glanced over to where my parents had been standing.

My father stood staring at us with eyes as hard as ice, and I realized among the crowd near the table, I was still clinging to Christophe's arm. With heat rising to my face, I felt that somehow I'd done something wrong. My father strode toward us with the same hard expression, and I let go of Christophe's arm.

"Nicole," my father said as soon as he was close enough to be heard. "It's getting late. It's time you were in bed."

Christophe had not seen him coming and turned quickly, his features tensing with anger. "It's early yet," he said carefully.

My father ignored him. "To bed, Nicole. Now."

"Yes, Father."

Christophe's jaw muscle twitched, but he said nothing.

Feeling like a chastised child, I hurried for the door.

* * * *

Long after our maid, Jenny, had unlaced my gown, seen me into bed, and then left the room, I lay awake, covered by a quilt, wondering what I had done to anger my father so.

What harm could there be in my dancing with Christophe and eating a bit of pheasant and peach tart? And yet, Father had treated me as if I'd behaved badly, as if I'd behaved disgracefully. Chloe might love a party with dancing, but I loved my family and I'd never attend a dance again if such an event would cause Father to see me as a disgrace.

Unbidden, two tears slipped down my cheeks. Perhaps tomorrow, I might speak to my mother and see if she could enlighten me about my father's censure. This thought gave me some comfort and I finally closed my eyes, drifting off to sleep.

I don't remember any dreams, but at what seemed much later, I was awakened by a strange sound, like that of someone gagging.

Sitting up, I realized the sound was coming from the adjoining room. The gagging was accompanied by the sound of choking, and I jumped from my bed, running across my room and jerking open the door that separated my room from Chloe's.

There, my sister was on her knees, still in her emerald silk gown, retching violently into a basin on the floor.

"Chloe!"

Running to her, I knelt and held her hair back. She was nearly weeping from distress, and she couldn't seem to stop retching even after there was no food left to come up.

Finally, her body began to calm.

"Oh, Chloe," I said. "You are so ill. I'll run and get Mother."

Our mother was a healer, a skilled practitioner in herbal arts.

But Chloe grabbed my arm, clutching me fiercely. "No!"

Taken aback, I stared into her pale face.

"Please don't," she said more calmly. "I had too much wine to drink at the banquet, and if Father finds out, he'll be displeased."

She'd drunk too much wine? Her concern made sense to me, but I was still worried for her health. "Are you sure? Mother wouldn't say anything to Father, and she might be able to give you something to settle your stomach."

Chloe still gripped my arm, but less tightly now. "I am sure. Just get me out of this gown and help me to clean up the mess. I'll be fine."

Nodding, I moved around to the back of her and unlaced her gown. As she slipped out of the gown, I carried the basin out into the hallway, peering right and left. No one was up, so I took the basin outside and disposed of its contents at the base of a tree.

Hurrying back to Chloe's room, I found her in bed, still pale, but looking otherwise recovered.

"Nicole," she said, "will you swear to keep this between us?"

"Yes. I swear."

Of course I would keep her secret. We were sisters, and sisters kept each other's secrets.

Chapter 2

The next morning I woke up hungry, as I'd hardly had a chance to eat anything at the banquet. But I knew my family and our guests would sleep in, so there would be no gathering for breakfast.

Rising, I donned a simple day gown of tan muslin that laced up the front and then brushed out my hair, pulling it back into a tail at the nape of my neck. But I was careful to be quiet for fear of waking Chloe in the next room. She'd been so ill last night that I wanted her to rest.

Once dressed, I headed for the kitchen, where our cook, Louise, was glad to make me a plate of scrambled eggs with diced tomatoes. And yet somehow, the light of day and the prospect of breakfast did not bring any relief over my father's anger with me at the banquet.

I sighed. Nothing would most likely bring relief except finding out what I'd done wrong, and that would have to wait until my family had awakened for the day. Until then, I'd need to find a way to occupy my mind, so after finishing my morning meal, I decided to follow my usual routine. Here at White Deer Lodge, I had three main duties: my herb garden, our henhouse, and the beehives.

No one had ever assigned me to any of these pursuits. My devotion had simply happened. My mother's need for certain herbs in her healing practices had led her to teach me about the growth and care of such plants, and I'd grown up with an affection for our hens and bees. Over the years, their care had gradually become my responsibility and no one—including me—ever gave this much thought.

Erik's duty was to protect our home, and for all his good humor, he took this duty seriously. He managed our guards. He was skilled with a sword and the best archer I'd ever seen. When he married, his wife would live here and someday Erik would be lord. His wife would be the lady and she would be the one to run the household.

Father sometimes looked at Erik and called him a son of White Deer Lodge, of this place and this land.

Chloe was beautiful and admired. She spent her days entertaining any ladies who came for extended visits, planning tea and embroidery parties. Mother appreciated this, as she had little interest in gossip and tea. But Chloe also paid attention when our mother went over menus with the cook or oversaw our stores for winter. Chloe was training to be the lady of a noble house. Long before the betrothal to Christophe, my parents planned to make a great match for her, and their efforts had not been in vain.

She would soon be the lady of Whale's Keep.

But me?

I would continue working with my mother to learn the arts of healing and remain here to care for my parents when they grew old. I would be aunt to Erik's children and live under his protection.

Father once said to me, "It is Chloe's destiny to make a great marriage, but you are a daughter of White Deer Lodge. Your life is here."

When he said this, I heard truth in his words. I was a daughter of White Deer Lodge.

So no one cared that I knew nothing of running a household and that I spent my days learning healing arts from my mother or working in my herb garden or tending to my beloved hens and bees.

This morning, as my family and all our guests slept, I left the kitchens and headed outside, going first to visit the large henhouse that had been built years ago behind the hunting hall. It was a cheerful henhouse, painted white with blue trim, with a fenced yard outside the front door.

As I approached and passed through the gate of the yard, clucking sounds greeted me from inside.

"Good morning, my girls," I said, opening the door and letting them into the yard. I kept them inside at night for fear of foxes and raccoons. One by one, they came out, clucking all the while. Currently, I had thirty-six hens, but my family and our servants required a number of eggs.

After scattering grain all over the yard, I changed out the water in their shallow basins, using one of our family's water pumps, and then I went inside the house to gather eggs into a basket. These I took inside to Louise, who thanked me.

Upon leaving the kitchen for the second time that morning, I headed off to see my bees.

The beehives resided in a lovely spot at the edge of a meadow out back of the log building that housed our guards. The meadow was alive with color at this time of year, with a variety of wildflowers, butterflies, and dragonflies. It was my favorite place in all the lodge.

Sometimes, I would bring my lunch and remain out here all afternoon. Standing near the hives, I let the sound of buzzing soothe me. Something about the bees at their work always soothed me.

"Nicole," called a voice from behind me.

Turning, I saw Christophe and my father walking toward me, but my father's face was tense, and he stopped at the edge of the building that served as our barracks and let Christophe continue onward to where I stood. This morning, Christophe was dressed in black pants and boots and a simple wool shirt. He hadn't shaved and a dark shadow covered his jaw.

He'd always liked my beehives and this meadow, and I normally welcomed his company here, but not this morning. Not after last night and with my father standing well away from us looking as if he held the world on his shoulders.

"What's wrong?" I asked as soon as Christophe had closed the distance between us. "Why is Father angry with me and why is he standing back there alone?"

At first, I thought Christophe's eyes were bleak, but then I looked at him more closely and thought perhaps he looked…desperate.

Motioning to the ground, he said, "Sit with me. I would speak with you."

A wave of anxiety passed through me. There was something terribly wrong here, and I had no idea what it was. "Christophe?"

"Just sit. Please."

Slowly, I sank down into the grass of the meadow and he sat down beside me. Twice, he began to speak and stopped, as if uncertain how to formulate the words.

"I went to see your father this morning," he said finally, "to ask that he change one clause in the betrothal contract."

My heart skipped a beat. "What? You'll not refuse to send soldiers to protect our coastline? Christophe, you promised!"

Blinking, he shook his head. "No. It's nothing like that. I would never—" He appeared unsettled by my fear. "You know I'm a man of honor. Why would you wonder about that?" After closing his eyes briefly, he opened them again. "I've asked your father to remove Chloe's name from the contract and replace it with yours. That is the only change I wish to make."

Had the ground behind him opened up and a flight of birds risen up from the hole, I could not have been more surprised or confused. I wasn't even certain I'd heard him correctly.

"You've never visited Whale's Keep and neither has Chloe," he said, the desperation in his voice increasing. "The keep is on an island, too far out for a bridge. The only way on or off is by boat and for much of the year, the crossing is not comfortable. All the nobles at court speak of Whale's Keep with such admiration, but few ever make a visit, and if they do, they rarely visit twice."

"I don't understand what you're trying to—"

"There is no society there," he rushed on. "There are no banquets with guests, no dancing, no noblewomen for tea, and my sister manages the household. We live apart from the world. What would Chloe do with her days? But you—you could be happy there. The ground is fertile and you could plant your gardens. I would build you beehives myself. I would build whatever type of henhouse you wished and paint it white with blue trim."

He was in earnest.

I stared at him. "You would put Chloe aside?"

"Listen to me!" he said in anguish. "I should never have agreed to marry her, but I was drawn to the connection with your family. You have always seen me as a kind of brother and I never imagined that you might see me as a man, not until last night, not until you laughed while dancing with me and you held onto my arm and ate food from my hand." He paused. "I have no wish to harm Chloe, but she would not be happy and in the years to come, she would blame me. In turn, I would blame her for a lack of love, and bitterness would grow between us. But you could be happy on the island…with me. Our bond would grow. We are suited for each other. Chloe and I are not suited."

Though I'd thought myself a woman, perhaps until that moment much of me had still been a child, and his words were a revelation. I saw the truth in them. To me, if a man and a woman married, they would naturally care for each other and care for each other's happiness—as my parents did. But the future Christophe painted for himself and Chloe could be all too true, as was the future he painted for himself and me.

"Oh, Christophe," I whispered, for a lack anything else to say.

He leaned closer and lowered his voice. "I love you. I know Chloe is your sister and you are of the same blood, but I want to make my sons and my daughters with you."

Bloodlines meant so much to him. This much I'd already known. To my shock, I began to imagine the life he envisioned for us, living on his island and raising our children quietly away from the rest of the world. I'd never planned to leave White Deer Lodge, but I cared for Christophe and I understood the things he was saying.

Was he right in this? Was his betrothal to Chloe a mistake for them both?

And yet...he had already signed a contract, and their betrothal was public knowledge.

"What does my father say?" I asked, looking back toward the barracks.

One look at my father's face told me what he thought. Beneath his tension, he was frightened. If Christophe broke the betrothal with Chloe for any reason, she would be shamed. But we needed Christophe's goodwill a great deal more than he needed ours. I suspected that were my father not in dire need of de Fiore soldiers, this conversation between Christophe and myself would not be taking place.

Christophe moved in front of me, in a crouched position, blocking my view. "I want to know what you say, not your father."

"Let me talk to him. Please."

For a moment, I thought he would not allow me to stand up and walk away, but then he rocked backward. "Talk to him, then."

Quickly, I rose and closed the distance between my father and myself. Christophe followed.

"He's told you, then," Father said immediately. It was not a question.

Again, we both knew there was a great deal at stake here, but my thoughts were for my sister. "What will become of Chloe if I accept Christophe's proposal?" I asked.

"If he puts her aside for you, there will be gossip," he answered. "In the eyes of the world, she is a better choice and he has already signed a contract. If he alters the contract now in favor of you, the nobles will believe she is damaged somehow. She will never make a great match. She will be seen as flawed."

This had been my suspicion, but I'd needed him to confirm it. In my mind, I continued picturing the life Christophe had painted for himself and me, and I was in near-disbelief by how much I was drawn both to him and to what he offered. I'd never seen him as more than a beloved potential brother. Now, I realized he was a great deal more, or he could be more.

But he was pledged to my sister and I'd never do anything to harm her. Though she might not be happy at Whale's Keep, she would be the lady of a great house and she would be respected. Chloe was proud and to her, respect was more important than happiness.

And yet, I had no wish to hurt Christophe either. I cared for him.

This was awful.

Turning, I looked up into his face, focusing first on his shadowed jaw and then his gray eyes. "You know I can't accept you at the expense of Chloe's good name."

My father exhaled in relief.

But Christophe's features shifted to panic.

"Nicole!" he said. "You're not thinking clearly. This is our only chance. If you refuse me now, we will both end up living the wrong lives."

His words were like blades and my throat began to close in fear that he was right.

"You heard her," my father cut in angrily. "I agreed to let you ask her, and you have your answer. Now I need to know if you intend to live up to the contract you signed. My lady has planned the wedding for the end of this month. Will your honor our agreement?"

Christophe stepped backward in defeat. "I am a man of my word. You know I'll honor our agreement."

"Good," my father said, breathing raggedly. "Whether you believe me or not, I do understand your reasons for proposing this change. Remember, when I was younger than you, I married a girl much like Nicole." He paused. "But I promise that Chloe will make a fine lady of Whale's Keep, and your blood mixed with hers will continue a strong de Fiore line."

Christophe wouldn't look at him, but nodded and turned away. "I'll be leaving within the hour. I'll return at the end of the month."

He walked away.

I stood in silence for a few long moments, trying to process all that had just happened. "Father, are you angry with me?"

"Angry? Why would I be angry?"

"I don't know. I just can't help feeling that I've done something wrong."

"You've done nothing wrong. I've worried this was a tenuous match between him and your sister since I signed the agreement. But it *is* a good match, and our people must have the protection of de Fiore's troops." He patted my back. "I knew you would think only of your sister, but I did fear that if you refused him, he might break the agreement."

"He'd never have done that."

"Perhaps not." My father's expression grew intense again. "No one can ever know what happened this morning, not your mother, not Erik, and certainly not Chloe. Can you be silent?"

His question offended me. "Of course I can. What do you take me for? I understand a good deal more than you think. I turn eighteen years old this coming winter and I am a woman."

He sighed. "Forgive me. Much as it pains me, you are a woman, and now you and I share a secret."

Yes, we did share a secret, one I would keep.

"You've not had breakfast, have you?" I asked. "Come to the kitchen, and Louise will make you some eggs."

* * * *

I tried to put Christophe's anguished words from my mind, and my own emotions confused me.

I pitied him.

I was angry with him.

As he was a longtime friend of my family—and engaged to marry my sister—it would never have occurred to me to view him as anything else. But now, after his pleading and his vision of what our future might have been, I could think of little else. Why had he done this to me? Surely, he could not have expected me to ruin Chloe's prospects by agreeing to his proposal. He indeed must have been desperate.

That thought only made me feel worse and my anger turned back to pity. I hoped he would be proven wrong and that he and Chloe could find happiness together, or at least some mutual contentment.

Two days after Christophe's attempt to alter the path of my life, I launched into helping the women servants of our household with our typical weekly laundry day. My mother always oversaw this event, but I liked to help as well.

Young Jenny was indispensable to us. She served as my personal maid on occasion, helping me dress and doing my hair—when such a need arose. But she served as Chloe's maid more often and she helped to keep our closets arranged.

Today, she was helping to wash clothing in large tubs.

Looking at the pile of evening gowns from the night of the banquet, she frowned. "Lady Nicole, I see the lavender gown you wore, but I don't see Miss Chloe's green silk. Might another of the maids have simply hung it back up? I do think it was in need of a cleaning."

Indeed it was in need of a cleaning. Poor Chloe had been so sick after the dance.

Quickly, I went through the pile. "You're right. It's not here. Let me run to her room and I'll see if it's in her closet."

Leaving the laundry room, I trotted out the back door and up the connecting path to a three-story building that served as our main residence.

Walking through a side door, I turned left down a passage and made my way to the rooms I shared with Chloe. She never minded me searching through her closest, and of course I would never have minded her searching through mine.

Hers, however, was much larger, almost a small room to itself, so upon entering her bedroom, I walked past the bed and dressing table, and through another door into her closet. Countless gowns hung there and most of them were either a shade of green or amber.

I began searching for her emerald green silk.

Only a few moments later, I heard the door to her bedroom open, followed by the sound of her voice.

"There is nowhere else safe to talk," she said. "Hurry inside and close the door."

"You take too much risk," a male voice answered. "You know what would happen if a servant walked in."

I froze. I knew the voice. It belonged to Julian Belledini. What was she thinking? Men were not allowed in our rooms. Even Erik stood in the doorway if he came to seek one of us for some reason.

"The servants are all busy doing laundry with Mother and we must talk. Besides…in a few moments, any worry of being caught in an indiscretion won't matter," Chloe said. Her voice sounded strained. I'd rarely heard her use any tone that wasn't calm and serene.

Julian's voice was agitated. "My love. What could you mean?"

His love? I held a breath. I should not be hearing this.

A pause followed and then Chloe said, "I'm with child."

"What?" He sounded horrified. "How could this have happened? We've been so careful. I've never spent myself while still inside you."

I could feel my face flushing red, and in spite of my shame at overhearing this private conversation, I moved up behind the open door of the closet to peer through the crack into the bedroom. Chloe was beautiful and pale, but she appeared stunned by his reaction.

"You are not pleased?" she asked. "Don't you see what this means? If we tell my father, he'll have no choice but to break my betrothal to Christophe. We can be married."

From where I stood, I watched emotions playing across Julian's face: fear, shock, and great disappointment.

Then his voice altered to a softer note, and he moved closer to grasp her hand.

"No, my love. We cannot tell your father. If we do, he will shame us both. Even if he did break your betrothal and allow you to marry me, what would your dowry be now? Nothing. You and I would be left with nothing, and how fair would that be to our child?"

She gasped. "What are you saying? You won't claim the child as your own? What of all our plans?"

He touched her face. "Our plans are lost. We cannot let your father know that we have…been together."

"Then we won't tell him I'm with child. We'll simply go now and tell him that we are in love and beg him to allow us to marry. He is not unkind. He may agree."

"And then what? Even if we asked his permission for an honorable marriage, it will take him time to break the contract with Lord Christophe. Compensations would have to be made. Then, your parents would wish a decent amount of time before our wedding, and by then, you would be showing. The truth would be known. Again, your father would shame us and leave us with nothing. Is this what you want for our child? To grow up in poverty?"

Reeling from the scene playing out before, I tried to get my head around the fact that Chloe had shared her body with Julian and had hoped to marry him. But other realities fought to the forefront of my mind as I watched the bitter disappointment in Julian's face. In spite of his words of concern for the welfare of the child, he had the look of a trapped fox. He had wanted to marry Chloe, but he also wanted my father's blessing and a large dowry.

He was certainly right that if my father learned Chloe was with child, he would most likely force a marriage and not give Julian one copper penny in wealth or lands. There would be no thousand acres of prime timberland for him. No yearly stipend.

Julian would have nothing but Chloe and the child.

And it seemed that now he wanted neither.

"Then what I am to do?" she asked.

He grasped both her hands. "For the sake of yourself and our child, you must go ahead with the marriage to Lord Christophe. That is the only way I see to protect your futures."

"No!" she cried. "You love me as I love you. What does it matter if we have no wealth? Your family would allow us to live with them. We would have each other."

"You say that now," he answered. "But soon, it would not be enough for you and it would not be enough for me."

She jerked her hands from his. "You liar. You made me believe you wanted to spend your life with me."

He stepped away from her. "And I did. I do. But not like this. Marry Lord Christophe. You have no choice now. In three years' time, you'll thank me."

Turning, he walked out of the room.

Chloe put both hands to her mouth to stifle a sob and I fought the urge to run to her. I could not let her know what I'd just overheard. Tears flowed down her face as she continued attempting to stifle sobs. The sight and sound was heartbreaking, but I remained in the closet.

Then a knock sounded on the door. "Lady Chloe?"

I knew the voice. It was Matilda, one of our kitchen maids.

"Please don't enter," Chloe managed to call back. "What do you need?"

"Cook asked me to come fetch you. She's wondering about changing tonight's dinner menu, and your mother is overseeing the laundry."

"I'll come directly," Chloe answered.

The sound of footsteps trotting away followed. Chloe took several breaths and wiped her face. She put her hands to her stomach. Then with effort, she forced her face back into its normal serene expression, and she left the room.

I stood shaking in the closet for some time.

Then, I allowed myself to walk out into her bedroom, crossing the floor to the adjoining doorway and entering my own room. Though I ached for Chloe's pain, a myriad of thoughts churned one upon another in my head.

She was pregnant with Julian's child, and he had just abandoned her. And she would marry Christophe. Of this I had no doubt. She neither loved nor cared for him, but she would marry him and allow him to believe the child was his. For a woman of our station, this was her only option.

My thoughts drifted forward. If the child were a girl, would the harm be so great? She would not be of Christophe's line, but he would never know and he would love her as his own. As a girl, she could not inherit the estate or his title.

But what if it was a boy? Christophe's belief in bloodlines was stronger than any man I knew, and if Chloe's child were a boy, he would inherit both Christophe's title and become the heir to Whale's Keep. The future lord of Whale's Keep would not even be of the de Fiore line.

Could I allow this to happen?

Should I keep this secret?

I loved my sister. I would do almost anything for her, but could I do this? Should I? And yet, what would happen if I revealed her secret and the betrothal contract was broken? Christophe would not send his troops to guard our coastline. Tears began flowing from my eyes. I could see no way to protect everyone.

The water in my eyes made the following moment even more uncertain than it might have been.

The air in the bedroom appeared to waver. Alarmed, I wiped away my tears, but the motion of the wavering air grew more rapid, and then… something solid began taking shape.

I took a stumbling step sideways.

There, only a few paces away from me, a great three-paneled mirror now stood where there had been only empty air an instant before. The thick frames around each panel were of solid pewter, engraved in the image of climbing ivy vines. The glass of the panels was smooth and perfect, and yet I didn't see myself looking back.

Instead, I found myself staring into the eyes of a lovely dark-haired woman in a black dress. Her face was pale and narrow and she bore no expression at all. But there she was, *inside* the right panel gazing out me. How could this be? Had my dilemma driven me mad?

"There is nothing to fear," the woman said.

Her words brought no comfort.

"You are at a crossroad," she continued, and as she raised her arms, material from her long black sleeves hung down. "And I am bidden to give you a gift."

I stood frozen.

"You will live out three outcomes to three different choices," she said. "Three paths await you. Three actions—or inactions—you might decide upon. Then you will have the knowledge to…choose."

"Wait! What are you saying?"

Lowering both hands to her sides, she said, "The first choice."

My thoughts went blank and the bedroom around me vanished.

The First Choice:
Telling Erik

Chapter 3

I was standing in Chloe's closet, feeling dizzy and disoriented, as if I'd forgotten something and needed to remember. Peeking out a crack between the closet door and the wall, I saw my sister, Chloe, standing in her bedroom with Julian Belledini.

"You liar," she said. "You made me believe you wanted to spend your life with me."

He stepped away from her. "And I did. I do. But not like this. Marry Lord Christophe. You have no choice now. In three years' time, you'll thank me."

Turning, he walked out.

Chloe put both hands to her mouth to stifle a sob.

Then I remembered. I'd come in here to find her dress from the banquet, so that it might be laundered, and I'd overheard that she was carrying Julian's child. Shock and fear of what this might mean washed through me in waves as I listened to her try to keep her weeping silent.

A few moments later, one of our servants called to her through the door. She composed herself as best she could and left the room. I remained in the closet, trying to let myself fully comprehend the ramifications of what had happened. The people of our lands needed Chloe to marry Christophe, and I believed she would follow through with the marriage as her only option.

But if her child were born a boy, he would inherit both Christophe's title and become the heir to Whale's Keep. The future lord of Whale's Keep would not even be of the de Fiore line.

Could I allow this to happen?

If I said nothing, the marriage would take place and Christophe would send soldiers to guard and protect our coastline, but should the child be a boy, I would be partly responsible for the de Fiores passing their ancient title and lands to a son of the Belledinis.

I could not betray Christophe like this.

And yet I could not betray Chloe either. What could I do? Taking long breaths, I realized I had to tell someone who could help decide what should be done. I needed someone who loved both Chloe and Christophe, and I knew of only one person: my brother, Erik.

The thought calmed me. He would never hurt Chloe, but neither would he hurt Christophe. Erik would know what to do.

Leaving the bedroom, I hurried down the hallway and outside into our circular courtyard. This time of day, he could normally be found at the barracks. Even though Christophe's troops would be coming, Erik had begun new training exercises for our own men. He and Father had also started hiring more guards.

Walking down the main path, I took a side path toward the barracks and then gathered myself as I opened the door. I never came in here, and the smell of leather and perspiration caused me to remain in the doorway. This building housed a world of men, and Corporal Devon stood not far inside the entryway, wearing his dark green tabard over chain armor. His eyes widened at the sight of me.

"My lady?"

"Is my brother here?" I asked. "I need to speak with him."

"Of course. You wait. I'll go and find him."

Beyond the corporal, I saw a large open room filled with tables and chairs. A few other guards were sitting around, drinking from mugs or playing cards, and I was glad for Corporal Devon's assistance. I had no wish to step further inside.

"Thank you."

Leaving me, he walked through the large room and out an archway on the far side. Thankfully, he wasn't gone long and soon returned with Erik at his side. Erik wore a wool shirt, chain armor, and a green tabard—but no sword this morning. Armor and weapons had always suited him well. Erik was a born soldier.

Striding through the entryway, he offered me a broad smile. "What are you doing here, little sister? Do you need my help deciding on tonight's dessert? I vote for anything with strawberries."

Is that what he thought of me? That I would only come to him to ask what he wanted for dessert? Well…perhaps that assessment was not entirely unfair.

Then he took in my face and stopped mid-step. "What's wrong? Is Mother ill?"

"No." I shook my head quickly. "But I need to speak with you, alone."

"Can it wait? I was about to start a drill."

"It cannot wait. Will you please come outside with me?"

Frowning, he stepped outside with me, and I cast around for someplace private, but this time of day, the courtyard was alive with guards and servants going about daily tasks. I could think of only one place.

"This way," I said, heading around the side of the barracks.

"Nicole, really," Erik said from behind, sounding annoyed now. "This isn't like you. I have men waiting on me."

Without stopping, I walked through the meadow out back and all the way to my beehives. There was no one else here and no sound but the buzzing of my bees.

Turning to face him, I said, "Chloe is with child."

His eyes searched my face as if he hadn't heard me correctly.

"It's true," I added.

"That can't be. She and Christophe barely speak."

"It's not Christophe's child."

At that, he went still. "What?"

"It's Julian Belledini's."

The color drained from his already pale face and he closed the distance between us, grabbing my wrist. "Why would you say that? Are you repeating gossip? Do you know what damage such rumors can do?"

His grip hurt and Erik had never hurt me, but his words hurt more. "Repeating gossip? I would do anything to protect Chloe! You know I'd strike the first person to whisper such gossip. I heard this from Chloe herself when she told Julian. I was in her closet and she didn't know I was there. I heard her telling Julian."

Erik let go of me and stepped back. He put both hands on the top of his head. "This is true? She's with Belledini's child?"

"Yes."

"What did he say when she told him?"

"He spurned her...politely. I think he was after the type of dowry Father offered to Christophe, but that prospect is over now. Should Father believe Julian seduced her, he would blame them both and there would be no dowry at all. So Julian has abandoned her." I heard the panic in my voice rising. "I believe she will go ahead with the marriage to Christophe."

Erik's eyes shifted back and forth.

Stepping forward, this time I was the one who grabbed his arm. "Erik, what do we do? If we say nothing and the child is a boy, we'll be placing a Belledini as the heir to Whale's Keep. But if we expose Chloe's secret, she will be shamed beyond imagining."

His gaze dropped to my hand on his arm. "Does anyone else know?"

"No."

"Are you certain Julian has abandoned her, that he has no intention of attempting to marry her himself?"

"He told her to marry Christophe and then walked out of the room." After pausing, I repeated, "What do we do?"

"I need to speak with Julian."

"With Julian?" I gasped.

"Intentions spoken in haste don't always last, and I need to know for myself what he plans to do. Then, I'll know what to do."

This seemed risky, to let Julian know that we knew. If he thought the secret was out, he might be less discreet. But after a moment, I began to understand Erik's reasoning. Once Julian thought on the idea of Chloe marrying another, it was possible he might change his mind. We needed to know his true intentions before we could try to help Chloe.

Erik was still thinking. "It's best I do this somewhere outside of the lodge, outside the gates." He looked down at me. "Go and tell Julian that I need him to meet me at the end of the first path on the river. Tell him I'm thinking of adding a ferry across, in case we end up needing to make a quick evacuation, and that I want his advice. He likes it when Father or I ask his advice."

"The river? Do you need someplace that isolated?"

"Yes. Go and tell him now. I'll go on ahead and I'll be waiting for him."

Something in his voice worried me, but I didn't know what. It was the cold way he'd said *I'll be waiting for him*. But I had little choice now. I'd employed Erik's help and I trusted him to help Chloe.

* * * *

Julian was not hard to find. During the day, he could normally be found at the barracks playing cards. I'd heard rumors that he owed several of our guards a good deal of money.

Once again, at the door of the barracks, I caught the eye of Corporal Devon and he came to the entryway.

"Would you please find Julian Belledini for me?" I asked. "Lord Erik needs to see him."

"Of course, my lady."

Corporal Devon was not gone long and returned with Julian—the sight of whom made my stomach turn. His handsome face and wavy blond hair did not affect me. But still, I adopted my best expression of politeness.

"Lady Nicole?" Julian said, sounding tenuous.

I'd never once sought him out.

"Forgive my intrusion," I said. "But Lord Erik has gone to the river. He's considering the best way to arrange a ferry across, in case an evacuation is needed, and he was hoping for your insights. Could you go and meet him at the end of the first path?"

"A ferry?"

"Yes. He would be indebted for your advice."

This was rather a brilliant stroke on my part, as I had a feeling Julian liked to have others indebted to him.

With a slight bow, he answered. "I'll leave directly. I had a losing hand anyway."

* * * *

I don't know what possessed me to follow Julian from a distance. I was not the type of woman who spied on others and until recently, I'd never had to keep a secret. But something caused me to need to know what transpired between him and my brother.

So, I let Julian walk ahead of me through the sprawling village, out the community gates, and down the dirt road leading to the river. In truth, I did not often come outside the wall surrounding the village and the lodge, but on occasion, Mother and I had come out to hunt mushrooms or wild herbs or even to travel to other villages when fever struck and healers were needed.

I knew the various paths to the river, so when Julian stepped from the road into the trees onto the first path—and out of view   I didn't worry. I had no wish for him to see me following, so I let him get a little ways ahead before jogging down the road and heading into the trees myself.

Not far ahead, the rushing of the current could be heard.

Slowly, I crept up behind a tree to watch Julian walk toward the bank to meet Erik, who was waiting. From where I stood, I could hear them both.

"You're thinking of installing a ferry?" Julian asked. "The current is too swift here. There are several better spots upriver, but those spots are nearer to the first bridge. Are you certain a ferry is even needed?"

Erik didn't answer and merely studied Julian's face.

"I hear that you've impregnated my sister and abandoned her," Erik said.

Julian's eyes widened and he nearly stumbled backward. "Is that what she told you?"

"What do you plan to do about it?" Erik asked.

For a long moment, Julian didn't answer and appeared to be gathering himself. Clearly, he'd not expected Chloe to breathe a word of this—but there was no way he could know that she hadn't.

"There is nothing I can do," he finally answered. "Should your father learn the truth, I'd be condemning Chloe to a life of penury, and I won't do that."

How noble he made himself sound. He was a selfish creature who'd tried to worm his way into my family by making Chloe fall in love with him. But now that she couldn't bring him a dowry of land and money, he'd discarded her like an unwanted toy.

"So, you're going to let her marry Lord Christophe?" Erik asked.

"What else can I do? That is her best chance for happiness."

"And out of your love for her, you'll be silent? You will swear silence, even if the child born is a boy?"

At this, something appeared to occur to Julian, and he titled his head in thought. "Of course. I would never place Chloe at risk nor tarnish the Montagna name, and I know how important this marriage is for your family. But perhaps in turn, you might do a favor for me?"

Erik stiffened. "And what is that?"

"You must know I've no wish to live as an officer. I'm much better suited for a place at court in Lascaùx. Perhaps you could convince your father to speak with the king's secretary? I'd not need a prominent position. Something like master of entertainments would suffice, at first."

"And if I don't wish to convince my father?" Erik asked.

"Well, I think it would be best if you did. Your family's honor and the safety of your people are at stake."

Listening to this exchange, I almost couldn't breathe. Julian's threat was clear. Either Erik would help him to find a position at court in the city of Lascaùx or he would not swear to keep silent.

"In this matter, I trust you'll know what do?" Julian asked.

Erik nodded. "I know exactly what to do."

In a flash, his right hand moved to his left sleeve and I saw a glint of steel. Then he rushed Julian, grabbed him by the back of his head, and rammed a dagger though the hollow at the base of his throat.

This all happened in the span of a blink, and Julian's expression registered shock as Erik continued pushing the blade deeper. Blood spurted, spraying one side of Erik's tabard, but he still kept pushing with the blade until Julian went limp in his hands.

I put one hand to my mouth at the sight of the rage and hatred on Erik's face. I'd never thought him capable of this level of sudden violence, much less such hatred. My brother was our protector, a warrior, but he was also a kind and playful soul, a man fond of laughter. This man on the bank of the river was a stranger.

With an angry grunt, he shoved Julian's body backward into the river and I realized the meeting here had required forethought. He hadn't wanted a private place so much as place where he could dispose of a body.

After wiping his blade in the grass, he stowed it back into a sheath on his left forearm. Glancing down at his tabard, he noticed the blood all over his shoulder. Pulling the tabard over his head, he tossed into the river.

Then he turned to head back for the path through the trees.

I stood there, frozen, staring at him, and he stopped.

Nothing could have prepared him for the sight of me, and his eyes flooded with a mix of anger and pain.

"Did you see that?" he asked, his voice ragged.

"You killed him," I whispered. I still couldn't believe it.

As he strode toward me, the sun glinted off his chain armor and I couldn't help shrinking away. I'd never in my life feared my brother. But I was afraid of him.

"I had to!" he shouted. "Did you hear what he said? Could you see his face? He was threatening blackmail, and he'd never have stopped with a minor position at court. So long as he was alive, he'd have power over us and Chloe would be in danger."

I began shaking and couldn't stop. I kept seeing him ramming the dagger through Julian's throat.

"What happens now?" I asked, like a child. "What will we do?"

"Nothing," he answered. "Chloe will marry Christophe, and Christophe will live up to his end of the contract. He'll send soldiers to guard our coastline."

"What if the child is a boy?"

"Then it's a boy." He shook his head as if I were simple. "Nicole, the prospect of one bastard child inheriting the de Fiore lands and title is a small thing compared to the lives of our people. What do you think we live on? Our people grow food and raise livestock, and we take a share for ourselves and for our taxes to the king. If our people continue to be killed or taken as slaves and our villages burned, what will become of us? Have you thought on this?"

He sounded as if the only thing that mattered to him was the comfort of our family and the preservation of our lands.

"Do you love Chloe?" he asked.

"Yes."

"Do you love me?"

I looked up into his face, into his blue eyes. There were spatters of blood on his cheek. He'd need to wipe those away. "Yes," I answered. I loved him. He was my brother.

"Then you and I will keep Chloe's secret, and you will keep mine." He glanced back toward the river.

I was beginning to hate secrets. Now, because of secrets, I would be complicit in Christophe's marriage to a woman carrying a child that was not his own, and I was complicit in hiding a murder.

But nothing in the world would cause me to bring harm to either Chloe or Erik.

Nothing.

* * * *

Three days later, a farmer found Julian's body downriver and brought it to the hunting hall.

When Chloe heard, she lost her serene composure and ran to the hall. I ran after her, but she was faster, and when I arrived, I saw Julian's still-wet body laid out on a table. His face and hands were completely white. Erik was holding Chloe to keep her away from touching the corpse.

After fighting him for a few moments, she sagged and wept into his chest.

The servants appeared taken aback by her raw sorrow, and both my parents were coming through the door.

Erik held Chloe and looked to my mother. "She's distraught. He had become a noble friend of our family, and now we must tell his father he died while under our protection."

Mother hurried forward and gently took Chloe from him. "Oh, my darling girl. You mustn't distress yourself. This was a tragic accident."

I stood back in silence, watching Erik.

My father strode to the body and looked down. "This was no accident."

Julian was a terrible sight with his white face bloated and the ugly wound at the base of his throat.

Erik looked down as well. "I've heard he owed several of the guards large sums of money. Would you like me conduct an investigation?"

Father glanced back at me and then to my mother and Chloe.

"Your sisters and mother should not be exposed to this sight," he told Erik. Then he spoke gently to my mother. "My lady, please take them both out."

Nodding, she drew Chloe toward the door. "Nicole, come."

Together the three of us went outside.

"Chloe is delicate and she should not have seen that," Mother said. "Nicole, are you all right?"

"Yes."

"Good. We will need your strength."

She and I had tended to wounded guards and villagers. She thought me strong. But today, I didn't feel strong. My brother was standing over the body of a man he'd killed, and he'd just offered to begin an investigation.

The only blessing here was that my parents thought Chloe's emotional state was due to shock. Together, Mother and I took her to her room and put her in bed. She'd stopped weeping, but she said nothing and her eyes drifted like someone lost.

"I'm going to the kitchen make her some tea," Mother said. "Stay with her."

Once Mother left us, I crawled onto the bed and lay down behind Chloe, wrapping one arm around her and pulling her close.

"I know you cared for him," I whispered.

"I loved him," she whispered back.

"I'm so sorry."

Reaching up, she gripped my hand.

* * * *

I made it through the next few weeks by caring for Chloe, and each day my resolution to protect her only grew. Erik had made the decision to protect both her and our family over Christophe, and now that this decision had been made, I was determined to follow it through.

The day after the discovery of Julian's death, my father and Erik placed his body into a wagon, and they rode out with several of our guards toward the Belledini estate. This type of news could not be delivered via proxy. But upon their return, my father explained that while Lord Belledini had been distraught, he'd not been overly surprised and related that Julian had long evaded other gambling debts.

Erik launched into questioning several of the guards to whom Julian had owed money. Nothing came of this and the mystery went unsolved. My father launched into overseeing a new barracks and stable built down near the beach for the impending arrival of de Fiore soldiers.

A week after this, Christophe arrived for his wedding.

We all met him in the courtyard, but to my confusion, only his own guards accompanied him.

"Your sister will not be attending?" my mother asked him, equally puzzled. "I've had the best guest room prepared for you and Chloe for tonight. But I reserved the second-best guest room for Mildreth."

I'd never met Lady Mildreth, as she had never visited, but she was all the immediate family Christophe had left. Surely she would come to his wedding.

"No," he answered. "She does not leave the island."

That might, we had a fine dinner of baked salmon and red potatoes in the gathering hall. Christophe barely spoke to me and the few times he glanced at me, I saw pain in his eyes. Chloe was serene and polite, but she spoke little and ate less.

Their wedding took place the following day.

Our gathering hall was decorated with dozens of white and yellow roses. A great feast had been prepared for a celebration after the ceremony. Father had brought in a magistrate all the way from Lascaùx, and a number of noble guests had traveled to see the happy event of this joining of the house of Montagna with the house of de Fiore.

Christophe wore the blue tunic with the silver thread that I'd made for him. Chloe chose the emerald green silk that she'd worn to the banquet, for the last time she danced with Julian. She was still as slender as a river reed.

They stood before a magistrate near the hearth of our gathering hall. All the guests stood behind them.

"Does anyone have any reason why these two should not be joined in marriage?" asked the magistrate.

My father and Erik both appeared tense.

I had a knot in my stomach. There were a number of reasons the marriage should not take place, including the fact that Christophe had formally asked my father to replace Chloe with me…that Chloe was carrying another man's child…and that Erik had murdered the other man.

Yet the most important reason was that neither member of the couple *wanted* to share a lifetime with the other.

Among our family, only my mother smiled. She knew Chloe was not in love with Christophe, but she believed they would come to treasure each other. My mother was possessed of a kind spirit.

When no one offered an objection to the marriage, the magistrate went on.

"Do you, Christophe de Fiore, swear to love this woman, to protect her heart, to give her your loyalty, and to care for her all the days of your life?"

"I swear," Christophe answered.

"Do you, Chloe Montagna, swear to love this man, to protect his heart, to give him your loyalty, and to care for him all the days of your life?"

She hesitated. These were sacred vows, and she was promising to protect his heart and give him her loyalty.

Standing beside me, my father watched her.

"I swear," Chloe said quietly.

They were married.

* * * *

Two days later, Christophe had Chloe's trunks packed into a wagon.

Out in our courtyard, the new couple said their good-byes.

"I'll have two hundred troops sent as soon as we arrive home," Christophe told my father. "They are good men, well-trained. Are the new barracks ready?"

"They will be," my father answered.

I hugged Chloe, holding her tight, not knowing when I would see her again.

"You will be the great lady of Whale's Keep," I whispered, "the envy of other women."

Pulling away to look at me, she tried to smile. "Yes. I will be that." But then she embraced me again. "Write to me often."

"I will. I swear."

Christophe lifted her onto a horse and mounted his own.

He glanced at me once, without saying good-bye, and I could still see pain in his eyes.

Chapter 4

Summer turned into autumn.

Word arrived from Whale's Keep that Chloe and Christophe were expecting a child in mid-spring. My parents rejoiced at this news. They sent gifts for the coming child and sweets for Chloe.

Autumn turned into winter. We celebrated my eighteenth birthday. Then, before I knew it, winter was on the edge of turning into spring.

I counted the months in my head.

Although I wrote to Chloe several times a week, I had to wait until my father needed to send a messenger to Whale's Keep before I could put my letters into a small packet for delivery. Still, when she wrote back, she always thanked me for having received numerous letters.

She did not write nearly so much to me of her daily life, but she always asked me for more news of the family and life at the lodge. I began to worry that even after months in her new life, she was missing her home more than she had expected.

And she was sorely missed here.

Her absence left a hole that Mother and I did our best to fill, but neither of us were skilled in entertaining other noblewomen—or at hosting tea or embroidery parties to gossip. I began to realize that most of the other women found us rather odd. They commented on my mother's "eccentric" habit of bringing medicines to our villagers. And Lady Richelle de Miennes once politely chastised my mother upon my obvious lack of education.

Though Mother did not retaliate, I could see the barb set her teeth on edge. Later she said to me, "My girl. You are far more educated in the things that matter than her useless daughter."

Was I?

As I found myself mourning the loss of Chloe, it would have been natural for me to turn to Erik for company and solace. But I didn't. Something between us had been altered and I didn't know if it would ever be altered back.

I'd watched him murder a man without hesitation and then dump the body into a river.

Keeping a secret was one thing. Living with it was another.

But he and I pressed forward as best we could. The truly unsettling thing was that I wasn't even sure he'd been wrong. Christophe's soldiers had proven as good as promised. They rode up and down our coasts, and since their arrival they had stopped three landings by the strange, tall raiders who wore furs. Deaths had occurred on both sides, but my father said this risk was in the nature of choosing life as a soldier.

Then one evening in late winter, not long before the dinner hour, a messenger arrived from Whale's Keep, and Jenny brought a letter to my room.

"Word from Lady Chloe."

"Oh, thank you, Jenny." Hurrying over, I took the letter and sat down to read it. I'd not heard from Chloe in weeks and had been growing concerned.

> *My dear Nicole,*
> *Although by Christophe's reckoning, the child will not arrive until mid-spring, I am growing heavy somewhat early and find myself a little fearful of the coming birth.*
> *It would be a great comfort if you could convince Father to let you come and stay with me.*
> *I know I could face what's to come if I had you with me.*
> *Love,*
> *Chloe*

I read this short missive several times. Chloe had never written me such a note. For her, this was the equivalent of begging. She was begging me to come. Closing my eyes, I thought on how alone she must feel, knowing her baby would arrive suspiciously early. Suddenly, I wished that before she'd left us last summer that I'd told her I knew, that I did not judge her, and that I would help her if need be.

Though she'd have been mortified at first, later, she would not have felt completely alone. She'd have known she had someone on her side.

Had I failed her by keeping my silence?

I would not fail her now.

At present there were no noble guests visiting the lodge—as few people traveled at this time of year—and so as opposed to eating in the gathering hall, our family had taken to meeting for dinner in our small private dining room near to the kitchens. None of us bothered to change into evening clothes, and Erik sometimes arrived in his armor and tabard.

After hiding the letter, I donned a cloak, left my room, and made my way down the passage and out the back door. Two of the great log constructions at the lodge served as residence for my family, and the dining room and kitchens were in the second building.

Going in the front doors, I headed through the entryway, past a staircase, and then through a tall archway into our dining room. Mother, Father, and Erik were already seated and I was the last to arrive.

"Am I late?" I asked.

"No, my girl," Mother answered. "It's been cold out today, and I think the rest of us were early."

"I've had a letter from Chloe," I said. Since Erik was here—and I would need him in this matter—I decided not to waste any time. "She would like me to come and join her at Whale's Keep until the baby comes."

My father blinked. "Travel to Whale's Keep? Now? Certainly not. You've no idea what the crossing from the shore will be like at this time of year. It's difficult enough in summer. I'll not risk one daughter for another."

I remembered Christophe saying the only way to reach the island was by boat, and that the crossing was not easy at certain times of the year.

But I turned my gaze to Erik and caught his eye. In a matter of seconds, the two of us spoke without needing words. He knew as well as I did that the child would come early, and Chloe would need someone there to help her convince the de Fiores nothing was amiss.

"The weather has been unusually calm this month," Erik said to my father, "and you know Chloe isn't one to ask for help. If she's asking for Nicole, she must be in need. I think we should allow Nicole to go. I can take a few days' leave and escort her myself. I'm good in a boat and I'll see her safely across."

Looking to my mother, I said, "Chloe is in a new home, surrounded by near-strangers and facing the prospect of childbirth. I can only imagine how she must feel. I would like to join her."

Though my mother still appeared somewhat uncertain, she nodded.

"My lord," she said to my father. "Erik will keep Nicole safe, and I agree Chloe would not ask unless she was feeling low indeed. She is in need of her sister."

Father frowned, but he seldom gainsaid my mother.

The following day, I made arrangements to have my hens looked after, and then I began to pack.

Mother came to help me and she brought a box of herbal medicines she'd made herself. "Take these along," she said. "You may have need of them when Chloe's time comes."

Mother and I had delivered many babies together and I knew what to do. "I will keep Chloe safe as her child comes into this world," I promised.

She grasped my hand. "I know you will."

* * * *

Father sent a messenger ahead with news of our impending arrival—lest Christophe and Chloe be caught unawares by guests in late winter.

Early on the morning of the third day following the arrival of Chloe's letter, Erik and I set off with fifteen of our own guards, led by Corporal Devon.

In spite of the cold air and in spite of my true reason for going, I found myself rather exhilarated as Erik rode beside me out the gates and up the northern path. I had never been on such a journey before.

As if sensing my mood, he smiled at me. "It's about time you saw something outside the lodge, or at least more than just villages filled with sick people."

I smiled back. I was grateful for his help in this, for his promise to protect me on the journey and to get me safely from the shore to the island. Perhaps we could become closer again. Nothing would ever be quite the same. I had seen him capable of violence, not on a battlefield or in self-defense, but of a personal nature. Yet he was on my side here, and on Chloe's side, and it was hard not to see him as an ally and a friend.

Whale's Keep was a full day's ride north.

As we traveled, we had the forest on one side and the ocean on the other.

"If there is still enough daylight when we arrive," Erik said, "we'll make the crossing by boat to the island. But if not, we'll need to sleep at the boathouse or the barracks and wait for morning. I won't risk crossing you over in the dark."

I was hoping to see Chloe tonight, but I understood his concerns for our safety.

Though the air was cold, the day was fine, with blue sky and white clouds.

When we stopped for lunch, though, as I began to dismount, I looked down to see Erik below me, reaching up.

"Put your hands on my shoulders," he said.

I was perfectly capable of dismounting a horse, but I followed his orders and let him grip my waist and lift me down. As my feet touched the ground, I realized why he had assisted me. My legs nearly gave way and I grabbed hold of him.

He flashed a grin. "You've never ridden for hours at a stretch and we've a ways to go. You'll be sore tomorrow."

"A small price to pay," I answered, trying to gain control of my legs.

After a light meal of bread and cheese, we mounted up and got back on the path. By mid-afternoon, my right hip was growing sore. In a sidesaddle, much of my weight was supported on my right side. But I offered no complaint.

I was still hopeful that we'd reach the Whale's Keep boathouse before dark, and that Erik could get me to Chloe tonight.

The afternoon wore on and then he pointed. "There is it, just ahead."

Coming around a tree, I looked out over the ocean and nearly gasped. Perhaps a mile from the shore, an island rose up from the water.

"However will we land?" I asked.

The sight was not at all what I'd expected. Though about five miles in length, the island was tall, with dark, rocky cliffs and no apparent shore.

"Around the south side," Erik answered. "There's a small but heavily guarded landing point." He glanced at me. "Did you never wonder why Christophe has no fear of his own home being invaded? There's only one place to land. The rest of Whale's Keep is impenetrable."

As I looked out at this forbidding place, I began to understand Christophe better. Gray waves with whitecaps crashed into jagged stone cliffs. Over the years, he'd often come to celebrate holidays with my family. It was little wonder he'd traveled so far. White Deer Lodge was a place of warmth and welcome.

This island almost seemed to shout, "Go away!"

As if hearing its voice on the wind, I could barely imagine Chloe living in such a place.

"There's the boathouse," Erik said, pointing to a small building up the shore—with a large adjoining stable.

At his words, a more pressing thought struck me. The sun was dipping. "Oh, Erik. Do we have enough light? Can you take me over now?"

He pulled up his horse. "You sound nearly desperate. Are you in such a hurry?"

"Yes. Please take me across. I want to see Chloe tonight."

For once, he didn't make a joke. Instead, he looked up at the sky. "All right."

As we headed forward again, I had a better view up the shore. The boathouse was larger than I'd first thought, made from faded clapboard with thick shutters covering the windows. The attached stable was wind worn and faded as well. But there was an enormous barracks and second stable built in a clearing in the trees behind the boathouse, and this was alive with activity.

Though there was no port or dock here, I counted seven longboats with oars pulled up onto the shore above high tide.

As we approached, Corporal Devon rode directly beside me.

Two men stood out front of the boathouse, talking. One of them was plump and somewhat grizzled, wearing boots, thick pants, and a canvas coat. The other was tall and perhaps forty years old, wearing chain armor and the light gray tabard of the de Fiores.

This man turned at the sound of our horses.

"Lord Erik," he said, and then glanced at me with some surprise.

Erik and Corporal Devon dismounted quickly, and Erik lifted me down with no warning. Then he strode up to the man. "Captain Fáuvel. It's good to see you." He motioned to me. "I don't believe you've met my youngest sister, the lady Nicole."

I did not wear jewels or an elaborate hairstyle, but my traveling gown was of fine red wool and my cloak was trimmed in white fur.

The captain nodded in respect. "My lady." But he still appeared nonplussed by our arrival.

"I've brought Nicole to stay with Lady de Fiore until the child comes," Erik offered.

"Oh, of course." The captain nodded in understanding. "Will you need lodgings until morning?"

"We'd like to make the crossing tonight," Erik answered. "I can help man one of the boats."

"Tonight?" The captain glanced up at the fading light.

"Please," I said quietly.

At the sound of my voice, he looked at me again. Then he turned to the grizzled older man. "Fetch Geoff and Marteen. I'll take Lord Erik and his sister across."

The other man grunted. "Suit yourself." Turning, he called into the boathouse, "Geoff! Marteen! Get your arses out here. Couple of nobles to haul across."

Ignoring these rude manners, Erik asked the captain, "Can you put up my men for a day or two? They've not had supper."

"Yes. Send them on back to the barracks. We've spare bunks now." With the ease of a soldier speaking to another soldier, the captain turned to Corporal Devon. "Ask for Sergeant Harper. He'll have your horses stabled and get you set up with supper."

The corporal nodded. "Thank you, sir." But before leaving, he unloaded my small trunk and carried it over.

"Should I put this into a boat, my lord?" he asked Erik.

"No, just set it down."

With that, Corporal Devon and our guards left us, heading off for the enormous barracks. Two rather shabby-looking men in their late twenties walked out of the boathouse with petulant expressions. Both had lank hair and wore clothing long in need of a wash.

"A crossing?" one of them asked. "Tonight?"

"Yes, tonight," Captain Fáuvel answered in a tone that brooked no argument. "Now grab this trunk, load it into a boat, and get the boat in the water."

The two men moved quickly into action. Erik and I followed them down toward the water, with the captain striding behind.

"It takes four men to handle a boat," Erik told me.

"But you've visited Christophe, so you've done this before," I said.

"Many times."

It had never occurred to me wonder about Erik's life when he was away from home. I worried for his safety, but otherwise I'd never really wondered what he *did* while away. I had certainly not pictured him rowing a boat through high waves out to an island.

After the two men loaded my trunk into a boat, Erik and the captain joined them to help push the boat forward into the water. Then Erik strode back to me, and before I could say anything, he swept me up in both arms and carried me into the water, depositing me at the back.

"You'll need to hold on tight," he said.

I gripped my wooden seat with one hand and the side of the small craft with the other.

All four men climbed in and set their oars.

Then we were off.

The sun had nearly set and dusk was upon us, but there was still light by which to see, and the men appeared to know how to oar the boat to the top of one wave and use its momentum to roll down the other side. While this alarmed me slightly at first—as it was a new experience—I soon caught the rhythm of their intention.

No matter what happened, I was determined to keep a brave face and sit quietly, as I was the one who had insisted on this crossing tonight. It did not take long for us to travel the mile between the shore and the island, but then the men kept rowing, and I remembered what Erik had said about the only entrance point being on the south side.

Erik called to me. "You all right, Nicole?"

The truth was that the reality of being trapped in a small boat on a vast ocean was a good deal more frightening than I'd expected. Water splashed inside the boat, spraying the bottom half of my cloak and dress.

"I'm well," I called back to him. "Press on."

My thoughts flowed to Christophe's words by the beehives.

All the nobles at court speak of Whale's Keep with such admiration, but few ever make a visit, and if they do, they rarely visit twice.

I'd not understood him then, but I did now.

As we rounded the corner of the south corner of the island, I saw a break in the cliffs and a rocky beach. All four men rowing our boat were panting as they heaved on the oars, and we rolled to top of one wave and down the backside, but looking over their shoulders, they steered us true.

There were men on the rocky beach and I could see a gatehouse.

As we neared the shore, the captain dropped his ore and moved to the front of the boat.

Putting one hand to his mouth, he called, "Kerock! Demargo! Get ready to catch us."

Two men ran into the water until the waves reached their thighs, and they grabbed the front of our boat as soon as it was close enough, pulling for all they were worth.

A moment later, Erik, the captain, and both men from the boathouse jumped out and helped pull the vessel up onto the rocky shore. I still clung to my seat.

Finally, the boat stopped moving and Erik was beside me, helping me out. Still panting with his clothing half soaked, he smiled.

"I told you I'd get you here safe."

"You did indeed." Though I was shaken, my voice sounded steady.

"But we're not done yet," he said, pointing to the gatehouse tunnel. "We need to pass through there and climb up."

Though somewhat confused by what "climb" meant at this point, of course I understood that we were at the bottom of the cliffs, and any dwellings would be higher. Darkness was falling, but looking ahead, I saw a raised portcullis.

"This way," the captain said, passing under the open portcullis and into the gatehouse tunnel. "I'll have the lady's trunk brought up."

Erik and I followed him down the gatehouse tunnel and then under another open portcullis. Once out of the tunnel, I found myself looking up at a seemingly endless set of stone stairs.

"How could you ever get a horse on or off this island?" I asked the captain.

"A horse?" he repeated. "We wouldn't even try. Is this your first visit?"

"Yes."

He nodded. "You'll see."

With that, we began our climb…up and up. My thoughts churned, keeping my mind occupied with anything other than the sheer effort it took to keep moving. What about food and supplies? Did everything have to be carried up these steps?

Finally, when my legs were nearly ready to give out, we reached the top and passed through another gatehouse, and then we stepped out to the sight of a thriving village, perhaps the size of a town.

All around us, as far as I could see in the increasing darkness, spread roads lined by shops and dwellings. There were taverns and small barns. Numerous people still bustled about, most likely heading home. Children and dogs hurried after adults. The ground sloped upward and looking to my right, I saw a great, four-towered keep at the top of the cliffs.

"Oh," I said, somewhat at a loss.

The captain spoke to a young guard. "Run up to the keep to give word that Lord Erik and his sister have arrived."

"Yes, sir."

Erik watched my face. "This place is astonishing, isn't it? Like a small world unto itself. The island has a twenty-mile circumference, so nearly everything they need is produced here. They raise chickens, sheep, and cattle. You should see the orchards. They even have a vineyard."

"Why did you never tell more of life here?" I asked.

He shook his head. "It wouldn't have done any good. Words aren't enough. You have to see it." He looked around and breathed the air. "To feel it."

For my jokester, warrior brother, this last statement waxed almost philosophical. But it was clear he had a fondness for this "little world unto itself" as he put it. I wondered how Chloe felt about the place.

For myself, I could already feel myself leaning toward Erik's view. From the shore, the island had seemed forbidding. But now, inside the cliffs, it seemed more safe and welcoming.

"The way," said the captain, leading on.

We followed him up through the town. The back of the keep was built over the cliffs, but a low stone wall bordered the front with a break at the center point, and we passed through the break into a courtyard.

But we'd barely entered the courtyard when two large doors of the keep opened and Christophe came jogging out, as if he'd not been able to wait.

"Erik," he called, picking up the pace to close the distance between us. He was not a man to offer embraces and yet, upon skidding to a stop, he grasped Erik's upper arm. "I am so glad to see you."

He was dressed simply in boots, canvas pants, and a black wool shirt. He'd not shaved in several days and the shadow on his jaw was a full stubble. But somehow, it suited him. The dark circles under his eyes did not.

"It's good to see you too," Erik said, also glancing at the dark circles.

I held in a breath. This was the only element of the journey that had concerned me. I wasn't sure how Christophe might feel about my presence. But as he stepped past Erik to greet me, I saw nothing in his face but gratitude.

"Nicole," he said. "I'm so glad you've come. Chloe's spirits rose the moment she read your father's letter telling her that you and Erik would soon be on the road. She has been awaiting your arrival."

"Have her spirits been low?" Erik asked.

Christophe hesitated before answering. "Yes. She's far from her home and carrying a first child, and you of all people know I'm not the most entertaining company."

This response was so open, so honest, that Erik patted his arm. "Well, we're here now, but I'll need to head back in a day or two."

"So soon?" Christophe asked. Both the regret and disappointment in his voice pulled at my heart.

"Yes, Father needs me now," Erik answered, "but Nicole can stay as long as Chloe needs her."

"Good," Christophe breathed. "Thank you."

I'd never seen him like this, in need of help and expressing gratitude for our company. I wondered what had gone on here over the winter.

But he turned to Captain Fáuvel. "Edward, thank you for helping to bring them across tonight. Will you join us for supper? I think our cook is baking a fish pie with that butter crust you like."

He spoke to the captain like a friend, on a first-name basis. Christophe had just invited the captain to join us at the table and knew what kind of food the man liked. I wondered if my father knew anything about the captain of our guards.

Captain Fáuvel nodded. "It would be my honor, but Lady Nicole here tells me this is her first visit, and I fear the crossing and the climb up have nearly done her in."

I was not quite done in, but neither was he entirely wrong and I shivered in the night air.

"Oh, forgive me," Christophe said in some alarm.

Quickly, he wrapped one arm around me and began guiding me toward the doors. Though I'd never have admitted it, I liked the feel of his arm, the same arm that held me on the dance floor at the banquet last summer.

Erik and I seemed to be mending the rift between us.

Perhaps Christophe and I could mend our rift too. He had long been my friend and I'd missed him.

* * * *

The bottom floor of the keep was square and solid, with crenellated turrets built into the second story of each of the four corners. The turrets rose into the air above the third floor.

To me, who had only lived in buildings constructed from logs, Whale's Keep seemed like a castle.

Christophe ushered us inside the enormous front doors into a square foyer. Passages led right, left, and straight ahead. He started to move forward when a voice from the left called out.

"Nicole!"

Turning, I saw Chloe coming toward me. She appeared to be trying to move quickly and gracefully at the same time, but her stomach was large with the child she carried, making her gait somewhat ungainly. Pulling out from under Christophe's arm, I ran to her. Upon reaching her, though, I was careful with my embrace. Something about her struck me as...fragile.

She hugged me back and did not let go. "I'm so glad you've come."

Then Erik was striding down the passage and she let go of me. Although those two were close in many ways, they rarely touched each other, but he clasped her to him, and she laid one side of her face against his shoulder.

"I knew you would bring her yourself," she whispered.

Watching this unexpected show of emotion, I took stock of her appearance. Though her stomach was swollen, the rest of her was thin. Her face was so thin there were hollows below her cheekbones.

I touched her arm. "Have you been well?"

She pulled partially away from Erik and looked at me as if she didn't know how to answer. But behind us, the front doors opened again and a guard came in carrying my trunk.

Chloe's eyes dropped to my damp cloak and skirt. "I am being selfish. You'll need to change before dinner and I'm sure you are hungry. I've had rooms prepared. We'll get you comfortable and then we'll meet for dinner in the great hall."

"You know I hate to make a fuss," Erik said. "Nicole's cloak may be wet, but the captain and I are both soaked from the waist down and I didn't bring a trunk. Any chance of spare clothing?"

"Don't be absurd," I answered. "You love to make a fuss."

But looking at his legs, a glimpse of the old Chloe came back. Standing straight, she said with regal grace, "Of course, brother. I'll see to it right away."

* * * *

I dressed simply for dinner, in gown of light blue wool, and then brushed out my hair. My guest room was on the second floor and it was a fine room, with a four-post bed and a cedar wardrobe. Yet, I barely noticed the furnishings.

The image of Chloe's thin face and the dark circles under Christophe's eyes troubled me. Something was wrong here. Of course, Chloe would be worried over the impending arrival of her child—which would come too soon after her wedding. But she was clever and the prospect of an early birth could be managed. She was not the type to stop eating and neglect herself.

And what was troubling Christophe? He had no idea the child she carried was not his own.

I needed to learn more.

As soon as I was dressed, I left my room and headed back down to the main floor. There, I stopped one of the house guards.

"Could you direct me to the great hall?"

"Yes, my lady. Continue down this passage to the main foyer, and then turn right. You'll soon see the arch."

"Thank you."

Following these straightforward directions, I walked to the foyer and turned right. Up ahead, I saw Erik passing through a stone archway at the end of another passage, and I followed him into the great hall.

The room was aptly named. It was enormous. Crossed swords, tapestries, and coats of arms decorated the walls. Twenty-four chairs surrounded a long oak table. At present, the vast chamber contained only one occupant. Chloe stood by a hearth so large several men could have easily stood inside it. Emanating warmth from the flames called to me.

Erik and I moved to join her and in spite of everything, I was glad for a moment for the three of us to be alone. Chloe wore an amber silk gown with the waistline let out, and she watched us approach with a grateful expression. I wanted to pretend this moment was one of days past, when the three of us had no secrets from each other.

"Good Gods, Chloe," I teased, "in at least one your letters, you might have warned me what it would take to reach you here."

At my joke, the slightest glint of mischief came into her eyes. "Did you manage to climb the stairs by yourself or did Erik have to carry you on his back?"

Erik laughed. "I rowed her across the sea. She could bloody well carry herself up the stairs."

"Yes, I managed," I answered, "but all the while, I kept picturing Lady Richelle de Miennes on a visit, huffing and puffing up those stairs while holding one of her great velvet skirts above her ankles."

Chloe rarely laughed, but her eyes lit even brighter at my description, and she kissed the side of my face. "Nicole, I am so glad you're here."

Just then, a cold voice sounded from behind me.

"The Lady Richelle de Miennes was a friend of my father's, and I would thank you not to speak of her with such disrespect."

At the sound of this voice, Erik's features tightened. Turning, I saw a woman and two children, a boy and a girl, standing in the archway. The woman was tall and gaunt, perhaps thirty years old. She wore a high-necked black gown with a starched white collar. Her hair was pulled into a severe bun at the back of her neck—so tightly it seemed to stretch the skin at her temples.

The boy was about ten, with dark hair and gray eyes like Christophe. The little girl was perhaps eight. Her hair was brown like mine, but it was pulled back into a bun as tight as the woman's. Both children wore serious expressions.

Chloe crossed toward them immediately. "Please don't mind us, Mildreth. We meant no harm. Lady Richelle was always a loved and welcome guest at White Deer Lodge."

Her words were not surprising. This would be a typical polite response from Chloe should someone have taken offense, but the tone of voice took me aback. She sounded more than apologetic, almost groveling, as if begging forgiveness for having smiled at a small joke.

Erik's jaw was still tight and I thought on the name Chloe had just used: Mildreth.

This woman was Christophe's sister.

"I don't think you've met my sister, Nicole," Chloe continued. Looking back to me, she said, "Nicole, this is Lady Mildreth, and her children, Jordan and Amanda."

"It is a pleasure to meet you," I said to Mildreth. "Lord Christophe has been so good to our family."

She ignored Erik completely and looked me up and down without speaking, as if trying to get the measure of me. I smiled at Amanda, who started slightly, as if uncertain how to respond.

Christophe and Captain Fáuvel came through the archway together, speaking of the rotation of the guards down on the lowest portcullis, but they stopped upon entering the hall and seeing everyone.

The captain bowed to Chloe. "My lady."

She appeared glad to see him. "Captain, I'm glad you've joined us for dinner. It is a treat for us to have guests tonight."

I asked Chloe quietly, "Is it rare for you to have dinner guests?"

"Yes. Normally, it is just the four of us."

Christophe walked over and took Chloe's hand. "Are you feeling well tonight?"

He sounded genuinely concerned, like a solicitous husband, and when she looked up at him, I saw warmth in her eyes.

"Yes, my lord. And I'm so happy to have my brother and sister with us."

"I am happy too."

Whatever was troubling them, it had nothing to do with a lack of fondness for each other. I could see that immediately. They may not love each other, but it appeared they had fostered at least a friendship.

Then what was wrong?

With Erik's input, the men again began discussing the watch rotation, and Chloe and I drifted to the other side of the hearth.

Mildreth walked over to join us, looking Chloe up and down. "Did I hear you say you were feeling well tonight?"

"Yes, sister," Chloe answered—and it rankled me to hear her call Mildreth by my title. "Just a little pressure on my hips."

Mildreth studied her with cold eyes. "That is due to the child moving downward nearer to the time of birth. It normally does not begin so early. I fear you will have an uncomfortable few months."

Chloe paled, but nodded. "Yes, I fear so too."

But I looked to Mildreth's face. She *knew*. Or at least she suspected. Had she been throwing subtle taunts at Chloe? Was she the real threat here? If so, why wasn't Chloe fighting back? Her whole life, she'd handled noblewomen with much greater tact than Mother or me, but her polite demeanor was a type of armor. In a lion's den of "ladies," she could more than hold her own.

I barely recognized this cowed young woman before me.

Several servants entered carrying trays of food. The smell of savory fish pie wafted through the air, and I realized I was hungry. Normally, the lady of the house would announce dinner, so I waited for Chloe to step forward.

But Mildreth straightened. "Dinner is served. Will everyone please take a seat?"

Chloe's eyes had dropped to the floor. This astonished me and I looked back to Mildreth.

She would bear watching.

* * * *

Dinner proved a somewhat strained affair and Chloe retired not long after.

As I'd been traveling all day, I also excused myself and no one found this impolite. The warmth and comfort of my guest bed was welcome. But in spite of my weariness, I tossed and turned for much of the night.

Chapter 5

The next day, mid-morning, Christophe, Erik, Chloe, and I met in the hall for breakfast.

"Will Mildreth not be joining us?" I asked.

"No," Christophe answered. "She rises early, so she can check on the kitchen staff and checks the daily menus."

Mildreth oversaw the menus? Thinking back, I remembered Christophe once having said something about his sister managing the household, but I'd expected Chloe to make her own position clear upon arriving. She was particular when it came to menus. If few guests visited here and Mildreth managed the household, what did Chloe do?

At present, I felt it best not to ask.

Instead, I asked Erik, "You'll be staying with us today?"

He nodded. "Yes. I can stay today. I'd stay longer, but Father needs me back."

He was probably delaying his departure only because Christophe wished him to stay.

"Well, then we should make the most of it," I said and asked Christophe, "Does your village have an open-air market this time of year?"

He seemed to find this an odd question, but he nodded. "Yes."

"Then the four of us should don cloaks and go visit. I've rarely seen a village outside the lodge, except when I go out with Mother to help those who've fallen ill when a fever passes through. I would enjoy having you and Chloe show me your village."

This idea might not have occurred to him, but it seemed to appeal.

Turning to Chloe, he asked, "Do you feel well enough? Please say if you don't. We won't leave you here alone."

I couldn't help a rush of affection for him. He was kind to her.

"No, I feel well enough," she answered almost eagerly. "I should like to show Nicole the village."

I smiled. "We can purchase sweets and gifts for Mother."

"Does anyone care what I think?" Erik asked.

"Not at all," I answered, "but I know you like a good open-air market."

So, the four of us dressed warmly and headed outside the keep to walk through the island village. Christophe came to life, explaining the history of the smith and the stables. He was clearly a beloved lord and people came out of shops to greet him warmly. I chatted with several of the merchant wives and they were delighted to see Chloe heavy with a coming heir.

Chloe basked in their kindness and she breathed in the fresh air.

"Don't you and Christophe ever do this by yourselves?" I asked.

Almost puzzled, she shook her head, "No, we've not…Over the winter, we just settled into the habit of staying inside."

"Well, you should at least take Amanda sometimes. I'm sure the child could use an outing."

"Amanda?" Chloe repeated. "Oh, no. Mildreth would never allow that."

Poor Amanda. It seemed Mildreth certainly liked things her own way. But I was determined not to spoil the day for Chloe and changed the subject. By the time we reached the market, it was mid-afternoon and so we stopped for lunch at an eatery first, dining on delicious sausages and fresh rolls and chatting of small things.

Then we went shopping.

Chloe and I labored over some purchases for Mother, deciding in the end on several ribbons and a box of sugared almonds. Erik bought a dagger sheath for Father.

I kept a close eye on Chloe. She was much closer to her delivery date than Christophe knew, and I made sure she didn't wear herself out. But as opposed to growing weary, she appeared to draw on the life and fresh air around her.

Before I knew it, the afternoon was waning.

Christophe looked up. "It's later then I realized. We should head back."

"It's been a wonderful day," I said. "I like your island very much."

He nodded with pride and I could see how much my words pleased him. He was proud of this place. But Chloe looked around as if such a thought had never occurred to her.

"It *has* been a lovely day," she said slowly.

We walked back to the keep, passing through the gatehouse and into the courtyard. By this point, Chloe was walking a little slowly and the rest of us slowed our pace. Still, I could see she was happy, and I knew we'd not done wrong to take her outside.

As we passed through the front doors into the foyer of the keep, she said, "I think Mother will like the robin's-egg blue ribbons best. She could use them to brighten up her tan muslin. It's been looking a little…"

She trailed off, her eyes fixed ahead, and I followed her gaze.

Mildreth stood in the center passage, in her black dress with its starched white collar, clasping her hands in front of herself. Her expression was tight, as if she'd caught us all committing a crime. She had two of the house guards standing behind her.

"There you are," she said. "I was about to send the guards searching. I had no idea where you'd gone."

Christophe walked forward. "We went into the village, but I'd not planned to stay out all day and I should have sent word. It was thoughtless of me not to."

She nodded tightly and he seemed to think the matter at an end.

"I'll go and clean up for dinner," he said.

"Me too," Erik put in, clearly eager to be away from Mildreth.

I reached out to Chloe. "We should go and change as well."

But once the men left, Mildreth walked straight to us, glaring at Chloe. "Men do not always think in such matters," she said, "but as you are carrying the next child in the de Fiore line, you might abstain from flouncing carelessly about the village where anything could happen."

Chloe dropped her gaze. "Yes, of course. I'm sorry." All the enjoyment of the day was gone from her face.

This was too much for me. Squaring off with Mildreth, I said, "We were hardly flouncing and Lord Christophe was with us the entire time. A bit of fresh air will do both Chloe and the child good. You might consider some for yourself."

Ignoring me, Mildreth kept her eyes on Chloe. "I trust you understand me."

"Yes. I do. Now I must go and dress for dinner."

Turning, she fled down the passage as quickly as her condition would allow. I glared back at Mildreth, but she walked away.

* * * *

Less than an hour later, I came to a decision.

Leaving my guest room, I asked a servant woman for directions to Chloe and Christophe's private apartments, hoping I might catch Chloe alone.

The question confused the woman slightly, but she was kind enough to escort me up one floor where the family kept their rooms.

"Thank you," I said by way of dismissal.

Once alone, I knocked. "It's me."

"Nicole?" Chloe said from the other side of the door. "Come in."

Upon entering, I found myself in a sitting room with thick carpets and low couches. In the far wall, I saw an open doorway into a bedroom. There was a white lace comforter on the bed and flowers in vases on the tables. I wondered if Christophe minded the feminine décor. Chloe sat on a low couch, wearing the same amber silk from last night.

"I've not let out enough gowns," she said quietly, as if she needed to make excuses to me. "I should have a few more altered."

Her gowns meant nothing in the moment. "You and I need to talk. Send word that the day's outing has made you weary, that you won't be down for dinner, and that you and I will eat on trays here in your rooms."

Hope passed across her features, followed by despair. "No. We could never do that. Mildreth would not approve."

Walking toward her, I said, "Chloe, *you* are lady of Whale's Keep. You can have dinner in your rooms any time you please."

She stared at me. Then she rose and pulled on a bell rope.

A moment later, the same servant woman who had helped me opened the door. "My lady?"

"Have Lord Christophe informed that I am a little tired from today's outing," Chloe instructed, sounding more like the woman I knew. "Assure him that I'm well, but would prefer to eat here in my rooms with my sister. Then have the cook make two dinner trays and bring them up."

"Yes, my lady."

Once the woman was gone, Chloe sank back down on a couch.

Sitting down beside her, I said, "There are things you need to tell me and things I need to tell you. Why do you not stand up to Mildreth?"

"You couldn't know what I've been through since arriving here, locked inside the place like a prisoner, constantly…fearing…fearing…"

"Fearing what?"

Perhaps she would tell me, and I wouldn't need to admit I already knew her secret.

"I cannot tell you," she whispered.

With a sigh, I realized I'd have to do this the hard way. Reaching out, I grasped her hand. "Chloe, I know."

"You know what?"

"I know the child is not Christophe's, that it is Julian Belledini's, and that you are now suffering in fear of discovery."

Her entire body stiffened, and at first she said nothing. She just breathed. Then she asked, "And how would you know any of that?"

"Because I was standing in your closet when you told Julian, and I heard everything you two said to each other."

She whirled toward me, her expression a mask of rage, but I was glad to see her anger. It meant she could still feel something besides fear.

But before she could speak, I grabbed her shoulders. "I have protected you! I have protected your secret. I'm here to protect you now. I would do anything to help you."

All the rage bled from her face. Her breath caught and her lip quivered. "Oh, Nicole. You have protected me, haven't you? You've kept this secret. I thought I was alone."

I pulled her close. "You're not alone." Then I drew back. "But you need to tell me what you're up against. Christophe seems a kind husband with no suspicions at all. You've had nothing to fear from him yet. What is Mildreth holding over you?"

"Holding? Nothing. But she hates me. Her own marriage is a travesty and her husband has no interest in their children."

"Husband? I assumed he was dead."

"No. She is married to Baron Phillipe de Caux. He's minister of finance to the king and for several years, early in the marriage, Mildreth lived with him at court. But for some reason she wished to give birth to Amanda here, so halfway through her pregnancy, she traveled here with young Jordan, but not her husband. Shortly after Amanda's birth, the baron sent a letter saying he didn't want Mildreth back. This was eight years ago. Christophe and Mildreth's father was still alive then, and of course he wished to protect his daughter and grandchildren. He put her in charge of the house. She has ruled as lady ever since."

"So, she feels her position here is all she has left, and that's why she won't share duties with you?"

"Worse," she said, shaking her head in near-despair. "Christophe had never shown interest in marriage before our betrothal, and I think she'd begun to hope he'd not marry. Without an heir of his own, Whale's Keep and the de Fiore title would go to Jordan, Mildreth's son."

Sitting back, I absorbed all of this. It was worse than I expected. Mildreth was not just jealously guarding her position as lady here; she viewed Chloe as an obstacle.

"But Nicole," Chloe went on. "When I first arrived, I was broken. I loved Julian and found myself married to another man. I cared nothing for the running of Whale's Keep and felt almost as if I were sleepwalking. It was months before I realized Mildreth was setting the course of my life for me—in which I had no power and voice. I tried to begin taking on some of the household responsibilities, but by then my waist was thickening and I was showing too early. I could see her counting the months in her head. She's said nothing to Christophe, but I grew afraid of her, afraid of angering her."

Some indelicate questions rose in my mind. "Chloe, how far along were you before your wedding to Christophe?"

"Perhaps two months."

"You said you felt broken when you first married Christophe, but how soon did you…?"

"Get him into bed?" she finished for me.

"Yes," I answered gratefully.

"Our wedding night at the lodge. I had the sense to act swiftly there. But he hasn't come to my bed since I told him I was pregnant."

"What do you mean? Doesn't he live in here with you?"

Our mother and father had always shared the same rooms and slept in the same bed.

"No. We don't have that sort of marriage. He keeps his own rooms. I don't think he wanted to marry me any more than I wanted to marry him. But he admires and loves our family so much, and he wanted an heir from his own line and our line." She put one hand to her mouth. "He's been so kind to me. I've been a misery to him and he's never been anything but kind, and now I might saddle him with a son, an heir, who is not his own."

"It could be a daughter," I said.

"Yes," she said, sounding calmer. "It could be. I am so glad you're here. I felt as if I were drowning in fear. Just having you here makes me feel as if I can breathe again." She paused. "And you've told no one, all this time?"

"Only Erik, but I knew we'd need his help. I wouldn't be here at the keep without him convincing Mother and Father. He loves you as I do and he'd do anything to protect you."

She wouldn't mind me telling Erik. He was our brother.

But her body went still again and she turned to look into my eyes. "Erik knows Julian was the father of this child? When did you tell him?"

"The same day I found out, the day you told Julian." Uncomfortable by her reaction, I glanced away.

"Nicole, look at me," she ordered. "Did Erik kill Julian?"

Nothing could have prepared me for her to ask this. Were our positions reversed, I would never have thought to wonder if Erik had murdered the father of my child. And yet this was the first thing to enter her mind. Did she know our brother better than I did?

No matter what, though, I'd never tell her the truth. Erik's was a different kind of secret and I would take it my grave. Chloe could never know. It would destroy her love for him.

"No," I answered. "Of course he didn't. How can you ask that?"

She closed her eyes in relief, but I felt only further guilt. This was something else given birth by secrets. They turned sisters into liars.

I had just lied to mine.

"What am I to do when the child comes nearly two months early and is fully formed?" she asked.

I had been giving that some thought. "Don't worry. We'll manage."

She gripped my hand.

* * * *

The next morning, I had an idea to help Chloe see how she might be able to carve out some happiness in this isolated place. I wrote three notes and paid a kitchen boy to deliver them.

Then, Christophe, Chloe, and I gathered in the courtyard to see Erik off. I was sorry to see him go.

Though he kept up a cheerful front with Christophe, as he hugged me good-bye he whispered in my ear, "Can you handle this?"

Could I? I hoped so.

"Yes."

"If you need anything," he said, "send me a message."

Then he was off, waving good-bye and walking through the gatehouse to begin the journey home.

"I'm a little tired this morning," Chloe said. "I think I'll go and rest."

We saw her back inside and then she started down the left passage. Within a few moments, she was out of sight and I found myself alone with Christophe. We'd not been alone since my arrival here.

But he looked down at me. "Come this way. I want to show you something."

Curious, I followed him all the way to the back south corner and he entered a stairwell.

"Where are we going?" I asked.

"You'll see."

One floor up, we emerged from the stairwell, but he turned almost instantly and we entered a turret with curving stairs leading up. I continued following him all the way to the top and then we stepped out into the wind at the top of the tower.

Walking to the other side, he gazed out through an open space between the crenellations. "Nicole, come and look."

Without hesitation, I went over and stood beside him, holding in a gasp. We were directly over the sea. White waves crashed into the rocky shore below, and the ocean stretched out as far as the eye could see.

Looking out, I felt insignificant and free at the same time.

"It's beautiful," I said. "I have never seen a view like this."

He turned his head to study me. "I knew you'd say that. I knew you'd understand this place. Most people don't."

The circles under his eyes were darker this morning. Given what had transpired months ago, back at my beehives, we were probably the last two people who should be baring our souls, but he didn't appear to have anyone else to whom he could talk. He couldn't speak to Erik on matters of the heart and certainly not to Mildreth, and Chloe was lost somewhere inside herself.

"Christophe, what is wrong?" I asked. "I can see you are troubled. Are you worried about the coming birth? Do you worry for Chloe's safety?"

At first, he seemed taken aback by the open questions, but then he answered, "No—yes, I do worry, but my main worry is Chloe's unhappiness here."

"You worry because she seems unhappy?"

Again, he hesitated. "You remember the things I said to you last summer?" Then he stopped, as if hesitant to tread on dangerous ground.

But I nodded. "Yes, of course. It's all right to speak of such things."

"My mother was a great deal like Chloe, lovely and admired. She grew up at court and she loved dancing and banquets and large gatherings. But she fell for my father and he brought her here." He paused and gazed back out over the sea. "Father watched her fade from the bright girl at court to a creature of misery. She saw no beauty and no thriving community. She saw herself cut off from all that mattered, a lonely prisoner in a stone keep. Soon Mildreth was born and then me. Father thought children might give her purpose, but she grew only worse."

I'd never asked how his mother died and a fear gripped me. "Did she grow ill from her sorrow?"

"No." He pointed to the turret across from this one, which was also high over the cliffs and sea. "When I was six years old, she threw herself from that tower. My father blamed himself and he never fully recovered."

"Oh, Christophe."

"So, when I asked you to marry me, I was not being selfish…or at least not entirely."

His words were hard for me to hear, but at least I understood him now. He did not simply fear his wife being unhappy. He feared her falling into a misery where death seemed preferable to life.

"What's done is done," I said finally. "You and Chloe are married and she lives here now. But she is more resilient than you think. We need to show her she can build a life here on her own terms."

"Is that possible?"

"Yes. You saw her yesterday at the market. She enjoyed herself."

"You think she needs to get out into the village more?"

I nodded. "And not only that. I have a few other ideas. Come to the great hall in the mid-afternoon and you'll see."

Something—perhaps a glimmer of hope—crossed his eyes. "All right."

* * * *

Not long after this, I was back down on the main floor and heading for the stairwell to go up to check on Chloe, when the boy I'd sent with my messages that morning came running up the passage.

"My lady."

I stopped. "Do you have replies?"

He handed me three notes. After reading them, I smiled and changed direction, heading for the kitchen. I'd not visited the kitchen of Whale's Keep before and found it a large area bustling with activity.

"You keep a close eye on that bread in the ovens," a large woman ordered a young girl. "I don't want it burned again."

"Yes, ma'am."

It was not difficult for me to spot the cook. The large woman turned with a scowl as I entered. But she took in my blue wool gown and loose, wavy hair.

"My lady?" she asked carefully.

"Do forgive me for intruding."

My apology surprised her. "You're not intruding."

Walking up to her, I said, "I am Lady Nicole, Lady Chloe's sister, come to help her until the child arrives."

"Her sister? Yes, I was told you were here. It's good of you to come."

There was warmth in her tone and I sensed kindness beneath her gruff manner.

"Thank you," I said. "I've invited a few of the merchant wives from the village to come for tea and embroidery this afternoon, and I was hoping you might allow me to use a corner of the kitchen to make some tarts."

"You want to make tarts?"

"Yes. I feel Lady Chloe needs the company of other women now, and I want to surprise her with a small gathering for tea. Are there any apples still to be had? She is fond of apple tarts."

The cook watched me for a long moment and then asked, "Does Lady Mildreth know of this?"

I straightened. "No."

This was the moment of truth. Mildreth held the power here. But my sense of the cook had been correct. "If Lady Chloe likes apple tarts," she said, "I'll make some. We've cinnamon and sugar, and I could bake some sweet dough twists as well."

"That would be perfect, but I'm glad to help."

"No, you'd best make yourself scarce in this kitchen. Leave it all to me. I'll have a proper tea ready by mid-afternoon. You send word and one of the girls will bring it all up."

I smiled. "Thank you."

* * * *

I waited until early afternoon to tell Chloe of my plan. But I wanted to give her time to choose a gown, should such a thing matter to her. At first she was dumbfounded. "Merchant wives? Here? For an embroidery party?"

"Yes, I enjoyed meeting the women yesterday in the village. They are all quite respectable and seemed taken with you. Your cook is preparing tarts and tea. We can arrange chairs by the hearth in the great hall."

"Tarts and tea?" she repeated.

"Yes."

Then she flowed into motion, choosing a green day gown and having me brush her hair. At the appointed time, we had chairs set in a half-circle near the hearth in the great hall. Chloe waited there, seated. I sent for the tea to be brought in and then I went out into the courtyard. My actions today were probably unprecedented here, and I wanted to make sure everything went smoothly.

Soon, four women came through the gatehouse, somewhat tentatively, and a few guards glanced in their direction. I walked to the women straightaway.

"Mistress Gabby," I said, holding out my hands to the woman in the lead. "It's so good of you to come."

Mistress Gabby was the wife of a wool merchant here on the island. She was in her late thirties and in the short time I'd observed in the village, she had seemed to command respect from the other women. She grasped my hands quickly and released them, still appearing tentative. And who could blame her?

"Thank you, my lady. We weren't sure what to think when your notes arrived."

The other three women were Mistress Judith, married to a wine merchant; Mistress Edna, married to a cheese maker; and Lacey, who was Edna's grown daughter.

Lacey looked around at the courtyard. "I've never been up here, my lady. And I didn't have no embroidery to bring, but I brought some socks I'm knitting. Will they do?"

"They'll be perfect. I don't have any embroidery either and I'll be working on a shirt for my father."

The women nodded and seemed to grow easier. I led them inside as we chatted. Upon our entry to the great hall, Chloe stood, and further greetings took place. Again, there was a little tension at first, but the women soon began asking how she fared, and she mentioned the baby was sitting low.

"Probably a girl then," said Mistress Judith. "Girls sit low."

Chloe smiled. "Please come and have some tea."

Two servants had set up a tea service. Apple tarts and cinnamon twists were arranged on porcelain platters.

"Look at this," Lacey said in delight. "Have you ever seen anything so fine?"

I poured tea and passed out small plates. Chloe asked polite questions about events in the village. Once we'd all eaten and sipped our fill, we pulled out various sewing or knitting projects. Chloe was working on a beautiful pillow cover of pink and sky blue roses.

I watched her when she thought I wasn't looking and I could see her coming to life. Perhaps these were not women of her class, but they *were* women and at their core, women understood each other. I wanted Chloe to see that even in this isolated place, she was not alone. There was company for her here should she choose to seek it out.

The six of us sewed, knitted, and visited for about an hour.

"So, Martha's husband hasn't been coming home at nights and he's been at the tavern," said Mistress Judith. "She near to fits trying to get him to come home. But—"

Just then, Christophe walked into the great hall and Judith fell silent.

He stood for a long moment taking in the tea and pastries on the table and the sight of us all gathered around the hearth.

"Nicole?" he asked me, but he sounded puzzled as opposed to disapproving.

"We are having tea and a good gossip," I answered. "And we could use a man's opinion. Do get yourself a tart and come gossip with us."

To his credit, Christophe walked to the table, got himself an apple tart, and dragged over a chair. All four of our visitors tensed up again. They'd probably not expected the lord of the island to join us.

"And what is the gossip?" he asked, sitting down.

Chloe said, "Apparently, Martha—from the candle shop—is having trouble with her husband. He has taken to staying late at the tavern and she doesn't know why. How do you think she might get him to remain at home?"

Christophe swallowed a bite of tart. "Has she asked him why he's staying away?"

"I'm not certain, my lord," Judith answered.

"Then she should ask him. He'll probably tell her a good deal more than she wants to hear."

The women broke into laughter and even Chloe smiled.

Christophe stretched out his legs and glanced over at Chloe's pillow cover. "That's pretty. I like the light blue roses."

She leaned forward to show it to him.

But as he pointed to a rose, Mildreth walked into the hall. At the sight before her, she froze. Her eyes settled first on Chloe showing Christophe her embroidery and then they moved to our visitors.

"What is all this?" she demanded.

Though Christophe normally seemed unaware of her cold tone, he frowned. "What do you mean?"

"I was not informed of visitors," Mildreth answered, her voice shaking with anger. She pointed to the tea service. "Where did all *that* come from?"

"All of what?" he asked. "Tea and a few tarts? Lady Chloe probably ordered it from the kitchen. Come and join us."

Suddenly, I was grateful for his presence. I thought Mildreth might be annoyed, but I'd not expected her to be enraged.

She glowered at Chloe in hatred.

"No. Thank you," Mildreth said. "Some of us have duties to attend."
Turning, she walked out.

The visiting women appeared stunned, but I shook my head at Lacey. "Not to worry. I forgot to tell her about our gathering and she prefers to be informed. Now, what were you saying about your new dog who eats too much?"

We continued visiting and sewing, but I knew Mildreth was against anything that might bring Chloe a scrap of happiness.

I knew she'd strike back.

I just needed to be ready.

Chapter 6

Though I expected some form of retribution from Mildreth, I didn't expect it to come so swiftly.

Dinner that night started out well enough. I arrived at the great hall to find Christophe, Chloe, Mildreth, Jordan, and Amanda already gathered.

"I hope I've not kept anyone waiting?" I asked.

"Not at all," Chloe answered.

As of yet, I'd not heard a word from either of the children and felt rather sorry for them. Mildreth did not strike me as a loving mother. Servants arrived carrying trays of food, but I'd eaten so many tarts earlier that I wasn't particularly hungry.

As we sat, I asked Christophe, "I've heard there are cattle on the island. From where did they come?"

"From where they came originally, or how they were transported, is unknown. Even my grandfather didn't know that story. We assume calves were brought over and carried up, but we've had cattle on the island for as long as anyone can remember."

"Do you keep horses?"

He nodded. "A few."

"Then are you teaching young Jordan to ride?"

Christophe blinked as if such a thought had never occurred to him. "To ride?"

"Of course. You are his uncle." I spoke directly to Jordan. "Would you like your uncle to teach you to ride?"

Jordan pulled back in his chair as if no one had ever spoken to him, but Mildreth offered me a level gaze.

"He is too young," she said.

"Erik told me he could ride before he could walk," Chloe said. "I imagine so could Christophe."

I don't believe she intended these comments as a slight, merely as an observation.

But hatred glowed from Mildreth's eyes. "And how are you feeling tonight after your…activities this afternoon?"

"I am well," Chloe answered carefully. "Thank you."

"I have been concerned for your health," Mildreth returned, "and feel it's best to employ a midwife now. I've spoken to a woman from the village, someone worthy of respect, and she has agreed to tend you."

Suddenly, I was on guard. "There's no need. My mother has served as a midwife since before I was born and I've assisted her many times. Part of the reason I've come is to act as Chloe's midwife."

"Of course, my dear," said Mildreth. "But Chloe may be carrying a boy, the heir to Whale's Keep. Such a birth happens only once in a generation. There is no reason why both you and a village midwife should not attend to Chloe." Turning to Christophe, she said, "Do you not agree, brother?"

Taking a bite of chicken, he said, "If you think it wise."

Chloe did not say a word through this exchange, but her eyes showed fear.

"I do," Mildreth answered. "More, this midwife would like to conduct an examination tomorrow, just to make sure all is well and to get an idea how soon the child might arrive."

And then I understood what she was doing. She was going to have a midwife in her own employ perform an examination that would most likely result in the revelation that Chloe's body was ready to give birth any day.

Even Christophe would have questions after that.

With bloodless lips, Chloe whispered, "I would prefer not."

"But it would be for your own good," Mildreth answered, "and the baby's."

When Chloe fell silent with her eyes on her plate, I realized that even at the height of her courage and strength, she would not have been able to give voice to objecting to the indelicacies of this situation.

But I was not squeamish about openly addressing elements of the human body.

Looking to Christophe, I said, "This would not be good for Chloe or the baby. Do you understand what Mildreth means by 'examination'? This midwife, a stranger, will put her fingers and possibly part of her hand up inside of Chloe."

Appalled, Christophe started at my blunt and rather vulgar description. Men were ignorant in such matters—but this was not their fault.

"As all seems well at present," I went on, "and Chloe seems to be heading toward a normal childbirth, I see no reason to subject her to such an indignity now. Do you?"

He shook his head. "No. I don't…" He trailed off and looked at Chloe. "What do you think?"

"I would prefer not," she repeated quietly and her distress was clear.

"Then, no," Christophe said. "Mildreth, tell your midwife that Nicole is skilled and she will see to the birth of the child."

Mildreth opened her mouth to argue, but closed it, staring at me. Her hatred had a new target.

* * * *

That night, after dinner, I sat with Chloe in her room, as fear caused her tremble.

"Mildreth knows," she whispered, sounding manic. "She *knows!*"

"She doesn't know," I said. "She only suspects."

"She's been taunting me for weeks now. She told me that Amanda was a little late in coming, but that Christophe held her the night she was born. Amanda had a full head of hair and tiny fingernails." Chloe's eyes shifted back and forth. "Then she told me Captain Fáuvel's wife had a child a month early. The child was not only small, but less formed, less developed. Christophe was on shore when that baby was born and he held it."

"What are you saying?"

"I'm saying Christophe knows the difference between an early and a full-term baby! And if Mildreth begins whispering poison in his ear, he will know the truth as soon as he sees my child."

I held a breath. I had known this would be Chloe's greatest danger, but I'd been contemplating a plan of perhaps having her fake an illness—which I would pronounce as contagious. I could say the illness brought on an early birth and I could use the fear of contagion to keep everyone away for at least a week, and then say that in spite of her illness, Chloe's milk came in quickly, and the child had been nursing well and was thriving. In this way, I believed we could keep Christophe from even questioning if the child was his.

But with Mildreth here, I doubted we could keep her or him away. She'd find some reason to come into Chloe's room—and to bring Christophe—as soon as the child was born. So if that plan would not work, something else would have to be arranged. Could I get Chloe out of the keep somehow? No. Christophe would never allow that.

If she couldn't be removed from the keep, perhaps…

Gripping my sister's hand, I said, "I have an idea, but it may take me a few days. Can you hold on a few more days?"

Still trembling, she touched her stomach. "I can. I just hope the child can wait." Her gaze drifted. "Nicole, do you know what the worst part of all this is?"

I shook my head, thinking the worst part would be fear of discovery.

"It's how much I miss home," she whispered. "Growing up, I couldn't wait to get away and go live my wonderful life someplace else. But every day now, sometimes all day, I ache for White Deer Lodge, our warm log home, my family, and our friends there. I miss Erik's laugh. I miss our mother and your meadow and your beehives. I long to go back there and never leave. How strange is that?"

Poor Chloe. I didn't find it strange at all.

But I wished she could see the beauty of this keep and this island.

* * * *

The next morning, I wrote a letter to Erik. At first I was worried about when I might be able to have it sent, but Christophe also had a letter for my father, so he had the messages rowed to shore after breakfast.

Around lunchtime, Chloe was resting, and so I wandered into the great hall to see if anyone might be gathering for a light meal. Christophe stood by the fire.

"Are you hungry, my lord?" I asked. "Should I ring for some bread and cheese?"

Turning, he said, "What? No tarts and tea and women from the village today?" But his voice was light and I could tell he was teasing.

I smiled. "Not today."

"I wanted to thank you for that gathering. It was kind of you. Chloe enjoyed herself."

"Mildreth was not pleased."

I wondered if I might broach the subject of Mildreth with him. She was capable of speaking poison in his ear. But perhaps I could plant a few doubts of her motives?

Before he could speak again, a man in his late twenties, wearing armor and a gray tabard—and wet up the waist—came striding into the great hall.

Christophe frowned. "Lieutenant?"

"Forgive the intrusion, my lord," the man said, "but I have news that couldn't wait. A party of raiders somehow got through our lines several miles up shore undetected. They made it all into Chastain."

"Chastain?" Christophe nearly gasped.

"Yes, my lord. The village was attacked. But word didn't reach Captain Fáuvel until the attack was well over and the raiders were gone. Their boats are gone. Anyone they took cannot be retrieved."

Christophe put the back of one hand to his mouth. "No," he breathed.

I could only imagine what he was feeling: That he had failed his people. Of course he'd done his best to protect them, but my father always felt at fault if any of our people suffered.

Christophe's gaze sharpened. "What about the village? What is the damage?"

"I don't know, my lord. The messenger who arrived was badly injured. He could only tell me what I've told you. Captain Fáuvel sent thirty men on fast horses immediately, but he's in the process of preparing a larger contingent to go and provide help to survivors. He wants to make sure we have adequate supplies to offer assistance when we get there, and we may not be ready until morning."

Nodding, Christophe said, "Good. I'll need to make some preparations here, but I'll take a boat over before dark this evening. We'll leave at first light."

As he spoke, a thought hit me like lightning and I saw my chance.

"My lord," I said. "There will be wounded people at Chastain. My mother sent a box of medicines and I can quickly put together some bandages. If you take me with you, I can work as a healer."

"Take you?"

"Yes, I would be safe riding at your side, under your protection." Guilt rose inside as I watched his eyes light up at the prospect of me riding beside him and needing his protection. But I didn't stop. "This is not a rushed or dangerous mission to cut off any raiders. It is a well-planned mission to go and offer food and aid. I could be of help to you."

I knew exactly what I was doing: Appealing to his love for me and painting an image of the two of us working together to help his people.

Still, he hesitated. "What of Chloe? She may need you."

"The child will not come this early and we will be gone only a matter of days. I would like to help and the people of Chastain will be in need of a skilled healer."

Slowly, he nodded and then turned to the wet lieutenant. "Take a boat back to shore and inform the captain that Lady Nicole and I will join him at the barracks before dark. Have him prepare a private room for her. We'll leave with the contingent in the morning."

"Yes, my lord."

The lieutenant walked out, leaving Christophe and me alone.

"I have a number of things to attend before I can leave," he said. "But we need to make the crossing before dark. Can you be ready?"

"I'll be ready."

Guilt and relief warred inside me, but nothing would make me stop now.

* * * *

Up in her room, Chloe's eyes widened. "You're leaving the island with Christophe?"

"Yes. We need to get him away from here for a little while."

"And you?"

"I have to go with him. On his own, he'd get back here as quickly as possible. If I'm with him, I can find ways to keep in Chastain. You are ready to give birth any time and I'll try to keep him away for a least a week, longer if I can."

"No! Nicole, you cannot leave me here alone with Mildreth."

Grasping her hand, I said, "You won't be alone. I've written to Erik this morning and I've asked him to either bring or send Jenny straightaway. He'll have her in a saddle as soon as he reads my letter."

"Jenny?"

"Yes. She's assisted Mother and me with births. She'll know what to do and she is loyal to you. More...her family lives inland but near the coast. She nearly wept in relief when Christophe sent those two hundred soldiers to help guard our coastline. She'd do anything to protect your marriage."

We were both standing, but Chloe sank down onto a couch. "You've thought this through."

"Yes. I've been mulling possible ways to get Christophe off the island, but this chance is better than any of my ideas. And if I'm with him, I can keep him away."

"What about Mildreth?"

Walking over, I sat beside her. "We can manage Mildreth too, but it won't be kind and you'll need to do exactly what I tell you."

She listened.

* * * *

Late that afternoon, not long before dusk, carrying a small chest of medicine and supplies, I hurried out into the courtyard to meet Christophe. I wore a thick wool gown, my fur-trimmed cloak, and leather boots.

Though he was waiting for me in the courtyard, wearing chain armor and a gray tabard, he was arguing with Mildreth.

"What you do mean, you're leaving?" she demanded, her voice carrying.

"Chastain was attacked. I must go."

"And you'd leave your lady, who may be carrying a son and your heir? Did Nicole put you up to this?"

"Put me up to what? Lady Nicole is coming with me."

For the first time since my arrival, Mildreth's face shifted to confusion. "She's going with you?"

I walked out to join them. "Yes. There will be injured in need of a healer."

Her confusion only deepened, but it was colored with suspicion now. "And you would leave Lady Chloe here in my care?"

"Of course," I answered. "I am comforted leaving her in such good hands."

Mildreth breathed slowly, clearly trying to figure me out. But she would not. I had planned for several contingencies.

To my surprise, Christophe leaned down and kissed the side of her face. "We must go, Mildreth. Take care of Chloe."

"I will, brother."

Christophe took the heavy chest from my hands. "Ready?"

"Ready," I answered.

We headed out the gatehouse and through the village, toward the stone steps leading downward.

Chapter 7

I felt safe with Christophe.

He and three other men rowed me to the shore. We had supper at the barracks with the captain and then Christophe went off to check on supplies being loaded into wagons for transport to Chastain. I was shown to a small, private room near the front of the barracks.

Alone in the room, I tried not to think on all that could go wrong. What if I was off in my counting and I kept Christophe away for a week or more, and Chloe had still not delivered when we returned? There would be little chance of getting him away from the island again.

But all I could do now was press onward. To me, my sister looked ready to give birth at any moment.

Though I feared I would not sleep, I dropped off almost right away and was awakened the next morning by male voices calling to each other.

"Get that load tied down!" someone called.

Quickly, I dressed and hurried out of my room and through the barracks. Stepping outside, I saw the boathouse and the sea straight ahead, but in-between, the cleared land was alive with activity. Twenty-one wagons had been piled with supplies of food, blankets, lumber, and tools.

At least a hundred soldiers were preparing to either ride horses or drive wagons.

Christophe stood conferring with the captain near a wagon loaded with casks and bags. At the sight of me, he broke off and strode over.

"Would you prefer to travel by wagon or ride a horse?" he asked.

"I'll ride a horse, but I'd prefer to ride near you," I answered, knowing that was what he wanted to hear. Then I looked around again. "Do we need all these men?"

"Yes. If necessary, they'll function as a work crew to rebuild homes. We take care of our own here."

So did my family, but I didn't say that.

Christophe pointed to a table near the barracks. "There's tea and biscuits. Be sure to eat before we leave."

"I will."

In a short amount of time, we'd eaten, tied down the remaining supplies, and were ready to go. My chest of medicines and bandages were in the first wagon. Christophe led a small chestnut mare to me and laced his hands together.

"Up," he said.

With rather a lack of grace, I stepped into his hands and clambered up.

Then he mounted a taller black horse and our large group headed up shore. In spite of everything, of all my deceptions of Christophe and worry for my sister, I couldn't help being affected by being part of this group setting off to help a village.

And looking up at the side of Christophe's face, I couldn't help admiring him. He was a good lord, a good leader.

"How far up shore will we go?" I asked.

"Only a few miles. Then we'll turn inland." He shook his head. "I cannot think how these raiders managed to land on shore, disembark, head inland all the way to Chastain, attack the town, and then get back to the shore without any of our troops ever seeing the boats."

I had no answers. "Where do you think these men come from?"

"I don't know. The captain believes they come from across the sea. And yet their boats do not seem large enough for sea passage."

I pondered this and we rode in comfortable silence.

Christophe and I were near the front of the caravan, and I knew we looked like a lord and his lady. Though I tried to stop such thoughts from rising, I couldn't help wondering how all of this might have played out had I accepted Christophe that morning at the beehives.

I *would* be his lady and the mistress of Whale's Keep.

Though I had never wished to marry anyone, Christophe was different. He was kind and strong and any woman would be beyond fortunate to have him for a husband. Why had I not seen this sooner?

Quickly, I pushed away these thoughts. It wasn't that I hadn't seen his qualities, but rather that I would never have done anything to injure my sister.

I still wouldn't.

A few miles up shore, I could hear the rush of a river flowing into the ocean. There was a bridge across and a narrow road leading inland.

We took the road inland.

"How far now?" I asked.

"A little over a half day's ride. We should reach Chastain by early afternoon."

I'd been hoping the town was further away. Once there, I'd need to start looking for reasons to keep Christophe from leaving.

* * * *

As he'd predicted, we reached Chastain in the early afternoon, but nothing could have prepared me for the sight. It had been a good-sized village, and at least a quarter of the buildings had been burned.

Some cleanup was underway, but there were dead cattle and horses lying about the outskirts. People still in shock were limping around as if uncertain what to do. The captain had sent some troops the day before, probably to make the people feel a little safer and to offer assurances that more help was on the way. Hope could do much in the face of tragedy.

Yet, as we arrived, people turned to watch us with dazed expressions. I could only imagine what had happened here.

A tall de Fiore soldier came walking from the edge of town, moving straight toward us. Christophe and the captain both jumped off their horses. The man stopped and nodded in respect to both of them. "My lord. Sir. We know how the raiders got through."

"How?" Christophe asked.

"They didn't leave any boats on the shore. They came straight up the river."

The captain breathed in sharply. "That's not possible."

"It is, sir," the man said. "People here are all giving the same account. The raiders came upriver in three boats, ravaged Chastain, and then headed back downriver and out to sea."

Christophe turned to the captain. "Boats that can cross the sea and move up rivers?"

This frightened me on more than one level. Back home, we had a river running right past White Deer Lodge.

Still on my horse, I said softly, "Christophe, my father needs to be warned."

Turning, his face awash with concern, he reached up to lift me down. "Yes. I'll have someone sent right away."

"Thank you."

Though I knew little to nothing of sea travel, even I had a difficult time imagining a boat that could cross an ocean and traverse a river.

Christophe spoke directly to the captain. "Some of the cleanup can wait. Our first two priorities should be distributing food and seeing to the wounded. You oversee distribution of food and I'll help Lady Nicole set up someplace where she can begin tending injuries. I'll try the common house first if it's still standing."

"Yes, my lord."

Walking to the first wagon, Christophe lifted my chest filled with supplies, and then he walked down the main path of the town. I trotted along behind. He appeared to know where he was going, and I followed him past charred buildings and people who were moving toward our caravan of supplies.

"It's still there," Christophe said in relief, leading onward to a large log building with a double front door.

"My lord!" a voice called.

A stocky man with silver hair limped toward us. He had a dark bruise on his forehead.

"Antoine, it is good to see you," answered Christophe, sounding even more relieved. "Nicole, this is Antoine de Portiers, Chastain's elderman. Antoine, this is the lady Nicole Montagna, my wife's sister."

The man offered an exhausted nod. "I wish we could meet under better circumstances."

"My corporal tells me the raiders came upriver in their boats," Christophe said.

Antoine de Portiers nodded. "There was no stopping them." He glanced at me, hesitated, and then said, "They took eleven of our women."

Christophe's body tensed. "We'll find a way to stop them if we have to block the rivers." After a moment, he collected himself and said, "Lady Nicole is a trained healer. I'm going to help her get set up in the common house. Can you spread word for people to bring their wounded here?"

As Antoine listened, his eyes were wet. "Yes. Good. I'm glad you've come."

"I'm sorry it took us until this afternoon. We were putting supplies together."

Antoine began limping away. "Don't be sorry."

"I'll want to look at his leg later," I said to Christophe.

Together, we went inside and I thought this space would work well. There were long tables and plenty of room.

"We're probably going to need splints," I said. "A slender chair leg can work well. I may need you to break up some chairs."

"All right."

Picking a table, I opened my chest of supplies and began setting up. For the time since arriving, I wished my mother were with me. Though I knew many of her skills, I did not know them all.

But I was determined to help here and do my best. Among the medicines my mother had sent, I was most glad for the bottle of poppy syrup to help numb pain; the jar of adder's-tongue ointment for cleaning wounds; and the mixture of ground garlic and ginger in vinegar, for staving off infection.

Not long after, people began arriving and Christophe began to pick out those in the most need and place them at the front of the line. Right away, I was faced with a mother carrying a five-year-old girl with a badly broken arm.

"My lord," I called, thinking it best to be formal among so many of his people. "I'll need two small splints." Holding up my hands, I illustrated the correct size.

He nodded and began breaking up a chair.

While he worked on that, I turned back to the mother and child. The little girl was frightened and her mother appeared caught between hope and caution. I needed to remember these people had been through a traumatic experience.

"Will her arm be crippled?" the mother asked.

Gently feeling around the break, I answered, "The bone needs to be set, but I think it will heal."

Opening the bottle of poppy syrup, I poured a tablespoon and held it near the girl's mouth. "Can you drink this for me? It will make you sleepy, but your arm won't hurt so much."

She swallowed the spoonful and I gave her another.

Looking up at the mother, I said, "We need to wait a little, to let the syrup take effect and dull the pain. Then I can set the bone."

The woman began to relax a little. "Thank you."

While the poppy syrup took effect, I glanced at the next two injured people, both with wounds that would need to be stitched in order to heal properly. But neither was bleeding badly—as any people with gushing wounds would have died the day of the attack. I tried not to think on that.

Christophe brought me the small splints and we laid the little girl on a table. He held her shoulders and talked to her quietly as I readied to set the bone in her arm. Glancing up at him, I nodded once.

"We brought some fresh apples," he said to her. "Perhaps your mother can make you a tart."

I snapped the bone into place. She jumped but did not cry out. Then I set the splints and began wrapping them to her arm. Once this was done, we took a curtain from one of the windows and used it to fashion a sling.

Touching the mother's shoulder, I said, "I'll check on her tomorrow, but so long as the splints remain secure, her arm will heal."

"Thank you," she said again.

After this, I began cleaning wounds with the adder's-tongue ointment, then sewing the wounds, and then applying the vinegar and garlic mix to stave off infection. I set and splinted three more broken bones. Christophe remained with me the whole time, and he did whatever I asked.

By sundown, we'd seen to everyone in dire need and I was exhausted.

"That's enough for now," Christophe said, looking at me.

"I'll want to check on most of these people tomorrow."

"I know."

After cleaning up, we headed back to the caravan of wagons and horses. The captain and his men had done a good job of distributing food, but rather than troubling the townspeople for lodging, the soldiers had set up a camp outside the town, and several of them were cooking pots of stew over open fires.

For supper, Christophe and I ate bowls of stew while sitting on the back edge of a wagon.

"Is the food all right?" he asked.

"It's the best thing I've ever tasted."

He smiled. His smiles were so rare that this one touched me.

"You were astonishing today," he said. "I've never seen anything like that."

"You should see my mother in action. Her stitches are better than mine."

"You did well."

His praise meant a great deal to me. I cared for his opinion and his feelings, and this only increased my guilt over the reason I'd brought him here.

That night, he pitched a small tent and had me crawl inside onto a bedroll. Then he laid his own bedroll just outside. "I'll sleep right here," he said. "You'll be safe."

I always felt safe with him.

* * * *

The next four days were a blur.

There was so much work to be done and I had no trouble keeping Christophe at the village. I checked on my patients every day to make sure wounds and bones were healing. He helped to clean out burned homes and shops and to start rebuilding new ones.

I helped to prepare and bury the dead.

We set up some communal cooking in the common house and I also helped with meals. The most confusing element of all this was that everyone called Christophe "my lord" and they all called me "my lady." None of them had ever seen Chloe and they viewed me as their lady, as the lady of Whale's Keep.

At first, both he and I tended to correct this, but then we just…stopped.

It was not uncommon for me to hear someone call, "Have you see my lady?"

I allowed myself to become lost in the illusion that I was their lady and that my place was at Christophe's side—and his place was at mine. Though I knew it was wrong, I could see him doing the same thing.

But then, on the morning of the fifth day, though, he said, "I think the captain has things under control here and I don't want to leave Mildreth managing everything and looking after Chloe for too long."

Mildreth.

Chloe.

The world waited. But I hoped to keep Christophe away from the keep as long as possible. If the child had come in our absence, every day that passed would make a difference.

"There's a woman here who is with child and near the time of giving birth," I said. "Her husband was killed in the raid and the village lost its midwife. Could we not wait a little longer?"

"Yes. Of course."

He agreed so readily that I wondered how much he wanted to go back.

The next day, the woman went into labor. I delivered the baby and then wanted to stay a few days to help them both. Christophe agreed.

In the end, I kept him away from the keep for eight days, but then we had to start back.

* * * *

As Christophe and three other men rowed us from the shore to the island, a knot began forming in my stomach. I'd had no contact with Chloe and had no idea what I was about to find.

Though quiet by nature, Christophe had been unusually quiet on the journey home, and my mind had been occupied with worry over whether or not my desperate ruse would succeed or fail spectacularly.

As the boat reached the bit of passable shore on the island, men came out to pull us partially in. Christophe jumped out and reached back in, lifting me out and setting my feet on solid ground.

"Are you up for the climb now, or do you need to rest?" he asked.

"I'm fine. Let's go up."

We passed through the gatehouse and started up. This time, the climb didn't feel quite so long—perhaps because I knew what to expect. Before I knew it, we were passing through the upper gatehouse and making our way through the village toward the keep.

Along the way, people greeted Christophe and asked about Chastain. He stopped several times to make assurances that everything possible was being done to help survivors and that he and the captain were making plans to ensure that such an attack would not happen again.

Finally, we made it to the courtyard and then through the front doors of the keep.

I drew in a long breath, anxious to learn what awaited us.

As we stepped into the foyer, two people came walking down the main passage toward us: Erik and Jenny.

Christophe stopped in alarm. "Erik—what is it? Have your people been attacked?"

Shaking his head, Erik smiled. "No, nothing like that. Nicole had written to me that Chloe was missing her maid, Jenny, so I thought to bring her. That's all."

"Oh," Christophe said in relief. "That was good of you."

"But there is news," Erik said. "You have a son. He came a few days after you left. We had only arrived that day ourselves."

A son. The knot in my stomach tightened.

For moment, Christophe didn't respond. Then his alarm returned. "Chloe delivered? So soon? Is she all right? Is the child all right?"

Erik held up one hand, still smiling. "They are both well. Chloe took a fall and it caused the child to come early, yet no harm was done."

"The child was small, my lord," Jenny put in. "But he was born nearly a week ago now and my lady's milk came in strong. He has been feeding and gaining weight."

Clasping Christophe's shoulder, Erik said, "I've been watching him put on weight every day."

"I'm so glad you were here," Christophe answered, embracing Erik. "I didn't know. How could I have known? I need to see them both."

He ran off down the passage and Erik met my gaze.

I should have been elated and wildly relieved. This could not have gone better. Erik and Jenny had arrived the day Chloe went into labor. Jenny had clearly delivered the baby and now she and Erik had said all the right words to Christophe: That Chloe had a fall to bring on early labor and the child had been born small, but had been eating well for days and putting on weight. Erik had been acting as guardian to the young heir of Whale's Keep. Christophe trusted Erik more than anyone in the world.

There would be no question in Christophe's mind that the child was his.

Slowly, I walked away, past Erik, and followed the path through the keep up to Chloe's room.

There, I walked into a pretty sight. She sat in a chair with the baby in her lap. Christophe was on his knees beside her, looking down with an expression of unconditional love.

"Look at him," he whispered. "He looks just like Erik and your father."

"He does," Chloe answered.

Entering the room, I went over to see the new arrival. He had a pale skin and head full of red-blond hair. Even as an infant, his features already resembled the men in my family. He was a son of White Deer Lodge.

"Where is Mildreth?" Christophe asked. "Did she help with the delivery?"

"No, I wish she had," Chloe answered. "Poor Mildreth. She's been ill, sick to her stomach for a week. She's not even seen him yet. But don't fear. I've been kept informed and she is recovering."

"I'll go and see her," he said, "but I want a few more minutes here."

So even that part of my plan had gone well. I'd instructed Chloe to dose Mildreth's tea with four drops of an areial roots mixture. One drop of this mixture could be used to make someone vomit—to help with a case of accidental poisoning. Four drops would make someone sick for a week.

"Could I hold him?" Christophe asked.

"Of course you can," Chloe said. "He won't break."

Carefully, Christophe lifted the baby and held him out for me to see. It was like looking at a tiny version of Erik or my father. I knew his eyes would stay blue. There was nothing of Julian Belledini in this child. Christophe's face was alight with love. "Chloe, have you named him?"

"No. I thought it best to wait for you."

"Gideon," he said instantly. "After your father. Gideon de Fiore. It's a strong name." He beamed at me. "Nicole, I have a son."

I tried to smile at him, but the knot in my stomach only grew tighter.

Planning a deception was one thing. Watching the result was quite another.

* * * *

Two days later, Erik said he needed to get back home—and that I should come with him. Though I was sorry to leave Chloe, I was not sorry to be able to go home and try to forget the part I had played here.

Shortly before we left, I went up to say good-bye to Chloe in her rooms. She sat in a chair, gazing out a narrow window. The room was quiet.

"Where's Gideon?" I asked, looking around for the cradle—which was nowhere in sight.

Turning her head, she seemed to take a moment to recognize me. "Where is Gideon? In the nursery, I think."

"You've put him in the nursery? So soon."

"I hired a wet nurse. She has him."

Walking in, I said, "Erik, Jenny, and I are about to leave."

"I wish you would stay."

"I know, but we all need to get back home. Mother has been missing me and I have duties at home."

"Yes. Home." She paused. "Thank you for everything you've done for me. No one would have stood by me as you did."

But she didn't sound thankful. She sounded alone.

"It's going to be all right, Chloe," I said. "Christophe already loves the child and he will be kind to you. Mildreth has lost and she knows it. Christophe would never hear a word spoken against you or Gideon now. Your honor is safe and you are safe."

She nodded. "Yes. Safe."

Not knowing what else to say, I kissed the side of her face. "I'll write soon."

Then I left the room and headed back down the passage.

Erik was waiting for me out in the courtyard and I made my way out of the keep directly, trying not to think of Chloe. Once outside, I breathed in the cold morning air, but paused at the sight of Christophe standing with Erik and Jenny. He turned his head at the sound of my steps and at the sight of me, his haunted eyes flashed such a look of longing and regret that I nearly backed up.

Then the look was gone.

"Your trunk is ready to be carried down?" he asked. "You've not forgotten anything?"

The words seemed so empty and I couldn't help thinking of our days at Chastain, working side by side as lord and lady.

"No, I've not forgotten anything," I answered.

Tightly, he nodded once, and I walked past him to join Erik.

"I'll join you at the lodge next month," Christophe told Erik. "We should do another full patrol of your lands, make sure no other raiders have made their way upriver."

"Agreed," Erik answered. "Come when the weather starts to warm a little. Send word if you can and maybe to stay a few days before we leave. Father enjoys your company."

Stay a few days.

I looked ahead at the years of my life, of Christophe coming to the lodge for polite family visits, of having to sit across from him at a table, knowing I'd betrayed him, that I'd help to make him believe another man's son was his own. Could I bear it? In my ears, I kept hearing his voice from that morning last summer at the beehives.

This is our only chance. If you refuse me now, we will both end up living the wrong lives.

Perhaps we were living the wrong lives, and I was the one who had brought this to pass.

But in my heart, I knew my actions had not been wrong.

In the grand scheme, this was the best possible outcome. Yes, I had deceived a good man, a man I loved. His heir was not his son and my part in that was unforgivable. But there was a great deal more at stake than the de Fiore bloodline.

My own people were safe, guarded by Christophe's troops.

Chloe was safe.

The child was safe... and Christophe loved him.

All things considered, I'd done the right thing.

* * * *

The courtyard around me disappeared. I found myself once again inside my bedroom and staring into the right panel of the three-tiered mirror.

Dropping to my knees, I thought on all that I had just lived through.

But the dark-haired woman was now looking out from the center panel.

"What was that?" I cried

"That would be the outcome of the first choice," she answered. "But now those memories will vanish and you'll go back to the beginning, to the moment of the crisis, to live out the second choice."

"Wait!" I cried. "I'll not remember anything of what I just saw?"

"Back to the beginning once more," she answered. "To live out the second choice."

My mind went blank and the bedroom vanished.

The Second Choice:
Silence

Chapter 8

I was standing in Chloe's closet, feeling disoriented, as if I'd forgotten something and needed to remember. Peeking out a crack between the closet door and the wall, I saw my sister standing in her bedroom with Julian Belledini.

"You liar," she said. "You made me believe you wanted to spend your life with me."

He stepped away from her. "And I did. I do. But not like this. Marry Lord Christophe. You have no choice now. In three years' time, you'll thank me."

Turning, he walked out.

Chloe put both hands to her mouth to stifle a sob.

Then I remembered. I'd come in here to find her dress from the banquet, so that it might be laundered, and I'd heard... I'd overheard that she was carrying Julian's child.

A few moments later, one of her servants called to her through the door. She composed herself as best she could and left the room. I remained in the closet, trying to let myself fully comprehend what had just happened, what I had just learned. Chloe now had no other option than to marry Christophe.

Could I allow this to happen?

Panic rose inside me. I couldn't betray Christophe and yet I could not betray Chloe either. What should I do?

Almost instantly, panic turned to anger. Why had I heard any of this? I should *not* have been in this closet. Had Chloe's gown not been hung back up by one of the housemaids, had Jenny not remembered that it needed to be washed, had I not heard Chloe retching on the night of the banquet and therefore been so determined to come find the gown, I would not have come here.

Had one small event played out differently, I would be ignorant of this awful truth and I would not be faced with the decision of what to do with what I had learned.

And then I knew the answer. This was not a decision for me to make. Were I not in this closet, I would be as blissfully ignorant as everyone else and fate would take its own course. I could not choose between Chloe and Christophe and therefore, I would not.

I would pretend that I'd never left the laundry room, that I'd heard nothing. I would keep this secret to myself.

* * * *

The following few weeks felt long, as preparations for Chloe's wedding were in full swing.

The worst moments came in the evenings, as Julian often joined my family for dinner, looking handsome as always, smiling as if all was right with the world, leaning back in his chair and stretching his legs out comfortably under our dining room table. I had to listen to him making polite conversation with my father and brother over the table. Chloe could barely look at him and when she did, her eyes shone with pain.

I was sure either my mother or Erik would notice.

But no one did, or if they did, they most likely thought it a harmless girlish crush, nothing so unusual with a man like Julian, and that Chloe would soon find her peace as the lady of Whale's Keep. Everyone wanted her to marry Christophe and no one was willing to say a word to interfere with that outcome.

Steadfastly, I held to my decision of pretending I'd heard nothing, that I knew nothing, for to acknowledge such truth would mean taking action and taking action would mean choosing between Chloe and Christophe. I could not choose one over the other.

The days passed.

Finally, the end of the month came and the wedding was upon us, and I breathed in relief. Once Chloe was married, this feeling of limbo would be over and events would be out of my hands. No matter how things played out after the wedding, it would be up to fate then and not up to me.

The night before the wedding, Christophe arrived at the lodge and we all met him in the round courtyard, but only his guards accompanied him.

"Your sister will not be attending?" my mother asked him, puzzled. "I've had the best guest room prepared for you and Chloe, for tonight. But I reserved second-best guest room for Lady Mildreth."

"No," he answered. "She does not leave the island."

That evening, we had a fine dinner of baked salmon and red potatoes in the gathering hall and a number of wedding guests joined us for the celebration. Christophe barely spoke to me and the few times he glanced at me, I saw a mix of anger and longing in his face. Julian sat across the table from him, inquiring about the troops that would be sent. Chloe spoke little and ate less. I wondered if my parents or Erik noticed that the evening hardly resembled a joyous meal on the night before a wedding. Could they be so oblivious?

But when the meal ended and we all filed from the gathering hall to head for our beds—as we had an early day tomorrow—Erik drew me back to speak to me alone.

"Nicole..." he began, sounding almost anxious. "Have you seen Chloe and Julian attempting to meet each other in private?"

I went still. This was the last thing I wanted him to ask me. He was not so oblivious after all. But I was determined to pretend that I'd not been in that closet. Telling Erik would mean taking an action, and I would not alter fate simply because I'd overheard something I should not.

"In private?" I repeated. "What do you mean?"

"Nothing. Forget that I asked." Leaning down, he kissed the top of my head. "I'll see you in the morning."

That night, in bed, I heard Chloe in the adjoining room, softly crying herself to sleep. What did she regret most: Losing Julian, being forced to marry Christophe, or that she would have to deceive her husband into accepting a child that was not his own?

I shed silent tears, wishing I could help her, but there was nothing I could do to fix any of this.

* * * *

The following morning, I barely saw Chloe, as I was busy overseeing food preparations in the kitchens and inspecting flowers in the gathering hall. I knew my mother would be busy helping Chloe to prepare and I tried to handle as many of the other duties as possible.

There were several small issues with our guests. Colonel Régnier and his wife had come all the way from Lascaùx to attend the wedding, but they could barely stand each other and after a single night together, they were demanding separate rooms.

Lady Richelle de Miennes was offended that she had been given a room so near to the servant quarters, but thankfully—since Christophe's sister had not come with him—I was able to change Lady Richelle's quarters and have her moved into the second-best guest room.

The wedding was scheduled for mid-afternoon, to give plenty of time for celebrating afterward and by the early afternoon, I found myself hurrying to the adjoining rooms I shared with Chloe to check on her.

I arrived to an unexpected situation.

Approaching the door, I heard my mother. "But, my dear…we had decided on your pale amber satin. Jenny spent half the night ironing the skirt." Her voice was tense and I'd never heard her use such a sharp tone with Chloe.

"No," Chloe answered flatly. "I'm wearing this one."

Entering the room, I found my mother, Chloe, Jenny, and two other maids inside. Chloe's fine amber satin gown lay on the bed. It was a lovely dress with a high, square neckline, capped sleeves, and a train. The color was light, almost cream, and it brought out a hint of red in her blond hair.

But she stood before her full-length mirror in the same green silk she'd worn to the banquet. While this gown was perfect for a dance, it had a low, V-shaped neckline and a simple skirt. It was not a wedding gown.

Besides, I'd been told green was bad luck for a wedding: the color of envy.

"You are so lovely in the amber satin," Mother pressed. "Please, just try it on."

"No," Chloe repeated. "This one."

Our mother sighed. "Very well. Sit down and let me put up your hair."

"No," Chloe said again. "Just brush it out. I'll wear it down."

And then I realized what she was doing. She wanted to appear exactly as she had on that night when she spent the entire evening dancing with Julian. I did not know why, but I wondered if this was her last act of defiance. She wanted to marry Julian, not Christophe. And yet she was trapped. Julian had abandoned her and she was not of a nature to become an object of pity, the cast-off mother of an illegitimate child, shunned from all society.

Christophe was her only option. Becoming the lady of Whale's Keep was her only option.

And yet, on the day of her wedding, she was dressing for Julian.

It was not a good omen.

* * * *

The wedding itself went smoothly for the most part.

Our gathering hall was decorated with dozens of white and yellow roses.

Father had brought in a magistrate from Lascaùx and a number of noble guests were with us to partake in this joining of the house of Montagna with the house of de Fiore. Julian stood in a place of honor near the front of the hall. He wore the same sleeveless black tunic from the night of the banquet.

Christophe wore the blue tunic with the silver thread that I'd made for him.

Though my mother had encouraged me to wear the lavender gown, I couldn't bring myself to put it on and chose a simple tan muslin instead. Upon walking into the hall and seeing both Christophe and Julian, I was glad for my decision. It wouldn't do to have all four of us wearing the same clothes from the night of the banquet.

Chloe was beautiful in her emerald green silk, slender as a river reed with her shining hair hanging down her back. With her head high, she joined Christophe near the hearth of our gathering hall. My family and all our guests stood behind them.

"Does anyone have any reason why these two should not be joined in marriage?" asked the magistrate.

Both Erik and my father appeared tense. Erik glanced at Julian and my father glanced at me first, and then Christophe.

I would not allow myself to even think on the question.

When no one offered an objection to the marriage, the magistrate went on.

"Do you, Christophe de Fiore, swear to love this woman, to protect her heart, to give her your loyalty, and to care for her all the days of your life?"

"I swear," Christophe answered.

"Do you, Chloe Montagna, swear to love this man, to protect his heart, to give him your loyalty, and to care for him all the days of your life?"

She hesitated. These were sacred vows, and she was promising to protect his heart and give him her loyalty.

Standing beside me, my father watched her.

"I swear," Chloe said quietly.

They were married.

A great feast followed the ceremony. Later, Christophe and Chloe were cheered as they were seen off to spend their first night as a wedded couple in the best guest room of White Deer Lodge. I could not help wondering what Julian was thinking as he watched them leave the hall.

Two days later, Christophe lifted Chloe onto the back of a horse, and they rode out of the courtyard.

Julian stood with my family to wave good-bye.

My sister was gone.

I was torn between mourning and relief. She had been in my life since the day I was born and I felt her loss keenly. But at least her fate was out of my hands now. She had made her own choices, and I'd allowed those choices to unfold without interference.

My decision to do nothing, to remain silent, had been correct.

What was done was done, and any part I might have played in all this was over.

Chapter 9

Christophe sent two hundred soldiers to guard our coastline. They were as skilled as promised, and for the first time in several years, I could see my father breathing easily.

Summer turned into autumn.

Word arrived from Whale's Keep that Chloe and Christophe were expecting a child in mid-spring. My parents rejoiced at this news. Autumn turned into winter. We celebrated my eighteenth birthday. Then, before I knew it, winter was on the edge of turning into spring.

I wrote to Chloe nearly every week, but sometimes it was hard for me to chat of daily life here at the lodge. Though I struggled not to, I found myself counting months in my head and wondering if Chloe carried a boy or a girl.

Still, she was sorely missed here.

Her absence left a hole that Mother and I did our best to fill, but neither of us were skilled in entertaining other noblewomen—or at hosting tea or embroidery parties to gossip. I began to realize that most of the other women found us rather odd, and they commented on my mother's "eccentric" habit of bringing medicines to our villagers.

Then one evening in late winter, not long before the dinner hour, a messenger arrived from Whale's Keep and Jenny brought a letter to my room.

"Word from Lady Chloe."

"Oh, thank you, Jenny." Hurrying over, I took the letter and sat down to read it.

My dear Nicole,

Although by Christophe's reckoning, the child will not arrive until mid-spring, I am growing heavy somewhat early and find myself a little fearful of the coming birth.

It would be a great comfort if you could convince Father to let you come and stay with me.

I know I could face what's to come if I had you with me.

Love,

Chloe

I read this short missive several times. Chloe had never written me such a note. For her, this was the equivalent of begging. She was begging me to come.

This left me feeling torn. Though I ached to comfort her, to help her, if I went to Whale's Keep, I would become part of her and Christophe's fates. But reading the letter again, I heard the loneliness and the fear between the lines.

I could not refuse. She was my sister.

At present there were no noble guests visiting the lodge, as few people traveled at this time of year, and so as opposed to eating in the gathering hall, our family had taken to meeting for dinner in our small private dining room near to the kitchens.

After hiding the letter, I donned a cloak, left my room, and made my way down the passage and out the back door. Two of the great log constructions at the lodge served as residence for my family, and the dining room and kitchens were in the second building.

Going in the front doors, I headed through the entryway, past a staircase, and then through a tall archway into our dining room. Mother, Father, and Erik were already seated and I was the last to arrive.

"Am I late?" I asked.

"No, my girl," Mother answered. "It's been cold out today and I think the rest of us were early."

"I've had a letter from Chloe," I said. "She would like me to come and join her at Whale's Keep until the baby comes. I should like to go."

My father looked over at me. "Travel to Whale's Keep? Now? Certainly not. You've no idea what the crossing from the shore will be like at this time of year. It's difficult enough in summer. I'll not risk one daughter for another."

Though I'd anticipated some resistance, I'd not expected him to refuse outright.

"Perhaps Erik could take a few days off and escort me?" I pressed. "I would be safe with him."

Taking a long drink of wine, Erik shook his head. "Sorry. I can't be spared right now. Father and I have hired some new men and I'm hip-deep in training drills."

He didn't know anything of what Chloe was facing. If he had, he would have found a way to take me to Whale's Keep. But it was too late to tell him now. I'd allowed Christophe to marry a woman who was carrying another man's child, and I had no idea how Erik might react to either the news or the fact that I'd said nothing.

Instead, I turned to my last hope. "Mother," I said. "She sounded so alone in her letter. I would be a comfort to her and I could help deliver the child."

My mother's eyes grew warm and she reached out to touch my hand. "You are a loving sister and I know you wish to be with her. I would like to be at her side too. But your father is right. The waves are high at this time of year and he's told me of the dangers of the crossing to the island. Chloe is not alone. She has Lady Mildreth and the midwives of Whale's Keep to help her. I know it sounds harsh, but there is no reason to risk your safety." She paused. "I will write to Chloe myself this evening and explain. She will understand."

My father nodded in agreement and that was his signal that the discussion was over.

I would not be allowed to join Chloe.

* * * *

Over the next four days, I began to question my initial decision to do nothing with the information I'd overheard. But every time I struggled to mull over choices of what I might have done, someone would have suffered. Had I spoken up and broken off the marriage, Chloe would have been shamed beyond imagining. Julian would not marry her without a dowry and Christophe would not only have refused the marriage, he might have rescinded his promise to send troops. And then what would have become of our people?

Had I taken some action to try to help Chloe, later I might have blamed myself for the marriage and for having taken an active part in deceiving Christophe.

My silence had been based on the fact that my presence in the closet had been an accident and I should not have been there. I should not have heard any of the exchange between Chloe and Julian and as a result, it would have been wrong of me to take any action.

As things played out naturally, the wedding *had* taken place. This had been none of my doing.

Or had it?

All I knew was that Chloe suffered now and she wanted me to come to her, and I did not know how to make that happen. My parents and Erik had refused and I couldn't fight all three of them.

On the evening of the fourth day following the arrival of Chloe's letter, I walked to the log building that served as our second residence. Upon reaching the dining room, I found Mother, Father, and Erik already there again, but none of them had taken a seat yet.

"What do you mean, 'he's vanished'?" my father asked.

"No one has seen him for days," Erik answered. "Nearly a week. I know he owes Lieutenant Toruline a good deal of money, but I doubt it was enough to make him run."

Of whom were they speaking? Who had vanished?

"Good evening, my girl," my mother said, offering me her usual warm smile. "I heard you have some new baby chicks. I'll come and see them tomorrow."

I was about to answer her when Corporal Devon walked into the room. He halted at attention and spoke to Erik.

"Forgive the intrusion, my lord. But Lord Christophe has just arrived in the courtyard, and he is uncertain about disturbing the family at dinner."

"Christophe?" Erik repeated. "He's here? Send him in at once."

As Corporal Devon left, my mother clasped her hands. "I hope nothing is wrong."

"If it was anything serious, he'd have come straight in," my father answered.

Though my father's words made sense to me, I still couldn't fathom what would bring Christophe back here with no prior message and no invitation. It wasn't like him.

Only a few moments later, Christophe walked into the dining room. He appeared road weary, as if he'd ridden hard, and he wore chain armor and the light gray tabard of the de Fiores. When I looked at him more closely, I saw a deeper weariness in his face and dark circles beneath his eyes.

His gaze locked instantly upon me, but I couldn't read his emotions.

"Is Chloe well?" my mother asked.

As if realizing how alarming his sudden presence must seem, Christophe raised one hand. "Yes, my lady—no, she is not…" He paused and drew a breath. "She is not ill, but she is not entirely well. It has not been easy on her, carrying a first child so soon, and in an unfamiliar home. She has been asking for Nicole. After reading your letter, telling her that you could not allow Nicole to come, she has fallen into a quiet sorrow." His voice held a note of recrimination.

"Oh," my mother said, reaching for the table as if needing to support herself.

My father began walking toward her swiftly.

But Christophe went on. "I came to see if you might now agree to part with Nicole until the child comes. I have brought several of my best men. Nicole will be well guarded on the journey and I will row her to the island myself." He looked to my father. "You know my skills in a boat. She will be safe."

Erik stepped forward as if he'd not heard correctly. "You came all the way from Whale's Keep to fetch Nicole?"

Christophe nodded. "Yes, and I'd like to start back in the morning." He spoke to my father again. "May I bring Nicole to Chloe?"

There were undercurrents here that could not be spoken. No matter the marriage and the new bonding of our families, we were obligated to Christophe. His men protected our people.

"Of course," my father answered. "You may take her. I did not realize Chloe was feeling quite so in need of her sister." He turned to me. "You would still like to go?"

"Yes." I nodded. "I'll be ready first thing in the morning."

Christophe closed his eyes and opened them again. "Thank you."

Erik ushered him toward a chair. "Come and sit. Our cook made breaded trout and corn cakes tonight. You love trout and corn cakes." He looked over to me. "Nicole, fetch him a goblet of wine."

I hurried to get the wine.

As Christophe sat, I heard him say to my father, "Oh, and young Belledini arrived safely. He's been staying at the keep, but I'll insist on sending him over to the barracks soon."

"Julian?" my father asked in what sounded like surprise. "He's with you?"

I half-turned toward the table.

Christophe frowned. "Yes. He said you sent him to me for further training."

My father glanced at Erik and Erik smiled quickly. "Oh, that was me. He owes my men so much money I thought it best to pass him off on you for a few weeks."

Christophe half-smiled. "How very big of you."

"See if your Captain Fáuvel can teach him how to use a sword," Erik joked. "I've had no luck so far."

But I knew he was covering. He and Father must have been discussing Julian when I'd first walked in. Julian had vanished from White Deer Lodge and now he'd turned up at Whale's Keep. Erik probably thought he was hiding out to avoid gambling debts, but he also did not know enough about the situation to cause possible friction by openly admitting that Julian had not been sent to Christophe. Instead, he'd opted for caution.

I knew there must be more to both Julian's departure from here and his arrival at Whale's Keep. The thought of him and Chloe in the same house was frightening.

* * * *

The following day, we left at first light. Christophe wanted to get an early start so that we'd arrive with enough light to make the crossing to his island before sunset. I'd had an uneasy night, wondering what this journey would bring.

But I was packed and ready when his men were ready to leave. They loaded my trunk into a wagon. My mother kissed my face and she sent a box of medicinal supplies to help with Chloe's delivery.

Erik led out a gentle mare with a sidesaddle and as he leaned down to entwine his hands, he said quietly, "Write to me tomorrow. Tell me what's happening with Chloe."

"I will," I promised, but I wasn't sure I would. I'd need to judge that for myself when I arrived.

Stepping one foot into his entwined hands, I took hold of the saddle and pulled myself up onto the mare's back.

Christophe rode a tall, black horse and I guided my mare up beside his mount. It seemed odd to be leaving my home on a journey with Christophe, and yet I was anxious to reach Whale's Keep and see my sister.

"Good-bye," I called to my father. "I'll be back once the child comes."

He nodded, but I could see that he didn't like any of this.

At Christophe's side and accompanied by ten of his men, I rode out the gates and into the world, up the northern path. I had never been on such a journey before.

Christophe glanced down at me. "Have you ever ridden a horse all day?"

"No."

"Whale's Keep is a full day's ride. I want to get there before dark, but if you need to stop, just tell me."

Even now, he was kind, putting the needs of others before his own.

We traveled with the forest on one side and the ocean on the other. Though the air was cold, the day was fine. We stopped once for lunch, but I sensed the urgency in Christophe and I did not ask to stop again, even when my right hip grew sore from the sidesaddle.

We rarely spoke, but as the afternoon waned, I couldn't help asking, "Besides low spirits, is Chloe all right?"

He didn't look at me. "I was hoping you could tell me. You'll see her soon."

I didn't press him further.

The afternoon wore on and then he pointed. "There is it, just ahead."

Coming around a bend, I looked out over the ocean and nearly gasped. Perhaps a mile from the shore, an island rose up from the water. Though about five miles in length, the island was tall, with dark, rocky cliffs and no apparent shore.

"Don't worry," Christophe said. "We'll land around the south side. You'll see."

Gray waves with whitecaps crashed into jagged stone cliffs. I could barely imagine Chloe living in such a place.

Up ahead, a boathouse with a large adjoining stable came into view. Around us, the light was fading as the sun dipped lower.

As we headed forward again, I had a better view up the shore and took in the sight of an enormous barracks and second stable built in a clearing in the trees behind the boathouse. There were no piers or docks, but I counted seven longboats on the shore. We headed directly for the boats.

"Sergeant Harper," Christophe said to one of his men, "have Lady Nicole's luggage loaded and then pick two men to help the two of us row."

"Yes, sir."

A flurry of activity began. Christophe dismounted and reached up to lift me down, holding me for a moment until I was steady on my feet. Then he joined several other men to help push a boat into the water.

After striding back to me, he carried me into the waves, settling me at the back of the boat.

All four men climbed in and set their oars.

The crossing itself was more unsettling and more frightening than I'd expected. But I felt safe with Christophe and I trusted him. As we rounded the south corner of the island, I saw a break in the cliffs and a rocky beach. There were men on the rocky beach and I could see a gatehouse.

As we neared the shore, Christophe dropped his ore and moved to the front of the boat. Two men ran into the water, grabbing the sides of our boat as soon as it was close enough, pulling hard. A moment later, Christophe and the other three men inside jumped out and helped pull the vessel up onto the rocky shore.

Finally, the boat stopped moving and then Christophe was beside me, helping me out.

"You all right?" he asked.

"Yes."

"We're not done yet. We still need to make the climb."

Though somewhat puzzled by what "climb" meant at this point, of course I understood that we were at the bottom of the cliffs and any dwellings would be higher. Darkness was falling, but looking ahead, I saw a raised portcullis.

"This way," Christophe said, passing under the open portcullis and into the gatehouse tunnel. "I'll have your trunk brought up."

I followed him down the gatehouse tunnel and then under another open portcullis. Once out of the tunnel, I found myself looking up at a seemingly endless set of stone stairs. As we began to climb, I thought of Chloe and I imagined her arrival in this place. It was so very different from home. How had she felt? What had she thought?

Following Christophe, I went up and up, and just when my legs were nearly ready to give out, we reached the top and passed through another gatehouse and then we stepped out to the sight of a thriving village, perhaps the size of a town.

All around us, as far as I could see in the increasing darkness, spread roads lined by shops and dwellings. There were taverns and small barns. Numerous people still bustled about. Children and dogs hurried after adults. The ground sloped upward and looking to my right, I saw a great, four-towered keep at the top of the cliffs.

"Oh," I said.

In the fading light, he stared at me. "What do you think?"

"It's beautiful up here," I answered. And it was.

"I knew you'd say that." He started forward again.

I followed him up through the town. The back of the keep was built over the cliffs, but a low stone wall bordered the front with a break at the center point, and we passed through the break into a courtyard.

Hurrying through the courtyard, Christophe ushered me inside the enormous front doors into a square foyer. Passages led right, left, and straight ahead. Only upon entering the front doors of the keep did I realize how wet and cold I was. But as so often happened, Christophe had been quite aware.

"Roweena!" he called to a young serving woman down the left passage. At the sight of him, her eyes widened and she trotted to him. "My lord?"

"This is Lady Nicole," he said. "Please take her to a guest room with a fireplace and have a fire built. Her trunk will be up directly. Help her to change for dinner and then bring her to the great hall."

"Yes, my lord."

He looked down at me. "You'll see Chloe at dinner."

Though a part of me wanted to see her right away, I was grateful at the thought of a fire and dry clothing.

* * * *

A little over an hour later, I was shown to the great hall of Whale's Keep, wearing a sensible gown of sky-blue wool. I had a feeling no one here would notice or care how I was dressed.

For my part, I just wanted to see Chloe.

When I walked through the archway, relief flooded through me at the sight of her standing near the great hearth, in a gown of amber silk, staring into the flames.

"Chloe."

At the sound of my voice, she whirled. "Oh, Nicole. He said he would bring you."

Quickly, I crossed the room to clasp her hands. Though she was heavy with child, everything else about her appeared fragile and thin, as if she hadn't been eating. Her blue eyes were haunted.

"I had hoped you would come right away," she said.

For some reason, these words brought guilt rising up inside me. It was now five full days since her letter had reached me.

"I'm sorry," I answered. "Mother and Father wouldn't let me come. But I'm here now. How are you?"

Her smooth brow wrinkled slightly, as if she was puzzled by the question. "How am I? I am—"

"Ah, the Lady Nicole," a voice said from behind. "We shall be blessed with even more beauty at dinner tonight."

Turning, I saw Julian Belledini in the archway with Christophe standing just behind him. Julian flashed me his most charming smile. Handsome as always, he wore a brown silk tunic and his dark blond hair curled around his ears to the top of his collar.

What was he doing here?

Striding over, he took my hand and kissed it. It took all my self-control not to jerk my hand from his. Then he kissed Chloe's hand. "My lady. I hope this evening finds you well."

Her hand trembled and her eyes were frightened. She feared him? What was happening here?

From the archway, Christophe watched all this in silence. Looking over, I willed him to come in.

And he did.

But before he reached the hearth, movement in the archway caught my eye and three more people entered the hall: a woman and two children, a boy and a girl. The woman was tall and gaunt, perhaps thirty years old. She wore a high-necked black gown with a starched white collar. Her hair was pulled into a severe bun at the back of her neck.

The boy was about ten, with dark hair and gray eyes like Christophe. The little girl was perhaps eight. Her hair was brown like mine, but it was pulled back into a bun as tight as the woman's.

"Oh, Mildreth, this is Lady Nicole," Christophe said, "Nicole, this is my sister, Lady Mildreth, and her children, Jordan and Amanda."

I thought it odd that he did not introduce Jordan and Amanda as his nephew and niece, but rather as Mildreth's children, as if they had no connection to him. However, I did not think on this long as Mildreth's cold gaze moved to me, assessing me up and down.

"Chloe's sister?" she said. "Our numbers at dinner continue to grow."

"Ah, but surely you have no complaints," Julian said lightly. "You have new voices to entertain you."

Her attention moved to him. "Oh, I can assure you, sir. I have found your presence here most entertaining."

Chloe watched all this with frightened eyes, but I could not tell who she feared more, Julian or Mildreth. This was more than worry over managing an early birth. A clever woman could find ways to explain an early birth—and Chloe was clever. But now, she looked like a cornered animal and I was at a loss.

Christophe walked over and took Chloe's hand. "Are you feeling well tonight?"

He sounded genuinely concerned, like a solicitous husband, and when she looked up at him, all fear left her face. "I am well, my lord."

Several servants entered carrying trays of food. The smell of baked chicken wafted through the air. Normally, the lady of the house would announce dinner, so I waited for Chloe to step forward.

But Mildreth said, "Dinner is served. Will everyone please take a seat?"

Chloe's eyes had dropped to the floor.

After a brief hesitation, I started for the table. Christophe sat at the head and motioned me to sit beside him. As everyone else took a place, Julian sat across from Chloe, leaning back in his chair and stretching his legs under the table. I found this penchant of his ill-mannered, as if he were lord of any room he occupied.

"So, how soon can we expect the happy event?" Julian asked Chloe. "Can you make a guess?"

Chloe went pale.

Mildreth sat straight in her chair. "We may have an answer to that soon. I've employed a midwife from the village. Perhaps she might be allowed to examine Lady Chloe?"

"A midwife?" I asked. "There is no need. I'm skilled and I've come to serve as midwife."

"There's no reason you cannot both serve," Mildreth answered. "We all want Chloe to receive the most care possible."

Chloe sat with her eyes on her plate and I had had enough of this. I needed to speak with her alone.

Reaching out, I touched Christophe's arm. He went still beneath my fingers.

"My lord," I said quietly. "No matter what Chloe says, she is not feeling well. Look at her. Might I please be allowed to take her upstairs to rest?"

She had heard me and looked over in a mix of surprise and hope. Her expression was not lost on Christophe.

"Would you like to go upstairs with Nicole?" he asked her.

"Yes, my lord."

Quickly, I stood and hurried to my sister. Then I ushered her from the great hall.

Chapter 10

As Chloe whispered a few words to provide directions, I took her upstairs and down a passage.

Upon entering the apartments, I found myself in a sitting room with thick carpets and low couches. In the far wall, I saw an open doorway into a bedroom. There was a white lace comforter on the bed and flowers in vases on the tables. I wondered if Christophe minded the feminine décor. Slowly, moving carefully due to the weight of the child inside her, Chloe walked over and sank down onto a couch. I went to sit beside her.

"Nicole," she said.

Then neither of us spoke for a while. I longed to tell her that I knew the reasons for some of her fears, that the child was Julian's, that he had abandoned her, and that she taken the only path left open: marriage to Christophe.

But the words did not come. Perhaps I had remained silent on this matter for so long that now I could not speak of it.

Finally, I said, "I would help you if I could."

"Would you?" She paused. "I have things to tell you, things that might make you walk away from me and never look back."

"I will *not* walk away." Of that, I was certain.

She was quiet for a few more moments. "The child I carry is not Christophe's. It is Julian's. I love him…or I loved him. He would not marry me and I married Christophe to save my honor."

"Oh, Chloe."

She had told me. I could no longer pretend that I knew nothing. I was part of this now. Reaching out, I grasped her hand.

"What is it you fear?"

"Discovery," she whispered. "I thought I could manage this, but I am trapped."

"By who?"

"By Julian."

This was the part I did not understand. "Chloe, what is he doing here?"

"He is blackmailing me. Or he is trying to blackmail me. He's told me that unless I give him the emerald bracelet and the diamond necklace passed down to me by Mother as my wedding gifts, he will tell Christophe the truth."

I gasped. "Blackmail?"

Of all the things I thought possible of Julian, this would never have crossed my mind. He loved Chloe, or he had claimed to. But then I thought on the rumors I'd heard of Julian's gambling debts. Could he owe so much he was in danger? The jewels he'd asked for were family heirlooms, worth a small fortune.

"You've not given the bracelet or the necklace?" I asked.

"How could I? They are family treasures." Her voice broke. "I am expected to pass them down to my first daughter at her wedding. How I could explain their absence? No one here would steal them and no one would believe I lost them."

My mind raced. Chloe and I possessed no money of our own. My father paid for my gowns and other needs, and Chloe's yearly stipend went directly to Christophe. Julian would know this and he'd asked for the only things of real value that Chloe might give him.

"Do you think he'd really tell Christophe?" I asked.

"I think him capable of anything." Her voice was bitter now. "He has hunted me here, threatened me, made veiled taunts in front of Mildreth. I think she was suspicious when I began to show early, but she did not know anything and could not prove anything. Now...I'm certain she knows that I am ready to give birth at any time. I can feel it. As soon as the child is born, she will pounce. If the child is a boy, she'll not have a pretender inherit Christophe's title."

I sat back against the couch. I had wanted to let fate decide the outcome of this quandary. I had been desperate not to be forced to choose between Chloe and Christophe. But that time was past now. I had to make a choice.

And I chose Chloe.

She was my sister.

An indelicate question rose in my mind. "Chloe, how far along were you before your wedding to Christophe?"

"Perhaps two months."

"After the wedding, how soon were you able to...?"

"Get him into bed?" she finished for me.

"Yes."

"Our wedding night at the lodge. I had the sense to act swiftly there. But he hasn't come to my bed since I told him I was pregnant."

"What do you mean? Doesn't he live in here with you?"

Our mother and father had always shared the same rooms and slept in the same bed.

"No. We don't have that sort of marriage. He keeps his own rooms."

That struck me as an odd arrangement, but I didn't think on it long.

Gripping her hand more tightly, I said, "Listen to me. All we need to do is convince Christophe that the child is his, make him believe it. After that, anything Julian does will seem like a desperate ploy. Few men seem to trust him and Christophe trusts him not at all."

Her chin lifted and she looked me in the face. "Can this be done? How?"

Several ideas rolled through my mind at once. Could we pretend an illness on Chloe's part, something contagious? I could act as her nurse. Once the child came, we could keep everyone away for a week or so.

But I quickly rejected this idea. It was too risky. If Mildreth was suspicious, she'd find a way to see the child the day it was born—or find a way to send Christophe into the room.

"I'll need to get Christophe out of the keep somehow and away from here," I said. "I'll keep him away as long as possible. If the child feeds well, upon our return, Christophe will not know the difference."

"You think you could get him away? But what about Mildreth?"

This was trickier and I didn't care for the only idea that occurred to me. "Do you think you could get three or four drops of an areial roots mixture into her tea?"

With a quick intake of breath, she said, "Areial roots?" Then slowly, she nodded. "I could."

"Do you have a maid you can trust? Someone who can help you with the delivery?"

This was even more risky, but she would need help and we had no other options.

"Yes, Roweena has been treated badly by Mildreth. She is loyal to me and values her position here."

"Good," I said. "Once I have Christophe away from the keep, wait until the very beginning of your labor pains. Then find a way to drug Mildreth's tea. Fake a fall to provide a reason for early labor. If the midwife Mildreth hired arrives, order that she be sent away. Julian is not family and he won't be able to come near you without your permission."

Her eyes shifted back and forth with hope as she listened. "How long do think you can keep Christophe away?"

"I don't know. I haven't figured that part out yet. But he doesn't believe you are due until mid-spring, and so if I can convince him that I am needed someplace else for a short time, I should be able to talk him into taking me. I'll try to keep him away for a week."

With a soft exhale, she leaned forward to press her head to my shoulder. "Oh, Nicole. I'm so glad you are here. I'm so glad to have someone on my side."

Reaching up, I held her close. "We will manage this, Chloe. We will."

* * * *

Late-morning of the following day, I left Chloe resting in rooms so that I might go outside into the cold air of the courtyard to walk and allow myself to think.

I was nearly in awe of the architecture of the keep. The bottom floor was square and solid, with crenellated turrets built into the second story of each of the four corners. The turrets rose into the air above the third floor. To me, who had only lived in buildings constructed from logs, Whale's Keep seemed like a castle.

But how could I get Christophe away from this place?

I'd heard from my mother there had been an outbreak of fever in the village north of White Deer Lodge. It was not yet serious enough for her to travel there. Perhaps I could tell Christophe that a message had been forwarded to me from home, and that the fever had grown worse and my mother could not attend; the people there needed me. This ruse would prey on his kindness and concern for others—which troubled me—but I believed he would take me himself.

Near noon, I braced myself to lie to him and decided it was best to act as soon as possible.

But a side door near the kitchens opened and someone walked out. I expected it to be a house guard, but then I saw who it was.

Julian.

He saw me in the same moment and smiled as he walked toward me. "My lady. What are you doing out here? The air is cold." He wore a heavy cloak that swung around his feet as he walked.

I was near the front wall of the keep. Glancing toward the main doors, I nodded. "Yes, it is colder than I imagined. I should go back inside."

Before I could take a step, he moved around in front of me.

"Wait," he said. "I would speak with you a moment."

"Please. It is rather cold and I should like to go in."

I stepped nearer to the wall to try to move past him, but he reached out and put his right hand against the wall, blocking my escape. Beneath his cloak, he wore a sleeveless tunic to show off the definition in his arms. What a vain creature he was. Any man with sense would be wearing long sleeves.

But still, I could not get past him and nervousness rose inside me. The nearest guards were out at the gates, a good distance away. I wished Christophe would come outside.

"It's good of you to travel so far to help your sister," Julian said. "The question is, my dear: How much help are you willing to give her?"

I kept my eyes level with his chin. "I don't know what you mean."

"Oh, I think you know exactly what I mean, or you wouldn't have come running when she called."

Pretense was futile and I was no good at clever word games. Raising my head, I glared at him. "You are a snake," I whispered, "to bully and frighten a woman who loved you."

He didn't react to my insult. "She's in no danger from me so long as she does as I ask. Perhaps you could help her to see this?"

How I hated him.

"She'll never give you those jewels," I said. "She couldn't if she wanted to. And you are playing a dangerous game. Your only thought is to terrify her enough to buy you off before she gives birth. But the child will come at any time now, and if Christophe sees the truth for himself before you've told him, you'll have more to worry about than a few gambling debts."

At this, a flash of rage passed over his face and to my shock, he grabbed my wrist, jerking me up against himself. "She still has days left before the child comes, possibly a week. And if she does not do as I ask, I will tell Christophe she has deceived him. I mean it."

He was hurting my wrist and his eyes were desperate now. Perhaps he owed money to someone more threatening than one of our family guards.

I didn't care.

"Get your hand off me," I said, "Or I'll call for those men at the gate."

His breathing was uneven and he gripped me for another moment. "Talk to her," he said. "Make her see reason. Or by the time I'm done, your family's honor will be in tatters. Everyone knows how much your father needed this marriage. He'll take half the blame."

With a slight shove, he let go of me, turned, and walked through the front doors of the keep.

Shaken, I leaned against the wall, trying to gather myself. My forearm would be bruised tomorrow, but that was the least of my worries. I did not know Julian's troubles, but he'd almost seemed in fear for his life, and he needed money—apparently, a good deal of money.

Forcing myself to calm down, I let my thoughts flow, trying to see the path forward, wondering if I should change tactics in light of this knowledge regarding the depths of his desperation.

But my original plan still offered the best chance of saving Chloe: Get Christophe away from here and incapacitate Mildreth. Then Julian would lose any power or leverage. I would ensure that upon Christophe's return, he would fully accept the child as his own and once that happened, Julian would have difficulty attempting to blackmail Chloe. At that point, if he tried, he would look like a desperate man trying to cover gambling debts by impugning a lady—and the consequences for Julian might not be pleasant. I gauged him as intelligent enough to reason this for himself.

Still, I would have to move quickly. Julian was wrong about one thing: Chloe did not have a week. I needed to act now.

Upon reentering the keep, I stopped one of the house guards.

"Can you tell me where I might find Lord Christophe?"

"In the great hall, my lady."

"Thank you."

Heading down the center passage, I walked through the arches of the great hall to find Christophe speaking with Julian.

Julian must have come straight here. Neither man saw me in the archway and both of them were frowning at the other.

"I just don't understand the rush," Julian said. "I've not even been here a week. Are you in such a hurry to be rid of me?"

"Of course not," Christophe answered, but the strain in his voice belied his words. "But you were sent here to train. You need to take a boat to the shore and arrange for a room at the barracks. Captain Fáuvel will assist you."

"At the Montagnas', I always lived in a guest room at the lodge and ate with the family."

"Yes, but Erik handles most of the training himself there, and the main barracks is part of the lodge. We operate differently here. Captain Fáuvel does our training at the barracks on shore."

"I've already been training for months. Surely you won't begrudge me a week or so of rest here in your home?"

How manipulative Julian was. He wanted to remain here so he could continue pressuring Chloe to give him her jewels. Each day closer to her delivery would cause her to panic more.

Just then, he saw me standing in the archway and he smiled. "And here is the lovely Nicole. She has only arrived at Whale's Keep and I've barely seen her. I should like a few more days here in her company."

I fought back a shudder.

Christophe's frown deepened. "Julian," he began and his tone sounded firmer now.

But before he could finish the sentence, a man in his late twenties, wearing armor and a gray tabard—and wet up the waist—came striding into the great hall.

Christophe frowned. "Lieutenant?"

"Forgive the intrusion, my lord," the man said, "but I have news that couldn't wait. A party of raiders somehow got through our lines several miles up shore, undetected. They made it all into Chastain."

"Chastain?"

"Yes, my lord. The village was attacked. But word didn't reach Captain Fáuvel until the attack was well over and the raiders were gone. Their boats are gone. Anyone they took cannot be retrieved."

"No," Christophe breathed.

I could only imagine what he was feeling, that he had failed his people.

"What about the village?" he asked. "What is the damage?"

"I don't know, my lord. The messenger who arrived was badly injured. He could only tell me what I've told you. Captain Fáuvel sent thirty men on fast horses immediately, but he's in the process of preparing a larger contingent to go and provide help to survivors. He wants to make sure we have adequate supplies to offer assistance when we get there, and we may not be ready until morning."

Nodding, Christophe said, "Good. I'll need to make some preparations here, but I'll take a boat over before dark this evening. We'll leave at first light."

As he spoke, a thought hit me and I saw my chance.

"My lord," I said. "There will be wounded people at Chastain. My mother sent a box of medicines and I can quickly put together some bandages. If you take me with you, I can work as a healer."

"Take you?"

"Yes, I would be safe riding at your side, under your protection." Guilt rose inside as I watched his eyes light up at the prospect of me riding beside him and needing his protection. But I didn't stop. "This is not a rushed or dangerous mission to cut off any raiders. It is a well-planned mission to go and offer food and aid. I could be of help to you."

I knew exactly what I was doing, appealing to his love for me and painting an image of the two of us working together to help his people.

Still, he hesitated. "What of Chloe? She may need you."

"The child will not come this early and we will be gone only a matter of days. I would like to help and the people of Chastain will be in need of a skilled healer."

Julian's head swiveled back and forth between us, and as if he were growing anxious. Then his gaze settled on me. He knew what I was doing: Getting Christophe away until the child was born and some time had passed.

"My lord," he said, sounding deferential. "You would not risk Lady Nicole needlessly? Surely, this village must have its own healer."

"Not like me," I answered and then looked to Christophe. "And I will be safe with you."

Slowly, he nodded and turned to the wet lieutenant. "Take a boat back to shore and inform the captain that Lady Nicole and I will join him at the barracks before dark. We'll leave with the contingent in the morning."

"Yes, my lord."

Relief flooded through me. But as the lieutenant turned to leave, I froze.

Mildreth stood in the archway. She'd been listening to every word. Her gaze moved first to Julian and then to me. Then she turned to the young lieutenant and gave an order, "Leave us, but don't go far. Remain within calling distance."

After glancing at Christophe, he nodded. "Yes, my lady."

She waited for him to leave. I didn't like this. What was she up to?

"Brother," she said slowly to Christophe. "Send Captain Fáuvel to assist the people of Chastain. You cannot leave the keep."

Confused, Christophe shook his head. "Why not?"

"Because your wife will give birth at any time, and you need to be here when that happens."

He walked toward her, speaking gently. "It's all right, Mildreth. Chastain needs me now and Chloe will not deliver the child until mid-spring."

"She will give birth soon and the child will be fully formed."

I could feel my hands going cold. Mildreth did know. She was not guessing.

Christophe halted in mid-step. "What are you saying?"

"I'm saying the child is not yours." Gesturing to Julian, she said calmly, "It is his. I've had him followed and I've had him watched. Several conversations between him and your wife have been overheard and reported back to me."

"Gossip gained from ears pressed to keyholes?" Julian broke in. "And you've walked in here to tell false whispers as fact?"

His voice was steady. I had to give him that.

But the coldness in my hands was spreading up into my arms. Could Julian not see what was happening here?

Mildreth continued speaking to Christophe as if Julian was not in the room. "He's been attempting to blackmail Lady Chloe by threatening to tell you the truth if she does not give him several family heirlooms of great value."

For the first time since her entrance, Christophe appeared to waver, as if actually listening to her words.

"Your wife has been deceiving you since the moment of your marriage," Mildreth went on. "And what's more"—she pointed to me—"this one has been helping her. Why do you think Nicole is so eager to take you away from home? How long might she be able to keep you away? Long enough for the child to be born and to feed, to grow pink and rosy as babies do, so that you would not question its good heath." She paused. "Trust me, brother. The child will come at any time and it will be fully formed at birth."

How awful she made Chloe and me sound, schemers and deceivers.

Christophe was breathing raggedly, but he shook his head again. "No, this is a mistake somehow, Sister." He turned to me. "Nicole, tell her. Help her try to make some sense of this. Tell her she is wrong."

But I stood frozen in place, wordless. Mildreth knew the whole truth—or her perception of the truth—and she was not mistaken in the facts. Julian was the father of the baby. Chloe would give birth at any time. And the child would be fully formed.

For me to lie would be pointless. Within a day or two, Mildreth would be proven right.

As he looked at me, my silence must have spoken volumes because all the color drained for Christophe's face. "Nicole?"

I couldn't speak and he grabbed the back of a chair for support. "By the gods," he whispered.

"Christophe..." Julian began, sounding nervous now. "Surely, you can't believe—"

But he was cut off as Christophe whirled toward him.

"Guards!" Christophe shouted.

Within an instant, the young lieutenant and one of the house guards came running into the great hall.

Christophe motioned to Julian. "Lock him up."

* * * *

Chloe and I remained in her rooms for the next two days, as a kind of informal imprisonment. Meals were brought into us, but the servants hurried about their business, either depositing or retrieving trays and then leaving. A few times, I tried to gain news of what was happening outside, but no one would speak to us.

Near the evening of the second day, Chloe went into labor.

Upon entering with a meal tray, one of the serving girls saw what was happening and she left quickly. Soon, a few other women from the house came in carrying water, blankets, and towels. They remained to help me with the delivery and I was grateful for their help.

Mildreth did not come.

No hired midwife came. She was no longer necessary to Mildreth.

For a first birth, the labor was not long and shortly after daybreak, Chloe gave birth to a fine son. I cut the cord and held him in my arms. He was perfect, with fingernails and a full head of red-blond hair. He looked like a tiny copy of my father and brother.

One of the serving women slipped from the room.

Normally, in a noble household, men were not allowed into a birthing chamber until all remnants of the painful, messy event had been completely cleared away. The new mother would be washed and dressed in a clean nightgown. Her hair would be brushed and she would be sitting up in bed, holding the freshly wrapped baby when her husband was finally allowed to enter.

But this was not a normal birth and I was not surprised when the door opened and Mildreth walked in with Christophe behind her. There were bloody sheets and towels all over the floor. The cord and afterbirth still lay in a basin. Chloe still glistened from pain and perspiration.

Mildreth walked over, took the child from me and laid him on the bed.

Christophe came to the bed and looked down. His face was impassive, as if he felt nothing. The baby kicked a few times. Christophe took in the sight of his hair and well-developed arms and legs. This had not been a premature birth.

Without a word, without even looking at Chloe or me, he turned and strode from the room. Mildreth followed him.

"What do think will happen now?" I whispered.

Chloe was silent for a moment and then she said, "I don't know."

* * * *

That afternoon, a serving girl put her head in the door and spoke to me. "His lordship wants to see you in the great hall."

Chloe was in the bed, holding the baby. After glancing at her once and seeing her eyes filled with fear, I left the room.

The walk was long. By rights, Christophe could legally have Chloe strangled to death. It was a capital crime for a wife to secretly pass off an illegitimate son as a nobleman's heir. Of course, Christophe would never go so far. He would not harm either of us, but this had played out in the worst of all possible ways, and I did not know how he would respond. Though Chloe had been a frightened, cornered girl seeking an escape from ruin, she now appeared every inch the deceiver.

Upon reaching the main floor of the keep, I headed down the main passage and tried to gather myself before reaching the archways. When I passed through and entered the great hall, I found Christophe there alone, standing near the fire.

I barely recognized him. All of the kindness I'd come to know was gone from his face, replaced by a hardness of depths I could not fathom. Walking across the hall, he stood close enough to tower over me. He was so tall that my eyes were level with his collarbones.

"Did you just learn the truth upon arriving here with me?" he asked.

With me.

The words cut like knives, but I wouldn't lie to him now. "No."

"Then how long have you known?"

"Since before the wedding."

A sound of pain came from the back of his throat and he half-turned away. "And you worked with Chloe to betray me?"

"No. Can't you see she was trapped? She fell in love with the wrong man and he abandoned her."

"And you chose her over me?"

How could he ask me that? "Christophe…she is my *sister*."

For some reason, that appeared the worst possible thing for me to say and he swung his head back toward me in a rage. "And I am more than your friend! I am more, Nicole! And you would have placed a Belledini as the heir to Whale's Keep." He staggered backward in disbelief. "You would have done this to me."

My heart was breaking—as everything he said was true—but I had never meant to hurt him, only to help Chloe.

Wildly, I tried to think of some way to explain this when a commotion sounded from beyond the archway. A moment later, Julian was dragged in by a guard, with two other guards following. Julian appeared disheveled, wearing the same clothing from the last time he'd been in this hall.

Christophe's rage faded, replaced by the same look of hardness I'd seen upon walking in.

"Congratulations," he said. "You have a son."

Julian jerked his arm away from the guard. "And what do you propose now, de Fiore? Some kind of manly duel?"

Perhaps I had overestimated his intelligence. Did he really think indignation would work here? And he wouldn't last a minute in a duel with Christophe.

"No." Christophe shook his head. "But I've written a letter to Gideon Montagna. I've explained how you seduced his daughter, how you impregnated her, how you abandoned her, and then came here to try to blackmail her."

Julian went completely still.

"If I were you," Christophe went on, "I would not ever set foot on Montagna lands again unless you wish to be tied to a stake in the courtyard and horsewhipped. I think you can be safely assured there will be no further actions on the part of Lord Gideon to gain you a commission. And since you are no longer welcome here, you have nowhere to go but back to your own father. Perhaps he'll take you in."

Julian's expression grew panicked and he stepped forward. "Christophe, please—don't send that letter. I cannot go to my father just yet. I'm in—I'm in a difficulty. The night of your wedding, I lost a hand of cards to Colonel Régnier, but there was more than money on the table. My father's will states that I'll inherit a vineyard on the west edge of our lands. I was out of funds and I had three aces in my hand. Three aces! I bet the vineyard and the colonel had four kings. How was I to know? I can't be blamed for that. But the vineyard isn't mine yet. I've been trying to raise the money to buy it back from the colonel, but if you send me home, he'll seek me out there and my father will learn what I've done. Please, don't send that letter to Gideon yet...or just let me stay here a few weeks. I'll live in the barracks. You'll never see me. I need a little time to raise the money."

Christophe didn't bother to hide his disgust. "I sent the letter this morning." He looked to the guards. "Take him down to the landing point and put him in a boat. Row him to shore and after that, he's on his own. Just make sure he leaves. I don't care which direction he goes."

All three guards moved forward and two of them grabbed Julian's arms. "Christophe, wait!" Julian cried. "Listen to me."

But he was dragged from the hall and soon we could no longer hear him. Christophe and I were alone again.

"What about us?" I asked.

The hardness in his eyes only deepened. "I sent two letters to your father, one in reference to Belledini's part in this and a second one in reference to yours and Chloe's. I've told him of your deceit and how you planned this betrayal together. I will handle having the marriage dissolved and have a copy of the documents sent to him." He paused. "I will give Lady Chloe time to recover from the birth and then my men will escort you both home. Your father can decide your fates from there. I want nothing more to do with either of you."

At this last sentence, the hardness in his voice was colored by pain and I felt as if I were breaking apart inside.

"Oh, Christophe."

"Stay out of my sight until you leave."

* * * *

I made my way back upstairs to Chloe and slipped inside her apartments. She sat on a low couch, still holding the baby.

"Well?" she said, but her voice held fear.

"He's written to Father, telling him what we've done. As soon as you're able to travel, we'll be escorted home."

She shook her head as if not having heard me correctly. "What? That is my punishment? To be taken home?"

I nodded, still feeling broken inside. "As soon as you can travel. Then he'll have the marriage dissolved."

She leaned back on the couch, gripping the child. "What about the soldiers he sent to guard the Montagna shoreline? Will he withdraw them?"

"I don't know. He didn't say."

"He said nothing about this at all?"

"No."

How could she be so callous? Together, we had damaged a good man, possibly destroyed him.

"And he's providing us with an escort?" she asked, sounding incredulous.

"Of course he is. Chloe, this is *Christophe*. He'd never put us on a road without guards."

She looked at me as if she thought me simple, as if she thought me a fool. But then she stood. "We'll leave tomorrow."

"Tomorrow? Have you lost your senses? You'll be bleeding for days. Think of the crossing to the shore. And you certainly can't ride."

"I'll be fine on the crossing and once on shore, I'll have Captain Fáuvel arrange for a wagon. I can ride in the back." The pale, frightened young woman was gone, but so was the serene young woman I had once known. She was someone else. "If Christophe is letting me go, I'm going home." Her tone was fierce. "I'm bringing my son home to White Deer Lodge."

Chapter 11

By dusk of the next day, Chloe, the baby, and I rolled into the courtyard of White Deer Lodge in the back of a wagon, surrounded by de Fiore guards. All around us stood the familiar log buildings and familiar pathways.

Chloe closed her eyes and breathed in the air. "I'm home," she whispered.

I doubt anyone was expecting us, because Corporal Devon came walking up in surprise.

"My ladies?"

Chloe reached out for him and allowed him to lift her out of the wagon. Then she reached back for the baby. I couldn't believe she was still on her feet, but she did not even seem weary. I climbed down behind her.

"Where are my parents?" Chloe asked the corporal.

"In the family dining room, my lady, about to begin supper."

"Good," she answered. "That's perfect. Please see that the de Fiore guards are given quarters and a decent meal. They will be heading back for Whale's Keep tomorrow."

"Yes, my lady."

With that, she headed toward our second residence—and the dining room. How could she be in such a hurry to face Father? Christophe's letter had most certainly already reached him, and I could only image what it had contained, how we had been portrayed. The two of us were coming home in more than just shame. I'd had all day to think more clearly and to worry a little less about Christophe and a little more about us. We had conspired to commit a capital offense and if Christophe chose to withdraw his soldiers, we would be responsible for the suffering of many of our own people.

What would Father say? What would he do?

But I followed Chloe as she strode into the dining room of our home.

Father, Mother, and Erik were already seated. At the sight of us, Father and Erik both jumped to their feet, their eyes blazing.

Chloe faced them without fear. "I am home."

No one spoke for a moment and then my father said raggedly, "You have brought nothing but shame upon your home."

Walking forward, Chloe laid the baby on the table and pulled back his blankets, completely exposing his small form. "Look at him," she ordered. "Look at every inch of him."

In spite of themselves, both my father and Erik looked down and their expressions began to alter. They could not help but be affected by the sight of the healthy child with his blond-red hair, blue eyes, pale skin, and strong legs. Again...he was a tiny copy of them.

"His name is Gideon Montagna," Chloe said, "and he is a son of White Deer Lodge. Look at him and try to deny it."

At first, Father couldn't take his gaze from the baby and when he raised his head, he appeared lost in thought.

But when Erik looked up, his anger returned. "You tried to deceive Christophe. You tried to convince him the child was his own. You must be punished."

"Don't play judge with me," Chloe returned. "Had Father known the truth, he might have stopped the wedding, but you'd have carried me to that magistrate yourself and taken my vows for me." Once again, she turned on our father. "And you! You knew I didn't want that marriage, and you traded me to Christophe for two hundred soldiers. How dare you let Erik speak of punishment? I have suffered enough."

To his credit, Father winced.

Quietly, my mother came to join us. Reaching out, she lifted baby Gideon. Holding him close, she rocked him in her arms. "He is a son of White Deer Lodge."

"And I am his mother," Chloe said, still speaking directly to our father. "You've never seen me as you do Nicole, but I am no different. I am a daughter of White Deer Lodge and this place is my home."

"Chloe is right," our mother said, still rocking the baby. "She is a daughter of White Deer Lodge. Our girls are home safe and our grandson is home safe, and there will be no more talk of punishment. Am I understood?"

Looking down at the baby, Father nodded.

* * * *

Late winter passed into spring. The documents arrived, finalizing Christophe's dissolved union with Chloe. For a noble divorce to be granted, a reason must be given. We never learned what reason Christophe had provided, but the king approved his request. Christophe and Chloe were no longer married.

News reached Erik that Julian Belledini's father had learned of the loss of the vineyard, that it had been gambled away. Julian had been sent off into the king's army as an enlisted man, not as an officer with rights or privileges.

My meadow bloomed, some of my hens hatched chicks, and my bees floated busily from flower to flower. My father and Erik waited tensely, but Christophe did not recall his troops guarding our shoreline.

Everything should have seemed the same as it was before, but it was not.

Chloe had come into her own power and I rejoiced for her. Though it had seemed likely she would be shunned from all society—a castoff from her husband under gossip-ridden circumstances—she was not. Christophe never said a word publically about why he had sent Chloe home or why he had dissolved the union.

And yet, my father had taken her back and given her son our family name. Should Erik decide not to marry, or should he marry and the marriage produce no son, young Gideon would inherit the family title and all our lands upon Erik's death. The child held a place of honor and this suggested Chloe had done nothing wrong. My father and brother doted on small Gideon and they could hardly wait to teach him how to ride.

To most people, the situation was a great mystery.

As opposed to society keeping away from Chloe, surprising numbers of noblewomen began calling upon White Deer Lodge on the flimsiest of excuses, such as to see the new baby. Noblewomen normally did not travel long distances to see a baby.

Chloe organized teas and embroidery parties, and the ladies were glad to have her back. She was much better at this sort of thing than my mother or me. A kind of game began in which women would carefully ask Chloe a question about her circumstances and see how she responded.

Only Lady Richelle de Miennes was more blunt with her questions. One day, over tea, she asked, "My dear, why did you leave Whale's Keep?"

Chloe took a graceful sip. "Have you met Lord Christophe's sister, Lady Mildreth?"

"Indeed I have."

"Then you already know why I left."

Laughter broke out, but this was all Chloe would say. She was home and finally flourishing in the knowledge that this was her place in the world. She was a daughter of White Deer Lodge.

I had never seen her so at peace with herself or so happy. But me? I could not stop thinking on what we had done to achieve this happiness for her, or on the man we had injured. It left me feeling low.

Spring passed into summer and this feeling did not lift.

I took some respite in caring for Gideon. He was five months old now, eating oatmeal, and able to roll around on his own. He was a sweet-natured child and I found comfort in his company. I'd taken to spending the early evenings, before dinner, in the nursery with him. We employed a young maid named Mina to care for him during the dinner hour, but she and I always spent time together with him first.

One night, in mid-summer, we spread two thick blankets on the floor of the nursery and laid Gideon on the blankets to let him roll around. He seemed to enjoy it very much and he smiled as babies do. We laughed as he rolled on his stomach and tried to push himself with his hands.

A shadow passed over me and Mina looked up at the open doorway. Her expression froze and she scooted back, as if frightened. Startled, I followed her gaze.

Christophe stood in the doorway, wearing chain armor and a sword.

He was not improved from the last time I'd seen him. He'd not shaved in days and his jaw was covered in a dark stubble. The circles under his eyes were worse. He appeared so tall standing there. Men did not come up to the nursery, not even Erik or my father, and Christophe's presence felt foreign, as Mina and I were two small women sitting on the floor with a baby while he stood watching us. I searched his face for the kindness that I had once so valued, but it was gone. Only the hard, brittle quality remained.

He walked inside the room and glanced down at Mina. "Get out."

In panic, she looked to me. I nodded and she fled the room.

Standing directly over me, with an impassive expression, Christophe studied Gideon as the child rolled onto his back.

"He looks just like Erik," he observed.

I had no idea what to say. His unannounced arrival here left me off balance. A part of me longed to beg his forgiveness, but I could not bring myself to broach the reason that I needed his forgiveness.

"I've heard your father has given him the Montagna name," he said, "and even placed him as the current heir."

"Yes," I answered quietly. "Father loves him. So does Erik."

Christophe nodded. "That's good. The child should not suffer for the crimes of the mother."

I stared down at the blanket, hoping to change the subject. "Is all well at Whale's Keep?"

"I don't know. I believe so, but I've spent the last month in Lascaux."

"Lascaux? Why?"

Christophe had never been one to visit court. It was a place of petty favor-seeking, and he had no interest.

"Looking for a wife, of course," he answered. "I need a son, and the woman I married tried to saddle me with a bastard."

The Christophe I'd known would never speak like this. He was a changed man. We had done this to him, Chloe and I.

"And did you find a wife?" I asked.

"No. Not that there weren't offers. I'd no idea how highly the de Fiores and Whale's Keep are thought of. Seven different noblemen dangled their daughters in front of me. Lord Shermaine offered a dowry of two thousand silvers a year if I'd take his daughter, Ilianna. Have you met her?"

I had. "Yes. Her family has visited. Ilianna is lovely."

"She is. Charming too. We spent a number of evenings at dinner together."

"But you will not marry her?"

"No."

"Why not?"

He stepped away, backing a few paces from the blanket. "Because I can't. No matter how hard I try to force myself, I cannot see my life with anyone but you. I tried to make you see this, back when I thought you innocent and free of deception."

This was too much. Any chance of marriage between us was long over. Had he come here to punish me further? All thoughts of begging his forgiveness vanished.

Standing, I squared off with him. "You have no idea what Chloe was facing. I had to help her. Christophe...she is my *sister*."

I'd said this to him once before and my words now brought the same reaction. His features twisted into rage, and I couldn't help shrinking away.

"Don't ever say that to me again," he bit off. "Ever." His voice was raw. "But I still cannot see marriage to anyone but you. When the years of my life roll out before me, all I see is you."

Something about this left me unsettled, even anxious. "I don't know what you mean."

"You will."

Anxiety turned to fear. Christophe no longer loved me. If anything, he despised me. Why did he keep talking of marriage?

"Why are you here?" I blurted out. "What are you going to do?"

"Do? What I should have done last summer. I'm going out into the village and I'm going to bring back the elder. He'll marry us tonight and you'll leave for Whale's Keep with me in the morning."

Crouching, I quickly lifted Gideon and backed away from Christophe. "No."

Following me across the floor, he leaned down. "You will agree to marry me tonight, or I'll withdraw my troops on your shoreline and leave your people to be slaughtered by those raiders."

As he waited for my reaction, I saw cruelty in his eyes. The Christophe I had known was not cruel, nor did he abuse his position of power over others. This man was a stranger.

"Don't do this," I begged. "Please don't."

Turning away, he said, "I'll speak to your father before fetching the village elder. Meet us in the hunting hall in one hour. We've no need for anyplace so large as the gathering hall."

He walked out.

* * * *

Less than an hour later, I was hiding in my room—when I should have gone down to supper—uncertain what was about to happen.

A knock sounded on my door and I opened it to find my father standing on the other side. His face was gaunt and drawn, as if he'd aged several years.

"He's told you then?" I asked, unnecessarily.

My father nodded. "He's in the hunting hall, with the village elder."

Village elders possessed the legal power to perform marriages.

For a long moment, neither of us spoke. Then my father said, "Chloe is right that I traded her for two hundred soldiers. I won't force you now."

Though his words meant a good deal to me, there was more at stake than one daughter of White Deer Lodge being forced into marriage.

"Do you believe he's in earnest about withdrawing his troops?" I asked.

"Yes. He is a changed man."

"Then I have no choice."

* * * *

Numb, I walked with my father down the path toward the hunting hall. Darkness had fallen and a few torches lit our way—and we both knew the path by heart. I had made my decision, or it had been made for me, and I was resigned.

But the family drama was not yet over. Erik ran out of our second family residence, followed closely by my mother and Chloe. By the light of a torch, they saw Father and me on the path and hurried toward us.

"What is happening?" Erik demanded. "We were told Christophe is in the hunting hall with the village elder."

My father did not stop walking and neither did I.

We all reached the hunting hall together and entered. Christophe and our village elder, Mason du Penne, stood inside. Elder du Penne appeared uncertain and unsettled. The walls were lined with spears, longbows, and the heads of animals. Somehow, it seemed an appropriate place for this wedding.

I had not bothered changing my dress and still wore the plain wool gown I'd been wearing in the nursery. I didn't think Christophe would notice.

"What is happening?" Erik demanded again.

"Nicole will marry Lord Christophe," our father said.

"No!" Mother gasped, looking wildly between him and Christophe. "What's the meaning of this?"

Chloe strode forward, speaking to Christophe. "Why would you do this? To punish me?"

For a moment, I thought he would pretend she didn't exist, but then he said coldly, "Not everything is about you, madam."

Her cheeks went red. "What threats have you made?" She whirled back. "Father, what has he threatened?"

"Chloe, move away from him," my father ordered.

Erik had been quiet through this exchange, but I could see his mind working. "What did he threaten?"

"It doesn't matter," I said quietly. "I've agreed."

"Agreed?" my mother repeated.

No one here besides my father, myself, and Christophe knew what had happened last summer in the meadow, that Christophe had once wished to marry me out of love.

"Father, you can't allow this to happen," Chloe pressed. "You cannot allow him to take Nicole. Look at him! Can't you see how angry he is?"

Yes, Christophe was angry and I was about to be wed to a man who not only did not love me, but who appeared to take pleasure at the sight of my suffering. And yet…I could not refuse.

"It's all right, Chloe," I put in. "As I said, I have agreed."

Mother was frightened now and Erik watched all this carefully. I believed if he knew of Christophe's threat, he'd walk me to the elder himself. Erik was determined to protect our people and I didn't blame him for that.

I was just as determined to protect our people.

Father turned to Chloe and my mother. "If either one of you says another word, I'll have you removed."

Mother stared at him.

Steeling myself, I walked to Christophe and Elder du Penne. The latter was an aging man with silver hair and a lined face. I'd known him since I was born.

He appeared at a loss. "You wish for this, my lady?"

I did not.

"Yes," I answered.

There was a large piece of paper on a table beside him: a hastily drawn marriage agreement with a place for four signatures.

With a tentative tone, he spoke to Christophe. "Do you, Christophe de Fiore, swear to love this woman, to protect her heart, to give her your loyalty, and to care for her all the days of your life?"

Christophe hesitated. Perhaps he'd forgotten he would need to swear to care for me and protect my heart. But if he didn't say the words, we would not be married.

"I swear." He bit them off as if they tasted bitter.

"Do you, Nicole Montagna," the elder continued, "swear to love this man, to protect his heart, to give him your loyalty, and to care for him all the days of your life?"

How could I swear to love him? In this moment, I felt I didn't even know him—and I was afraid of him. But again, there was no choice.

"I swear."

"Then by the power of the state and of the king, I pronounce you husband and wife." Elder du Penne motioned to the piece of paper. "I will need you both and Lady Nicole's father to sign."

One by one, we did. Then Elder du Penne signed.

Christophe gazed down at me as if waiting for me to realize something—and then I did. We were married and this was our wedding night.

My mother seemed to realize this in the same moment, and in spite my father's earlier threat, her dignified voice carried across the room. "Forgive me, my lord. I was not allotted time to prepare a proper wedding suite."

Christophe's head swiveled toward her.

I believed he saw himself as a greatly wronged man, exacting justified revenge upon a family that had injured him. It was clear that she saw him as an angry lord abusing his power over others to take what he wanted.

They were both right.

But Christophe had always admired my mother and seeing himself through her eyes, he wavered.

"No need for apologies, my lady," he said. "I will sleep in my usual guest room. Lady Nicole may sleep where she pleases." He started for the door and then paused. "But we leave for Whale's Keep in the morning."

Chapter 12

The following day was a blur.

As I'd already made the journey to Whale's Keep once, I knew what to expect and time passed more quickly than before, even though we were somewhat delayed by one of the horses going lame. We reached the shore across from Whale's Keep well after the dinner hour, but Christophe still loaded me into a boat and helped row me across to the island. The darkness did not seem to hinder him. Once we'd reached the landing, he walked ahead on the long climb up to the village, and we had not exchanged a word all day.

I followed him through the village and into the courtyard. My skirt was wet from the crossing, but the hood of my fur-lined cloak was up, keeping my head warm. He opened the front doors to the keep and walked inside.

Again, I followed.

Mildreth was walking down the center passage toward us and I remained behind him with my hood up.

"Brother," she said, sounding tentative, almost as if she feared him. "I'd heard you returned. Was this mad quest of yours successful? Have you brought back a wife?"

"I have."

He stepped aside and she watched me as I drew back the hood of my cloak.

Her mouth fell half open. "What is the—You cannot mean you have—?"

"The lady Nicole is my wife," he said. "It is done."

"This betrayer? You've brought her back into our home?"

When he turned on her, she drew back, and I realized I'd not been wrong. She was afraid of him.

"I am tired," he said. "Go to bed, Mildreth. We will speak of this in the morning."

With her body held tightly, she left us with as much dignity as she could muster, walking down the east passage.

But Christophe was watching me now.

"You will sleep in your sister's old apartments. I trust you know the way," he said. Then he leaned closer. "Shall I come up and join you there?" With this taunt, one side of his mouth curled into a snarl and again, I found it hard to believe him so easily capable of cruelty. He had been stoic and perhaps too easily hurt before, but he had never been cruel.

Still, it made fighting back easier, as I was assuaged of any possible guilt. Standing straight, I held my head as high as possible. "As my husband, that is your right, *my lord*."

He flinched.

In this matter, I was beginning to realize that I had little to fear. Given the current state of things between us, I would never give myself to him and he would never force himself on me. He may have changed, but in my heart, I did not believe he had changed to that degree.

I wasn't wrong.

Without another word, he walked away.

* * * *

And so, I became the lady of Whale's Keep.

After a restless night, during which I wept several times, the next morning I dressed and brushed my hair and walked down the great hall. Even in summer, a fire had been lit, as the wind from the sea could be cold. Several servants bustled about, sweeping and hauling away ashes.

They curtsied to me politely. "My lady."

"Where is Lord Christophe?" I asked, not sure I wanted to know.

"I believe he's gone to the shore to confer with Captain Fáuvel, my lady," a middle-aged woman answered.

"He does that at least once a week," came a voice from the archway. "It is one of his duties, but he'll be back for dinner."

I knew the voice without needing to look: Mildreth.

She had her children with her and they both carried several books. In spite of my own self-pity, I could not help but pity them. Jordan looked to be about ten years old. He never spoke or smiled. Amanda was eight, and as cowed and serious as her brother.

But Mildreth was assessing me.

"Children," she said, "begin your studies and I will return directly." Looking to me again, she said, "Come. I want to show you something."

Raising an eyebrow, I could not help my curiosity and followed her. She led the way to the back south corner and then entered a stairwell.

"Where are we going?" I asked.

"Just come."

One floor up, we emerged from the stairwell, but she turned and we entered a turret with curving stairs leading up. I continued following her all the way to the top and then we stepped out into the wind at the top of the tower.

Walking to the other side, she gazed out through an open space between the crenellations. "Come here and look."

As the sea wind swept my long hair about my face, I went over and stood beside her, holding in a gasp. We were directly over the sea. White waves crashed into the rocky shore below, and the ocean stretched out as far as the eye could see.

She watched me with contempt. "You see? This place is no warm lodge where we host tea parties for useless noblewomen. I don't know how you managed to turn Christophe's head, but just like your sister, you will soon regret it."

I did not respond.

She gazed back out over the rough sea. "As far as you're concerned, this is the far edge of the world and only the strongest survive here." Leaving my side, she walked back toward the doorway. "Think on that as you contemplate your coming days."

Then she was gone, leaving me at the top of the tower.

But she was wrong about me. I turned my face into the wind and breathed in the sea air. I was not put off by the crashing waves. I found this place wild and cold and beautiful. If she thought to bring me to despair, she was mistaken. Her words had actually helped me to understand my true place here.

I was now the lady of Whale's Keep. And it was Mildreth who should worry about her coming days.

* * * *

Upon leaving the tower, I made my way straight to the kitchen. During my previous stay here, I'd not visited the kitchen, but it was not hard to locate. Once there, I found the place a beehive of activity with a large, scowling woman giving orders.

"You girls get those pots clean this time, or I'll have you dismissed."

At the sight of me, she fell silent, taking in my gown.

"You are the cook?" I asked.

"Yes, my lady," she answered cautiously. "I am Amelia."

I nodded. "I am Lady Nicole, your new mistress."

Though I had no idea if the servants knew their lord had brought home a new wife—a scarce five months after divorcing the previous one—she did not appear surprised, so I assumed she must have heard something.

"I should like to go over the menus for the coming week," I added.

At this, her eyes widened. "The menus? Oh, no, my lady. The lady Mildreth plans all the menus."

I raised one eyebrow. "If Lady Mildreth takes issue with any changes I make, you may send her to me." I paused for effect. "*I* am the mistress of Whale's Keep."

She nodded. "Yes, my lady."

* * * *

Retribution came swiftly, but I expected it.

That night at dinner, Christophe appeared in the great hall, wearing a long-sleeved wool shirt and damp boots, as if he'd just returned from shore and had not bothered to change. Thankfully, he'd shaved at some point since the previous night.

But Mildreth followed on his heels with both children in tow.

I stood by the fire and braced myself.

Christophe glanced at me and then pointedly looked away.

"Brother," Mildreth began immediately. "We have long decided that I manage the household?"

"What?" he asked, sounding tired.

What a fool she was in some ways. Could she not see that he was weary from his day? He'd not even sat down, nor taken a drink of ale, and here she was accosting him like a harping fishwife. Her fear of him from the night before seemed to have vanished. Perhaps she was too indignant to worry about anything else.

"The household," she repeated. "I have managed the household and the servants and the menus for the past eight years."

"Yes, of course," he said, taking a seat and reaching for a cup of ale. "And you've done a fine job."

"Thank you," she responded quickly. "Then you will you kindly tell your new wife that I am in charge of the menus."

With a frown, Christophe shook his head. "What?" he said again.

"The menus! She has taken over the planning of the menus!"

"I am lady of this keep," I said quietly.

The situation finally appeared to dawn on him and his expression grew cautious.

Mildreth ignored me. "May I point out that her…predecessor had nothing to do with the running of the household."

I felt myself stiffen. No, Chloe had been shut out of management of the household because she lived in constant fear of discovery and she had catered to Mildreth's every whim. I was not Chloe and I had nothing to lose here.

Christophe shifted uncomfortably in his chair. "I see. You two will need to decide shared duties between yourselves."

"There is nothing to decide," I answered, looking him directly in the eyes. "I am your wife. I am the mistress of this keep."

He stared back at me. He was the one who'd forced this situation and perhaps now he was getting a little more than he'd bargained for.

With a sigh, he said, "Mildreth, in essence, Nicole is right. She is lady here."

Mildreth's mouth dropped half-open. "You're taking her side?"

He slammed the cup of ale on the table. "I take no one's side! I only want to eat dinner in peace. Now sit down."

She drew away from him and I had a feeling that before the night of young Gideon's birth, he'd never spoken to her like this.

With great purpose, I looked to the nearest servant. "Please have dinner served."

Mildreth glared at me in hatred, but she took her chair, as did the children. I was sorry they'd had to witness this scene.

We ate our meal in silence and I could not help thinking on my family back at the lodge, how Erik always kept us entertained through dinner, and how we enjoyed our meals in mutual affection for each other.

Even before the night of Gideon's birth, I had not felt affection among this family. Christophe barely noticed the children and he and Mildreth had seemed more like business partners than brother and sister. But I was beginning to realize that for better or for worse, this was my home now, and I could choose not to be miserable.

As the last of the dishes were cleared away, I asked Christophe, "Have you decided where you'll build my henhouse?"

He blinked. "What?"

"Last summer, you promised to build me a henhouse here, and that you would paint it white with blue trim."

At my reference to last summer, his features flattened and he stood up. "That was before."

He walked away and Mildreth shot me a look of pure triumph.

* * * *

The next day, I went to the keep gates and met a middle-aged guard, whose first name was Jerome, who oversaw the daily guards at the gates. He seemed somewhat daunted to speak with me and although I'd rarely used it in my entire life, I was aware of the effect that a tiny, pretty young woman with long, waving hair might have on a man.

"Would you please escort me just outside the gates?" I asked.

"My lady?"

"Just outside for a few moments, please."

"Of course."

He was of medium height with peppered brown hair, a heavy bone structure, and he wore his armor well. True to my word, we walked only a few steps outside the courtyard. The village spread out around us.

But outside the gate, I found a spot of open ground.

"Can this spot of land be used by his lordship?" I asked.

Jerome seemed to find the question odd. "The entire island belongs to his lordship."

Well, yes, technically that was true, but many people here owned the land upon which their businesses had been constructed.

"Could I have a henhouse built here?" I asked.

"I see. Yes, of course."

"Good. I'll need you to arrange some things for me."

* * * *

The following day, construction began. Jerome helped me to hire a carpenter who brought wood and supplies. I worked with the carpenter to explain exactly what I wanted and how I wanted the nests arranged.

Once the structure was built, a few of the guards from the front gate came out to help with the painting: white with blue trim.

Then, we started on the fence.

This all took about a week and during that time, I continued handling the menus and I took over the overseeing of the laundry, but I left all issues with the servants and the cleaning schedule to Mildreth. I was busy with the henhouse and I thought it wise to leave some of the household management to Mildreth. I had made my point to her and it wouldn't do to leave her with nothing.

For one, it would be unkind—and I had no wish to be unkind to her—and two, a bored Mildreth could be a dangerous Mildreth. I had no wish for her to be unhappy.

On the eighth day, one of the women from the village brought me some baby chicks and as I sat with them in the fence yard of the henhouse, a first true feel of happiness sparked inside me. Perhaps I could build a life here.

The morning only improved when I looked over to see Amanda watching me. The day was windy and some of her hair had escaped its tight bun. At first, I was alarmed.

"Amanda, does your mother know you're out of the keep?" I asked.

But her gaze was on the yellow bit of fluff in my hands.

"Jerome told me you had baby chicks," she said. This was the first time I'd heard her speak.

I smiled. "Come and join me."

Entering the fence yard, she sat beside me and I placed a chick in her lap. Stroking its back carefully, she asked about their care and I promised to let her help me feed them. One of the guards was still working on painting the trim of the henhouse, and my feeling of contentment grew until a shadow passed over us.

Christophe stood there, inside the fence, his expression one of near-disbelief as he gazed from the guard with the paintbrush down to Amanda, the chicks, and me.

"What is all this?" he demanded.

"I should think that would be obvious," I answered. "It is a henhouse. I had it built."

"You had it built? How much did it cost?"

"I've no idea. I'm having all the bills sent directly to you."

He stared at me. Then, to my astonishment, he crouched down beside Amanda. "You like chicks?" he asked her.

She nodded. "They are soft and they peep. Nicole says I can help her feed them."

Perhaps it was my imagination, but something in his face seemed to alter and for an instant, the hardness faded. Once again, he took in the sight of the new henhouse.

Then he sighed, as if in resignation. "Nicole, where do you want the herb garden?"

* * * *

He helped to choose a spot not far from the henhouse and we began work on the herb garden, first clearing and tilling the area. This took a few days and then he and I began work on a rock border.

Amanda visited in the mornings to help me with the chicks, and then she went inside to do her lessons. I wondered what Mildreth thought of this, but she did not stop the child from coming. Christophe seemed affected by Amanda's presence with us, as if he'd never noticed her before, and something about this caused me to think on Jordan.

Through Christophe and I worked easily together, we had not spoken much since beginning our mutual project of the herb garden. But on the afternoon of the third day, as we worked on the rock border, I asked him, "Christophe, how old were you when you first learned to ride?"

He was crouched beside me, setting a stone deep into the dirt. "To ride? I don't know. My earliest memories are of sitting on a horse with my father. Not long after I could walk, he bought me a pony."

"And what of using a sword? How old were you when you began learning to use a sword?"

He tilted his head thoughtfully. "I was six when I started training with a wooden sword, and I was around ten when my father had me switch to a metal short sword. He had me swinging that blade for hours. He said in a battle, it wasn't skill that would keep me alive, but stamina."

I sat down in the dirt, not caring about my dress. "So, you could ride before you can even remember, and you were training with a sword by the age of six?"

"Yes. Why?"

"Well…Jordan is at least ten years old. I'm not sure he's ever been on a horse, much less held a sword."

This turn of the conversation caught Christophe off guard and his expression closed up. "His father will decide when he should learn those skills."

"His father isn't here. You are his uncle, his closest male adult relative. If he's to learn horsemanship and swordplay, you will need to teach him."

"His father works in finance. He may not care if Jordan can use a sword."

"Perhaps not, but Jordan will need to survive in a world of men, and he'll need to know how to ride and defend himself. Don't you agree?"

He did not answer, but I could see him thinking.

* * * *

Two days later, I was ready to begin planting. Though summer was halfway done, I still had time to get the perennial herbs such as lavender, thyme, and oregano started. As I did not need Christophe's help with planting, I set out with Amanda that morning.

She helped me to care for the baby chicks and then she hurried off to do her lessons.

While setting about planting the lavender, I grew so focused on my work that I lost track of time. When I looked up at the sky, I realized it was past lunchtime. Standing, I stretched my back and headed back to the keep.

But I passed through the gates to an unexpected sight.

There, in the center of the courtyard, Jordan was up on the back of a horse. He was in a saddle and holding the reins of a bridle in one hand. Christophe had the horse on a lead and it was walking in a circle around him.

"Good," Christophe called. "Just feel your weight in the stirrups and don't pull on his mouth."

Mildreth stood to one side, wringing her hands in worry. But she did not interfere. For once, she looked like a concerned, loving mother. Jordan was beaming. He was not remotely afraid and sat on the horse quite well for a first lesson.

"All right," Christophe called. "I'm going to break him into a trot. Just move up and down in the saddle like I showed you."

He made a clucking sound and the horse began to trot.

Quietly, I moved up beside Mildreth. Jordan rose slightly and then let himself sit again, over and over, with the rhythms of the horse's trot. He did not pull on the animal's mouth and I knew the horse would respond to his easy manner.

"He's a natural," I said.

Mildreth did not answer, but she stopped wringing her hands.

The horse trotted a good ten minutes and then Christophe said, "Now, you pull him up yourself, Jordan. Do it softly."

Jordan pulled slightly on the reins and the horse slowed to a walk.

I clapped in applause and called out, "Well done!"

Christophe turned his head to see me standing there and to my amazement, he smiled.

* * * *

That night at dinner, Amanda informed me that some of the baby chicks had begun molting and Jordan chatted about how he wanted to let the horse canter next time.

"Mama," he said, "Uncle Christophe says that next week, he'll start teaching me to use a sword."

"Yes, I heard," Mildreth answered, but she was not disapproving. If anything, she seemed relieved. Perhaps she had come to some of the same conclusions as me.

Tonight, we almost sounded like a normal family at the dinner table. Perhaps the illusion is what caused me to drop my guard, because I thought on the large supply of oregano I would need to plant tomorrow and while contemplating how long this would take me, I turned to Mildreth as I would have my mother or sister.

"Mildreth, I'd like to get an early start in the herb garden tomorrow, and it's the first day of the new week. Would you mind going over the menus with Amelia in the morning? I don't think I'll have time."

And then I went still, realizing that I'd not only just asked Mildreth for a favor, I had offered to relinquish one of the duties I'd commandeered. Bracing myself, I waited for her withering reply.

She did not answer at first, and then said, "No, I don't mind. I'll see to it first thing after breakfast."

I was stunned. "Thank you."

An ember of hope glowed inside me. She and I would never be friends and we would certainly never be sisters. But perhaps we could become something other than enemies.

Jordan yawned.

"You have had a busy day," Mildreth said, rising. "It is time for bed. Come now, both of you."

Obediently, they both rose and followed her from the room.

"Good night," I called.

"Good night, Aunt Nicole," Amanda called back. "I'll see you in the morning."

Aunt Nicole.

I watched her walk through archway, but Christophe was watching me. The servants had cleared the dishes and we were alone.

"You did well with Jordan today," I said. "From the stories I've heard, my father was not so patient with Erik."

Christophe stood and walked to the hearth, looking into the flames. "I've long thought on ways in which I'd teach my own son to ride."

Standing, I moved to join him, but stopped as a shadow crossed his face. I did not know what he was thinking, but I guessed his mind had gone back to the months prior to Gideon's birth, when he believed his own son was soon coming.

Unwanted guilt washed through me and I tried to push it away. Perhaps it was time Christophe and I finally spoke of matters between us. After all, we had been married for nearly two weeks.

"Do you plan to have a son, my lord?" I asked.

A muscle in his jaw twitched. "And what does that mean?"

"Given the state of matters between us, I don't see how the creation of a child is possible."

He swung around to face me. "What would you have me do? I have longed for you, ached for you. But now, every time I look at you all I see is someone who chose her sister over me, someone who would have betrayed me and willingly stopped my line."

This was the crux of his inability to forgive me. I knew the importance of bloodlines to him and how badly he had wanted a child of his own bloodline and my family's. He was not wrong that I had conspired to make another man's son the heir to Whale's Keep. But I had not done so out of a spirit of treason, only out of a need to save my sister.

Once again, the words formed in my mind and I wanted to shout them. *She is my sister!*

But I held them back and did not speak them. Instead, it occurred to me that these words had been my only response on the two occasions we'd spoken of my betrayal. I had never asked for his forgiveness.

"Of all the people in the world," I began, "you are the last one I would wish to hurt. When I first learned that Chloe was with child and that Julian had abandoned her, I did not know what to do. Before the wedding itself, I did nothing because I could not choose between you and Chloe. I couldn't choose. I thought to let fate decide. But then when I arrived here and found Julian preying upon her...." My own words sounded weak, even to me.

Christophe's body was completely still.

"You couldn't choose between me and Chloe?" he asked.

"Of course not!" I cried. "I loved you both. But I found myself caught up in trying to save my sister and I am sorry. Christophe, I am so sorry for what I almost did to you. Please forgive me."

His body looked like a coiled spring now and he was breathing hard. But he closed the distance between us in a few strides and grasped the back of my head. His mouth pressed down on mine and at first, the sensation was so shocking I almost drew away. Then I felt pleasure from the soft pressure and moved my mouth against his. Reaching up, I wound my arms around his neck while kissing him, taking as much as I gave.

Wrenching his mouth away from mine, he still gripped my head and whispered, "I love you."

"Come to my rooms."

* * * *

In the middle of the night, I lay in his arms. We were both naked, but he was finally asleep. I listened to the sound of his breaths and felt his heart beating. I thought on all we had done together this night, joining our bodies without speaking another word, and I regretted nothing.

For better or for worse, I was Christophe de Fiore's wife.

* * * *

Three days later, the two of us took a walk out of the south side of the village, looking for a place to build my beehives. Christophe had not wanted the beehives too close to the keep's front gates, for fear of the guards being stung.

He led me to a meadow around the south side.

"What do you think?" he asked.

It was not beautiful as my meadow at the lodge. The grass was more tan than green and there were not so many types of flowers. But it would serve us. It was far enough from the keep and yet an easy walk for me.

"Perfect," I said, even though it was not perfect. It did not need to be perfect.

I thought back to that day at the lodge, out in the meadow, when Christophe had first told me of his love and his vision for us, and he'd pleaded with me to marry him. How changed we were from those two people.

I had viewed him as both kind and selfless, and he had viewed me as his guileless love. Now, I knew him capable of cruelty and abuse of power. He knew me capable of great betrayal. We had damaged each other in ways beyond repair and neither one of us would ever be the same.

We could never start over. But perhaps we had a new place to begin.

* * * *

The meadow around me disappeared. I found myself once again inside my bedroom at the lodge and staring into the center panel of the three-tiered mirror.

Struggling to breathe, I thought on all that I had just lived through.

The faces of Christophe, Chloe, Julian, and Mildreth swam around me. But the dark-haired woman was now looking out from the left panel.

"That would be the outcome of the second choice," she said. "Now you'll go back to the beginning again, to live out the third choice."

"Wait!" I cried. "Give me a moment."

I needed to think.

"To the beginning once more," she said. "To live out the third choice."

My mind went blank and the bedroom vanished.

The Third Choice:
Telling the Family

Chapter 13

I was standing in Chloe's closet, feeling disoriented, as if I'd forgotten something and needed to remember. Peeking out a crack between the closet door and the wall, I saw my sister standing in her bedroom with Julian Belledini.

"You liar," she said. "You made me believe you wanted to spend your life with me."

He stepped away from her. "And I did—I do. But not like this. Marry Lord Christophe. You have no choice now. In three years' time, you'll thank me."

Turning, he walked out.

Chloe put both hands to her mouth to stifle a sob.

Then I remembered. I'd come in here to find her dress from the banquet, so that it might be laundered, and I'd overheard that she was carrying Julian's child.

Moments later, one of her servants called to her through the door. She composed herself as best she could and left the room. I remained in the closet, trying to let myself fully comprehend what I had just learned. Chloe now had no other option than to marry Christophe.

What should I do?

If I remained silent, Chloe and Christophe would be married and if the child were a boy, the heir to Whale's Keep would not even be of the de Fiore line. Could I do that to Christophe? And yet, if I spoke up, Chloe could be ruined. I couldn't stand the thought of hurting either of them. I could not choose between them, but in this moment, remaining silent seemed the same as choosing Chloe.

This was not a decision to be made alone. I needed help. I needed help from people who loved Chloe and who cared for Christophe.

In my mind, I began to locate my family. Mother was still in the laundry room and Erik would be at the barracks. At this time of day, Father would most likely be in his private study. He was particular about not being disturbed there, but this matter could not wait.

Leaving the closet, I walked out of Chloe's bedroom and started up the passage. To my gratitude, Jenny was trotting down the passage toward me.

"Was the gown not in the closet, my lady?" she asked. "I came to see if I might help."

"Jenny," I breathed. "Please go to the barracks and find Lord Erik. Tell him to come to my father's study straightaway."

Her eyes widened. "The barracks?"

"Yes, tell him it is urgent."

At the word "urgent" she nodded. "Yes, my lady."

Together, we went outside. She headed off for the barracks and I hurried down the path toward our second residence, to the large laundry room. There, I found my mother overseeing the wringing of the sheets and I walked straight to her.

"Mother," I said. "I've just heard some news that must be shared in private. Will you come with me to Father's study? Jenny has gone to find Erik."

Straightening, she frowned—which was unusual. "We cannot disturb your father in his study. You know that."

"He'll understand. Please, Mother. Come with me."

Perhaps it was the frightened quality of my voice, but she turned to speak to the women. "Carry on without me. I'll return directly."

As she followed, I led us out of the building and back up the path to enter our main residence. Father's study was on the main floor, near the south end. Mother and I were nearly at the end of the passage when the far outer door opened and Erik ran inside, wearing chain armor and a dark green tabard.

He saw us instantly. "Nicole, what's happened? Has Father taken ill?"

"No," I answered, turning to knock on the study door. "Father, it is us." Without waiting for an answer, I turned the knob and entered. The study was a good-sized room with leather-covered chairs and tapestries on the walls depicting hunting scenes. My father sat behind an oak desk with ledgers in front of himself and a quill in his hand.

He was taken aback at the sight of me. No one knocked on his study door at this time of day, much less opened it without being invited.

"What are you—?" he began.

Quickly, I cut him off by ushering my mother and Erik inside and then I closed the door. They were all staring at me as if I'd taken leave of my senses.

Perhaps I had. But I could not keep this information to myself. I was not wise enough to know what to do. My mother, father, and brother would know how to solve this, how to help both Chloe and Christophe.

But how to begin? As I stood there, Erik grew annoyed. "Nicole, what is this about? I left men waiting for me at the barracks."

My father was more than annoyed and I could see his expression growing darker. Had there been some emergency, such as a fire, I would have blurted it out well before now.

"I was in Chloe's closet," I said, trying to keep my voice steady, to explain this clearly. "She did not know I was there and she came into her room with Julian Belledini."

"In her bedroom?" my mother gasped.

"She told him that she carried his child," I continued, sorry to tell Chloe's secret, but knowing I was doing the right thing.

Reactions around the room were starkly different. My father jumped to his feet. My mother sank down in a leather-covered chair, and Erik closed the distance between the two of us and grabbed my arm.

"You heard her wrong," he said angrily. "What exactly did she say?"

His fingers hurt, but so did his words. Did he think me likely to share such damaging information as a misinterpretation?

Looking up into his face, I answered. "She told him that she carried his child and they would need to tell Father, so that Father could break off the betrothal to Christophe. She thought Julian would marry her. But he told her that he would not marry her, not like this. He feared what would become of them both. He told her to marry Christophe."

Mother put one hand to her mouth. "Oh, my gods. My poor girl."

Erik's head swiveled toward her. "Poor girl? Don't you see what she's done? She's placed all our people at risk!"

I'd not expected Erik to be angry. He loved Chloe and cared deeply for Christophe. I expected him to help us find a way to help them both.

My father stood in silence, taking in the news.

Erik let go of my arm and walked toward him. "Father, this can be managed. If she is only a month or so along, we can move the wedding date closer. Julian will need to be silenced unless you think he can be trusted enough to be bought off."

My father stared at him. "What are you saying?"

"I'm saying all is not lost. This can be managed."

"You still seek to marry Chloe to Christophe?" my father asked in disbelief. "To dupe him into thinking the child is his?"

"What other choice do we have? We need those soldiers. You've finally given me the funds to hire and train new men, but it will be years before we have a force as large and skilled as Christophe's. Years!"

"And what of our honor? I will not play Christophe so falsely!"

"You speak of honor?" Erik shouted. "When it's your fault that we've gone groveling to him in the first place! If you had acted as his father did ten years ago, we'd have our own private force by now!"

Father's face tinged with red.

Mother and I watched this in horror. They were shouting at each other. Of all the things I'd expected, this was not it. I wished I had not spoken at all now.

Ignoring Erik, my father came around the side of his desk. "Nicole, where is Chloe now?"

"In the kitchen, I think," I answered quietly.

Striding to the door, he opened it and looked out into the passage. "You!" he called.

"Yes, my lord," a voice answered.

"Have someone sent to the barracks to fetch Julian Belledini. And have someone find Lady Chloe. Have them both sent here. Now!"

"Yes, my lord."

Father left the door half-open, but his breaths were coming fast. I had never seen him so openly angry.

"What are you going to do?" my mother asked him. "Do not be unkind to Chloe. Julian seduced her. You have seen him with her."

My father did not answer.

We all waited in silence, but the wait was not long.

Soon, Chloe arrived, walking through the half-open door. "Father?" she said, coming inside. Then she saw the entire family waiting. "What has happened?"

Before anyone could speak, Julian walked in. "My lord?" He stopped at the sight of us all. He was shockingly handsome, as always, but a flicker of uncertainty crossed his features. "Is something amiss?"

Erik glared at him in hatred. Mother sat in distress with her hands clasped.

Chloe began turning pale. "Father, why have you called us here?"

Father turned on Julian. "You have seduced my daughter and she carries your child."

Silence followed and Julian's expression turned to that of a cornered animal. For once, he was speechless. I wanted to sink under the floor. This was not what I had wanted. I had wanted help to know the right thing to do for both Chloe and Christophe. Now Father and Erik were at odds and Chloe was being humiliated before the entire family.

"Father—" Chloe began, her voice shaking.

"Do not speak!" he roared and then he swung back toward Julian. "You will marry her as soon as a ceremony can be arranged."

At that, Julian managed to gather himself and his voice took on its usual charming tone. "Of course. That was my intention. She and I simply had not decided how to speak to you yet. Perhaps you and I could privately discuss the dowry?"

"Dowry?" Erik jerked a dagger from his left sleeve and started toward Julian.

But Father held up one hand to stop him, while still speaking to Julian. "I will write to your father today to tell him of your actions here. He will arrive directly and you will marry Chloe. There will be no dowry and no stipend. There will be no family heirlooms placed into her keeping. You and she have both brought shame onto your families."

Chloe was stricken at his words about shame, but when she looked to Julian, I saw something else in her eyes: relief. She wanted to marry him.

Julian's voice lost all of its charming quality. "And how do you expect your daughter to live? How will we support a home? Do you wish her and your grandchild to live in squalor? What kind of father are you?"

The red tinge in my father's face turned a shade of purple. "Get out!" he shouted, "or I'll let Erik run that dagger through your ribs."

Julian walked from the study.

"Father—" Chloe began again.

"Out!"

She fled the room.

Erik's glare was now on my father. "You've just killed half our people."

But Father's attention was on me. "No. I have not."

* * * *

Over the following days events moved swiftly.

My father sent a letter to Julian's father. Within a week, Lord Belledini arrived at the lodge and he and Father had several meetings behind closed doors. Lord Belledini was a good man, nothing like his youngest son. He and Father had long been friends and between the two of them, they came to an arrangement that was a bit kinder to the young couple than my father had first suggested.

A letter was sent to Whale's Keep, summoning Christophe.

I admitted my part in this to Chloe, but I explained why I had shared her secret and she was not angry with me. In fact, she was almost grateful. Because of my actions—my betrayal of her secret—she would not have to marry Christophe and would be allowed to marry Julian.

I did not point out that Julian was being forced.

Two days after the letter was sent to Christophe, I was with my hens when I heard hoofbeats in the courtyard and I knew he had arrived. Leaving the henhouse, I walked to my meadow and to my beloved bees.

I thought he and Father might be speaking for a long time, so I waited. However, the wait was not long.

Less than a half hour after his arrival, Christophe came striding around the side of the barracks, pausing only briefly at the sight of me before closing the distance between us. He had come to me here just over a week before, telling me things that altered the scope my world.

I watched him coming toward me now, dressed in his armor and de Fiore tabard. With his short, dark hair and clear gray eyes, I found him far more attractive than Julian Belledini.

He stopped a few paces away. "Your father has released Chloe from her betrothal to me."

"Yes," I answered.

"And he's given me permission to ask you for your hand."

This startled me. I'd not been under the impression that I would be *asked* anything in this arrangement. Christophe had made no secret of his feelings for me, and I knew full well what would be the price of his soldiers.

As if reading my face, he took a step closer. "This is entirely your decision," he said. "I've told your father that no matter what you choose, I'll supply your family with a large contingent to guard your shoreline. I will sign documents in this regard."

"You will?"

"I'll not have you look back later and see yourself sold into marriage. You marry me out of choice or you don't marry me at all." He sank down into the tall grass, on his knees. "Will you?"

I thought back on his vision of our lives together, of him building me a henhouse and the two of us finding happiness together at Whale's Keep. Over the past few days, I had become resigned, but to my quiet surprise, I wanted to marry him.

"Yes," I said.

Instantly, he was on his feet again, clasping one of my hands in his. "Yes?" I nodded. "Yes."

Exhaling slowly, he said, "I could hardly believe it when your father told me why he'd called me here. I can still hardly believe it." He leaned down. "Marry me tonight. Let me go into the village and get the elder. I want to start our life together as soon we can."

This was awkward, but I did not draw my hand away. "Christophe, we will have to wait a little."

He frowned. "Why?"

"Did Father tell you why he released you from the betrothal to Chloe?" Slightly uncomfortable, Christophe nodded.

"He was very angry with Chloe and Julian at first," I went on. "But he and Lord Belledini have talked at length, and they both wish to preserve family honor and do the right thing. Lord Belledini will allow the new couple to live in a cottage on Belledini lands, near a vineyard that Julian will some day inherit. Though there will be no great dowry or family jewels, my father has agreed to provide Chloe with a small yearly stipend, enough to support a household. They will not lose their place in society."

Christophe nodded impatiently. "Yes, that is good of both fathers and only right. But how does it affect us?"

"If we're to preserve honor and make this appear more of a planned marriage, Chloe and Julian will need a wedding. We will need time to announce the change of Chloe's betrothal and to celebrate her wedding to Julian. Do you understand? She is the elder sister and she should be married first. Once this is done, you and I can make our plans."

Thinking on this, he relented. "Yes... I do see. When will their wedding take place?"

"At the end of this month, and of course we want you there."

"All right. I can wait. I'll need to go home, but I'll be back for the ceremony."

I knew he would understand. Christophe was a kind man and he always put the needs of others first.

* * * *

When Chloe learned that I was to wed Christophe, she grew alarmed, fearing that my father and Erik were now using me in their bargaining for soldiers. But I assured her that I was not being forced. It took me a while to convince her. She could not seem to imagine any woman *wanting* to marry Christophe.

I found this ironic, as I couldn't imagine any woman wanting to marry Julian Belledini.

But preparations for their wedding occupied life at the lodge.

At the end of the month, guests began arriving. At first, eyebrows had been raised over the change in grooms, but as Christophe had raised no objection and both my family and the Belledinis were sanctioning the marriage, in the end, everyone who was invited attended.

I knew there would be a little more gossip when a seven-month child arrived, but such things were not uncommon. So long as the couple was married and had the support of their families, the other nobles would smile and wink.

The evening before the wedding, Christophe arrived and I was so glad to see him. My parents held a dinner that night for our guests, serving salmon and baked potatoes and a good cask of wine. Christophe and I sat together, eating off the same plate. Chloe had always loved a celebration in her honor and it was a wonderful night.

I could see she was deliriously happy. Even though I had initially regretted my decision to tell my family her secret—given the explosion this news caused—now I was certain I had done the right thing. I remembered Christophe's words from the first time he'd asked me to marry him, that if I refused, we would be living the wrong lives.

Perhaps he had been right and due to my betrayal of Chloe's secret, I had somehow shifted everyone's path and we were all living the correct lives.

The next day, as I helped Chloe to dress for her wedding, only one thought troubled me: Julian. For the ceremony, Chloe had chosen a beautiful gown of pale amber silk. In her room, she stood before a full-length mirror, admiring it as I laced up the back.

"Chloe..." I said carefully.

"Yes." She turned slightly, so she could see the profile of her gown in the mirror.

"Julian is happy about the wedding, is he not?"

If she heard the caution in my voice, she didn't appear to notice. "He couldn't be happier. He's so encouraged by Father's agreement to provide us with a small stipend, and he's sure that soon, Father will relent even more and increase the sum."

I found it worrisome that Julian's main reason for happiness was my father's agreement to provide money, but I didn't mention this.

"More, he'll be allowed to stop training with Erik," she went on. "Julian was never suited for the military and I don't know what his father was thinking. We'll live in the cottage, on Belledini lands, and Julian will begin to study the art of wine-making. He's quite taken with the idea."

Again, I said nothing. I only hoped that Julian would apply himself more to the study of making wine than he had to the study of using a sword or a bow.

That afternoon, Chloe walked into the gathering hall to the sound of soft gasps. She made the loveliest sight in her pale silk gown with her hair up and long, curled tendrils hanging to her shoulders.

Standing with Christophe, I watched her make her way through the hall toward Julian and a magistrate that Father had brought all the way from Lascaùx. Chloe was radiant and I thought Julian the luckiest of men.

As the two of them swore their vows, Christophe reached down with one hand and laced his fingers through mine.

* * * *

The next day, our guests began leaving, as did the magistrate from Lascaùx, but Christophe remained at the lodge and he asked Julian and Chloe to stay a little longer before leaving for their cottage. Three days following their wedding, Christophe came to me as I worked in my herb garden.

"Nicole," he asked, "do you need a large wedding like Chloe's or would something smaller suit you?"

I thought on that. I'd never cared to be the center of attention in a crowd. "Something small."

"Good. I could bring the elder from the village and we can take our vows by the hearth in your family's dining room. If your father agrees, would you marry me tonight?"

That sounded perfect and I smiled. "Or course I would."

That night, we were wed exactly as he described, surrounded by my family, in front of our hearth in the dining room. He wore the blue tunic with silver thread that I'd sewn for him and I wore my lavender gown. When I swore my vows to always care for him and to protect his heart, I meant it. And when he swore his vows, I heard truth in his voice.

Afterwards, my mother embraced us both and said, "I've had the best guest room prepared for you."

* * * *

Alone with Jenny, in our best guest room, I let her undress me and slip a white nightgown over my head. She brushed out my hair. A few moments after she finished, the door opened and Christophe came inside. Quickly, Jenny picked up the hairbrush and left us.

Christophe glanced around the room. My mother had decorated it with glowing candles and vases of roses and lilacs. A down-filled comforter adorned the bed. Then his eyes moved to me.

But he did not come further into the room and I could see he was uncertain—even nervous.

Thankfully, I'd not been kept in ignorance, as were many young noblewomen. I'd delivered enough babies to know exactly what went on between men and women. In addition, my mother was not embarrassed by speaking of such things, of the natural needs and functions of our bodies. She had told me that for a husband and wife, coming together in the bedroom was meant for much more than the creation of children, that the act formed a unique bond between them. As she and my father shared a clear bond, I believed her.

Christophe stood there, watching me nervously. I could see the desire and longing in his face, but I had no idea how to begin. Finally, he took the few steps between us and leaned down to touch his mouth to mine. The gentle pressure was pleasant. Yet when I tried to kiss him back, he drew in a sharp breath and pulled his head away.

"I want this," he said, "but I don't want to hurt you."

What a good man he was, kind and gentle. I loved him so much. Reaching up, I touched his face.

"You won't hurt me," I whispered.

He kissed me again.

Chapter 14

Only one day later, I faced a new reality, of saying my good-byes.

The courtyard of White Deer Lodge was alive with activity. Christophe and I were preparing to leave for Whale's Keep up the coast, and Chloe and Julian would be heading inland, toward Belledini lands. There were wagons, horses, and guards everywhere. The de Fiore guards would escort Christophe and me, and my father had arranged an escort of our own guards for Julian and Chloe—as Julian's family had left several days before, taking all the Belledini guards with them.

My parents and Erik were also in the courtyard to oversee the packing and see us all off.

But as our luggage was loaded and tied down, a feeling of loss began to weigh upon me. I had wanted this marriage and I wanted to go to Whale's Keep with Christophe, but I was about to lose everyone else whom I loved— or at least that was how I felt. I'd slept in a room adjoined to Chloe's my whole life. I'd never been without Erik or my father for more than a few weeks at a time, when they were off on patrol or collecting taxes or seeing to our villages. I had never been without my mother.

And now Chloe was leaving, and I was leaving, and everything was about to change.

Thankfully, Christophe understood without being told and he did not rush me.

Chloe, however, could not seem to wait to be gone from this place. The summer day was warm and she wore no cloak over a tan muslin traveling gown. The moment her last trunk was tied down, she hugged me.

"Good-bye, little one. I will miss you. Write to me often."

Her words were comforting, but they felt rushed. Julian was in especially good cheer this morning, shaking hands with all the men.

"He seems in high spirits today," I noted.

Chloe smiled. "He is. Several of the wedding guests gifted us with money, and he'd not expected that. Christophe gifted us with two hundred silver pieces." She shook her head in wonder. "Considering the circumstances, I thought that most generous of him." Her voice lowered to a near whisper. "Julian had several...debts here, among our guards. He was able to repay them and we can begin our lives with a clean slate."

Again, something about this worried me. She never talked about Julian being happy with her, only that he was happy that the marriage had supplied him with a cottage, a small yearly income, a way out of training for the military, and gifts of money to pay his gambling debts.

With effort, I pushed down my worries. Of course he valued Chloe. What man wouldn't?

Then, Erik was standing beside me and I buried my face in his chest.

"My girl," he said, kissing the top of my head.

"You'll come to the keep soon?" I asked. "To visit? You promise?"

"Yes, I'll come soon."

When he spoke, I believed him.

Mother and Father embraced Chloe and me and they said their farewells to Christophe and Julian. Mounting a horse, I rode beside Christophe.

I was off to my new home.

* * * *

Early in our journey, Christophe prepared me for how the day would progress. He made certain I would not be shocked at my first sight of the island, and he explained how we would row over in a boat and how we would land.

All day, he was concerned for my comfort, but I assured him I was fine and that he could set a faster pace if he chose. He listened to me and we made good time, stopping only once to eat and a few times to water the horses. Although he was a difficult man to read, at several points I had a feeling he wished to say something to me, and then changed his mind.

We arrived at the shore across from the island before dark. He and three other men rowed me across and we landed on the south side. There was a long climb ahead, but again, he had prepared me and so I knew what to expect.

Following Christophe, I went up and up, and just when my legs were nearly ready to give out, we reached the top and passed through another gatehouse and then we stepped out to the sight of a thriving village, perhaps the size of a town.

All around us, as far as I could see in the increasing darkness, spread roads lined by shops and dwellings. There were taverns and small barns. The ground sloped upward and looking to my right, I saw a great, four-towered keep at the top of the cliffs.

"Oh," I said. "It's beautiful up here."

"I knew you'd say that."

I started forward, but he stopped me. "Nicole…"

Again, he seemed to wish to tell me something.

"Christophe, what is it?"

We were alone on the edge of the village.

He shifted his weight between his feet as if uncomfortable. "You know that I live with my sister, Mildreth?" he asked.

"Yes, I know." A thought struck me. "Oh, will she be upset at having missed our wedding?"

"No, she does not leave the island. But I want you to know some things about her before we go up to the keep." He hesitated. "She is married, with two children. Her husband is Baron Phillipe de Caux, and he is minister of finance to the king, and she lived at court for a while. But she and her husband are no longer…together. Eight years ago, she brought her small son here and shortly after, she gave birth to her daughter. Not long after this, her husband made it clear that he did not want her back."

"Oh, I am sorry."

"My father still lived then and he placed Mildreth in charge of the household. She has managed the house ever since." Again, he hesitated. "Even before the break with her husband, she was not a warm person, but over the years, she has built walls around herself. People think I don't notice this, but I do. Trust me when I say, she is a difficult person for whom to feel affection."

"But you love her?"

"Yes. In my own way, I do. Another reason I was reluctant to marry Chloe is that Mildreth would never have accepted her, even felt threatened by her. They'd have been oil and water. But you and Mildreth might be friends. Whatever you do, don't show her pity. She'd not forgive that, but perhaps you might be willing to share the duties as mistress here?"

At last, I understood what he was trying to tell me, and I commended his concern for his sister.

"Of course, Christophe. I've not been trained to run a great household and I should be glad for both her help and her guidance. I'll not try to take her place."

He breathed in relief. "Thank you. I've been trying to broach this all day."

I followed him up through the village. The back of the keep was built over the cliffs, but a low stone wall bordered the front with a break at the center point, and we passed through the break into a courtyard.

After walking through the courtyard, Christophe ushered me inside the enormous front doors into a square foyer. Passages led right, left, and straight ahead. Only upon entering the front doors of the keep did I realize how wet and cold I was. But as so often happened, Christophe had been aware.

"Roweena!" he called to young serving woman down the left passage.

At the sight of him, her eyes widened and she trotted to us. "My lord?"

"This is Lady Nicole, your new mistress" he said. "Please take her to her rooms and have a fire built. Her trunk will be up directly. Help her to change for dinner and then bring her to the great hall."

"Yes, my lord."

Christophe walked away, calling over his shoulder, "My lady, I'll change for dinner and meet you there."

Though glad for a chance to stand before a fire and change into dry clothing, I wondered about the reference to my own rooms. He and I were married now. Should we not be living in the same rooms?

* * * *

Not long past darkness, I left my new rooms wearing my lavender gown. It was my first evening here and I wanted to look well. Roweena showed me to the great hall and as I walked in, it dawned on me that I was mistress of this vast keep.

Near the hearth, Christophe stood waiting. Beside him stood a woman and two children, a boy and a girl. The woman was tall and gaunt, perhaps thirty years old. She wore a high-necked black gown with a starched white collar. Her hair was pulled into a severe bun at the back of her neck.

Both the children wore serious expressions.

At the sight of me, Christophe's expression softened. "Mildreth, this is Lady Nicole, my wife," he said. "Nicole, this is my sister, Lady Mildreth, and her children, Jordan and Amanda."

I thought it odd that he did not introduce Jordan and Amanda as his nephew and niece, but rather as "Mildreth's children," as if they had no connection to him. But I did not comment and smiled at Mildreth.

"I am so glad to meet you."

She didn't respond and looked at me in surprise. After a moment, she said, "You both must be hungry. I will have dinner brought in."

We sat and I waited for her to ask after our wedding or my parents, or even Erik, who had visited here often. But she did not speak and neither did Christophe or the children. Servants brought in trays of roast beef, green beans, and gravy.

"This looks delicious," I said.

Christophe began to eat and he took a long drink from his cup of ale. I preferred water, but sipped at some wine, becoming more baffled when no one spoke. With children at the table, I assumed the chatter would be nonstop.

"When will you begin building my henhouse?" I asked my husband.

A slight smile touched the corner of his mouth. "Not for a few days. Tomorrow, I need to go to the shore and get a report from Captain Fáuvel."

"What is this about a henhouse?" Mildreth asked.

"Nicole kept hens at White Deer Lodge," Christophe answered. "I promised her a henhouse."

For the first time, Amanda seemed interested in what was happening around her.

I smiled. "Do you like hens?"

She drew back in her chair, as if unused to being asked a question. Then she answered softly, "I like baby chicks."

"Oh, good," I said. "Then when I bring the first chicks in, you can help me care for them."

Her eyes were like saucers at the prospect and she looked to Mildreth. "Could I, Mama?"

"We'll see," Mildreth answered.

Somehow, we made it through dinner, and Christophe said he was tired and would walk me to my rooms.

Mildreth made no response.

* * * *

Christophe brought me back up to the apartments on the second floor, where I had changed for dinner. The rooms were well furnished with low couches, vases of fresh flowers, and a large bedroom. But I was still puzzled about the arrangements.

"You're not too tired?" he asked me. "You don't mind if I stay?"

Flustered, I responded. "What do you mean? Are these not your rooms too? Where are any of your things?"

"My things? They are in my rooms."

"Do you mean to tell me you expect us to live in separate apartments?"

He shook his head. "I don't understand."

"We're married. My parents have always lived in the same rooms together."

Nonplussed, he said, "That is not typical."

"It's not?"

"No. Couples of our station keep separate rooms. I've never heard of a noble couple sharing the same apartments."

"That's absurd. How does anyone make a child with that arrangement?"

This seemed to embarrass him. "The man comes to visit the woman in her apartments when he wishes."

I stared. "You mean to tell me that we are never to sleep in the same bed unless you wish it, and you decide to come here? I am not fond of that that idea at all, are you?"

He thought for a moment. "No...I'm not."

"Then we should live in the same apartments. Will you move in here?"

He shook his head. "You should move into my apartments. They are bigger." Reaching out, he gently grasped the back of my head. "Tomorrow. We'll sleep here tonight."

* * * *

The next morning, Christophe left early to take a boat to shore and confer with the captain. After dressing and eating a light meal in the apartments, I wondered what I should do with my day. While taking stock of the medicinal supplies my mother had sent with me, I noted she'd sent no cough syrup.

Roweena came in to fetch my breakfast tray and I asked her, "Where are the kitchen gardens located?"

"Not far from the kitchen itself, my lady. If you go out the back door, there is a space of land between the keep and the wall that gets enough sun. Our cook, Mistress Amelia, keeps a good garden."

"Are there roses?"

"Yes, my lady."

"Good. I'll follow you down and you can show me the door."

And so I began my life at the keep. I did wonder that Christophe had not remained even one day to show me around and get me acclimated, but I knew he had many duties and as a result, he was a well-respected lord.

I followed Roweena past the kitchen, and I found some shears and a basket and headed out the back of the keep.

She had not been wrong. A plot of land outside sported a fine kitchen garden with peas, potatoes, tomatoes, onions, green beans, and other lush vegetables. To the back of that, I saw a flower garden with an abundance of roses.

Carrying my basket, I began clipping heads and harvesting petals.

I'd clipped only a few when the back door opened and Mildreth walked out. She stopped in mid-step as if not expecting to find me here.

"Good morning, Mildreth," I said. "Did you need me?"

"No, I came to check on the onions. They've not been growing as they should this year." Walking over, she looked into my basket. Her entire body was tense. "What are you doing?"

"Gathering rose petals to make cough syrup. We'll need a good supply for this coming winter."

"You know how to make cough syrup?"

"Yes, and once I have my herb garden growing, I can make a number of other syrups and ointments. My mother is a healer and she taught me."

Lifting her gaze from the basket, she said, "You are not all what I expected."

This puzzled me. "What did you expect?"

"We have visitors here from time to time and I've heard much of your sister. I expected you to be something like her: vain, decorative, and useless. Spending your days organizing tea parties or in fittings for gowns and yet fancying yourself as the lady of the house."

It should have angered me to hear of my sister or myself described in such oversimplified terms, but she spoke with such dispassion, as if discussing the weather as opposed to being critical.

Then her eyes narrowed. "But you are not useless, are you? The question between the two of us is, how useful do you wish to be?"

At this, I felt thankful for Christophe's warning the night before. He'd been wise to tell me of her situation.

"Mildreth," I said. "Christophe has told me that you've managed the household, as mistress, for eight years and that you've done a fine job. You are right that I cannot abide to be idle and I have no talent for tea parties. At home, I had many duties, but I've been neither trained nor prepared to run a great house like this one. While I would like to be included in some matters, such as planning the menus, I have no wish to take your place."

She studied me, as if uncertain whether or not to believe my speech. "Why did you marry my brother?"

"Because I love him. He is the best of men."

Somehow, this was the right answer and the tension in her body eased ever so slightly.

"You and I are sisters now," I added, "and for years to come. It would be best if we could be friends."

The walls she'd created around herself were thick, but she continued to study me. "Perhaps."

* * * *

Summer passed into early autumn.

During the harvest season, Christophe was away from home a good deal, but I'd expected that, as my father and Erik were often out visiting villages and checking harvests at this time of year.

I wrote to Chloe several times, but she answered only once, saying she was busy with her new life. Erik did not come to visit. This hurt a little, but I was finding my place in my own new life.

Christophe and I chose a spot for the henhouse right outside the keep front gates, with a space for an herb garden nearby. He brought me to a meadow outside the village and we decided on this for the beehives.

As promised, he built the henhouse himself, and together we painted it white with blue trim. Young Amanda showed interest in my new chicks and she began to accompany me every morning. Mildreth did not appear to mind and I noticed the girl coming out of her quiet shell more and more.

This caused me to encourage Christophe to spend time with Jordan, teaching the boy things he would need to know. For some reason, this had never occurred to Christophe, but he began teaching the boy how to ride and defend himself.

While busy with my hens, bees, and gardening, I left much of the running of the household to Mildreth, and she was gratified enough to confer with me on the menus. I did not believe we would ever become sisters, but it seemed that perhaps we were becoming friends. Without ever showing her an ounce of pity, I understood that her position here was a tenuous one—as sister of the lord and not his wife—and I had no wish to cause her fear of losing her place in the world.

She, in turn, seemed quietly grateful for Christophe's interest in Jordan. Although I missed my mother, father, Erik, and Chloe, I found myself becoming more and more part of my new family.

Christophe made no secret of his love for me and this was seductive unto itself. When he looked at me, he saw perfection. I was coming to need to see myself through his eyes, and I could tell he needed to see himself through mine. I thought myself the most fortunate of women and did not hide this when I looked at him. My husband was kind and devoted and always put the needs of others before his own.

Only one thing troubled me. I spent every night in a bed with Christophe, taking pleasure in joining my body with his, and yet my courses continued to come each month. I was not yet with child.

Autumn passed into winter. When winter was just on the edge of spring, we faced a shocking tragedy. Somehow, raiders from the sea made their way to a de Fiore village called Chastain and they ravaged it.

Christophe and I joined Captain Fáuvel and a large contingent of guards to travel there to offer our assistance. The people had suffered greatly and eleven young women had been taken. Christophe blamed himself when he learned the raiders had rowed their ships upriver. He'd not foreseen ships that could cross both the sea and traverse a river.

We stayed at the village for over week, where I offered myself as a healer and Christophe worked to rebuild homes. Upon returning home, he launched into plans to block the rivers from passage via the sea.

But for as much sorrow as the event brought to us, working side by side to help his people—who were now my people—this also brought Christophe and me closer together in ways we had not experienced before.

And yet, I wanted to give him a child. Spring was arriving and we had been married in the previous summer. Upon our return from Chastain, I felt my hopes begin to rise. My courses were late and I had been feeling some queasiness in my stomach. I began to believe that I might finally have a child growing inside me.

Then in the early evening, I was in the rooms I shared with Christophe, preparing to dress for dinner, and I felt a cramp in my stomach. Checking my undergarments, I found spots of blood. The sight was crushing. I had been so sure, so full of hope. Unable to stop them, tears flowed down my cheeks.

While I crouched on the floor, weeping, Christophe walked in. At the sight of me there, he ran forward in alarm.

"Nicole!"

Pressing one side of my face against his shoulder, I told him of my sorrow. I let my pain pour out.

He rocked me back and forth like a child. "Is this what's been wrong lately? I've known something was wrong. You should have told me. Please don't worry. My parents were married over a year before Mildreth was conceived. It is not unusual."

I knew this. In my mind, I knew this, but *knowing* something and living through it are two different things. Still, I felt better after talking to him. As always, Christophe offered kindness and comfort.

About a month after this, I received a letter from my mother.

> *My sweet girl,*
> *Forgive me for being so remiss in writing to you of late. I think of you every day.*
> *I have news. Last month, your sister gave birth to a fine son. She and the child are both well, and she has named him Gideon, after your father.*
> *In two weeks' time, she and Julian will be traveling to White Deer Lodge for a visit. I know the baby is young for a journey, but she does so want for us to see him. I suggested that your father and I go to her, but she prefers to come here.*
> *Might you and Christophe join us? It would make my heart glad to have everyone together under one roof for even a short while.*
> *Sending love,*
> *Your mother*

I loved receiving letters from my mother. She wrote with the same warm affection with which she always spoke. I could hear her voice as if she stood in the room. The letter made me want to see her, but more, I wanted to see Chloe and know for myself that she was all right.

That night, I showed the letter to Christophe.

"Might we go?" I asked.

His brow knitted. "I don't know. We're heading into tilling season and I may be needed here to help decide the distribution of community equipment. You would not believe some of the squabbles that take place."

Gripping the letter, I said, "Please, Christophe. She is my sister."

At the longing in my voice, he reached out and touched my arm. "Of course. I'll make the arrangements."

Chapter 15

We arrived in the courtyard of White Deer Lodge a few weeks later with a small contingent of de Fiore guards.

The sight of the familiar log structures, built all around us, filled my heart with joy. My place was at Whale's Keep, but perhaps I would always think of White Deer Lodge as home. Erik came running from the barracks, straight to my horse. Without a word, he reached up and lifted me off, holding me against himself with my feet still off the ground.

It was rather undignified and I struggled. "Put me down."

The instant my feet touched earth, I made a fist and struck his chest. "You have not come to visit."

He didn't seem to notice the blow and kissed the top of my head. "I know. I'm sorry. I've been training men every day."

Christophe dismounted and they greeted each other with affection. I think each one viewed the other as the closest he would ever have to a brother. My parents came hurrying out to greet us. I hugged my father first and then found myself lost in my mother's arms. I did not want to let go of her, but I asked, "Is Chloe here? Where is she?"

"Not yet arrived," my mother answered. "But she will be here before dark."

Belledini lands were about as far inland as Whale's Keep was to the north—a full day's journey. But Christophe and I had made good time and dusk was nearly an hour away. I could wait.

Going inside, Mother and I left the men to their talk of training soldiers. We sat by the fire in the dining room and she asked me many questions about my life at Whale's Keep. It was so good to talk to her.

But then darkness came. Chloe, Julian, and the new baby had still not arrived. The men came in to the dining room to join us and I could see my father was worried. He did not like the idea of Chloe on the road after dark, even with guards. Mother announced we would delay dinner.

I was becoming concerned myself, when we heard the sound of hoofbeats, horses, and voices out in the courtyard.

Mother smiled in relief. "There they are."

A happy group, we all walked out to greet them. But as I emerged into the courtyard, two things struck me: First, the guards around Chloe were not wearing the red tabards of the Belledinis. They were our own family guards, led by Corporal Devon.

Second, Chloe rode in a wagon, holding a bundle in her arms, but Julian was nowhere to be seen.

Christophe reached the wagon first, reaching up. "My lady, hand me the child."

Through the darkness, I followed on his heels. She handed him the bundle. He passed it off to me and I held my nephew in my arms for the first time, looking down into the blanket to see his blond-red hair and blue eyes. He was a tiny copy of Erik.

"Oh," I breathed, at a loss for other words.

Christophe carefully lifted Chloe down, as if she might be made of glass, and then my family was greeting her.

"Where is Julian?" Father asked.

"He could not make it, but sends his love," she answered, her voice strained. "His duties at home were too great at this time of year."

Julian had sent her off by herself?

By the light of a torch, I took my first clear look at Chloe's face. Her skin was stretched thinly over her cheekbones. Her complexion was sallow. Her shining hair had lost its luster. Had the birth been more difficult than I'd been led to believe?

Christophe appeared more puzzled by her escort. "Where are the Belledini guards? Lord Belledini employs a good force."

Chloe did not answer and my mother broke in. "They could not be spared just now, so Lord Gideon sent some of our own men."

This made no sense at all. One of the main purposes of employing guards was to provide protection while traveling. My father had sent our own men all the way to Belledini lands to escort Chloe and Julian—and Julian hadn't even come?

Apparently, the situation made no sense to Christophe either, and he was about to ask another question, when my father said, "Let us all go inside for dinner."

* * * *

Dinner was a strained affair and strained affairs were unusual at White Deer Lodge. My mother appeared determined to pretend that all was well and she fussed over the baby, begging my father to allow young Gideon to remain with us at the table, instead of being taken to the nursery. Father readily agreed and we should have been a merry party, but we weren't. Chloe said little. Late in the night, as I lay pressed up against Christophe's right arm, I whispered, "There is something wrong with Chloe. I think something is wrong in her marriage."

"I know," he whispered back.

"I don't know what to do. Should I ask her?"

"For now, just be kind. Not all marriages are like ours. You need to remember that."

His words were not helpful.

The next day, I awakened determined to help my sister, or at least to find out what was wrong. Of course, Christophe dressed quickly and headed off to the barracks to find Erik. I had a feeling I would not be seeing much of either of those two on this visit.

Christophe and I had been housed in the guest quarters building and Chloe was staying in her old room in the main house. After dressing, I made my way to the main house, hoping to find her with baby Gideon, alone in her rooms, but as I opened the outer door on the south side, near to Father's study, I heard raised voices.

"And don't you try appealing to your mother again!" Father shouted. "You knew full well what kind of man you married. He's done this to himself! You tell him to find his own way out."

Peering through the door, I saw Chloe flee from our father's study. She did not see me and she ran down the passage and out the other side of the building. Quickly, I closed the door and hurried down the path around to the north side. There I saw her running toward the kitchen. I ran after.

But she never entered the kitchen. Instead, she stopped near my herb garden and let out a sound of pain. Running to her, I motioned to a small, iron bench beside the garden. She seemed almost unable to walk now and I helped her over to sit down.

"Chloe, tell me, please. What is wrong?"

She gripped my hand, but would not look at me. "Nicole, I don't know how to tell you. I was so happy when Julian was able to pay off his gambling debts after our wedding, and we were beginning our lives together with a clean slate. I thought that since he had a wife and a coming child, he would take advantage of his father's generosity and apply himself to making wine."

"But he didn't?"

"No," she whispered. "He began gambling again almost as soon as we set up our new home. Within a month, he'd lost the yearly stipend Father had given him for my dowry. There won't be another payment from Father until summer. We've been living on promises to pay our meat and bread bills."

"Oh, Chloe." I could hardly believe it. "How much was the stipend he lost?"

"Two hundred silvers."

I didn't know much about money, but I remembered that Christophe had given Julian the same amount as a wedding gift. "And you came here to ask Father for an advance?"

"No. It's worse."

How could it be worse?

"Last month," she went on, "we were invited to a dinner at Baron du Bonnè's estate. They are close neighbors of the Belledinis. I was near to my time of giving birth, so I did not attend. While there, Julian lost a card game to one of the baron's captains, but as he had no money and could get no credit, he bet the vineyard that his father left to him in the will."

Her voice broke and I went still.

"Julian has gambled away his inheritance?" I asked in disbelief.

"He does not even own the vineyard and he lost it. His father does not know yet and Julian has been madly trying to keep this quiet. Not long after Gideon's birth, Julian came to an arrangement that he could buy the note back for one thousand silvers. The vineyard is worth more, but the captain has agreed."

"And Julian sent you to ask Father for the money?"

"Sent me? No! He came out against it. His father and our father are friends. He did not believe our father would help and might even speak his own on the matter. If Lord Belledini learns that Julian lost a vineyard he does yet own... in a card game, there is no telling what he'll do. He may throw us out of the cottage and wash his hands of us." She took a quick breath. "I had to do something. Julian refused to even give me an escort, so I asked Mother and she had Father send Corporal Devon with Montagna guards."

Something about all this sounded rather calculated on Chloe's part. She had told Mother this visit was to share the sight of baby Gideon with the family. But I could not judge her. She sounded desperate and rightly so.

"I'm such a fool for coming here," she said. "I was certain Father would help us. I thought once he saw young Gideon, he'd not let his grandson suffer."

"Father won't help?"

"No. He said that Julian has made this mistake, and he must take the consequences and solve it himself. He said Julian would not learn otherwise." Her voice broke again. "Julian cannot raise the money on his own and I don't know what to do."

"I would do anything to help you."

"You? You are dear to say that, but there is nothing that you..." She trailed off for a moment and locked her gaze into mine. "Father paid your own stipend last summer as well, didn't he? It was a thousand silvers."

I started slightly. "That much?" Why was my stipend so much larger than Choe's?

"You didn't know? The marriage contract was the same as the one father arranged when I was to marry Christophe. I read mine in detail."

I hadn't known. But I'd never asked. Christophe handled all the money.

"Nicole, listen," she went on. "Christophe doesn't need your dowry. He owns one of the most prosperous estates in the nation and he has a private military to protect it. Father only offered him so much as a matter of honor, but he doesn't need it."

There was the answer.

"Of course," I said. "I will speak to Christophe. I know he will give it to you."

Her face lit up with relief and joy. "Thank you. I cannot begin to thank you."

Movement caught my eye and I looked to see Father step around the side of the building that housed our kitchen. His expression was a mix of anger and disbelief. He stood only ten paces away from us.

"And how did you come to be there?" Chloe asked, as if he were in the wrong, but her voice shook.

"I followed you," he answered. "I thought perhaps I'd been too harsh and sought to speak with you further, but then I saw Nicole and I feared what you might say to her. I wanted to be sure." He shook his head. "I hoped I was wrong. For you to bring this sordid business to your younger sister, to ask her for her own dowry, when you know she would give you anything."

"Father, no!" I cried. "That's not what happened."

Striding closer, he leaned over her as if I hadn't spoken. "You've brought shame to this family more than once," he said to her, "and I'll have no more of it! Do you understand? No more! You wanted that wastrel of a husband and you've got him. Go home and live with him." He turned to walk away and paused. "And I will speak with Christophe myself. He will not give you a penny."

As I sat in shock, my father walked off.

Chloe put her face into her hands and she began to weep silently.

* * * *

That evening, Chloe did not come down to dinner.

Later, in our room, when I tried to explain her plight to Christophe, his expression closed up.

"Do not speak to me on this matter. Your father has made me promise not to pay the debt."

Chloe left the next day. Again, my father provided a contingent of guards to escort her home.

I couldn't help feeling angry with both my father and Christophe. I suppose I should have focused my anger at Julian, but Chloe was in real trouble and I could not fathom my father and Christophe's refusal to help her.

We stayed at the lodge a few more days, but our visit had been ruined. Regarding Chloe's plight, my mother agreed with me, but Father and Christophe would not even discuss the matter. Erik appeared to have no opinion. Sometimes, I wondered if he thought of anything besides guarding our shoreline.

By the morning that Christophe and I were in the courtyard, packed and ready to leave, he and I were barely speaking. This was the first real difficulty between us in our marriage and I didn't know how to solve it.

We said good-byes to Father, Mother, and Erik.

Then we left, heading for Whale's Keep.

For nearly an hour, Christophe and I rode north in silence, with his horse walking beside mine.

"I don't like this," he said suddenly and I heard hurt in his voice. "I don't like us at odds with each other."

Sighing, I answered, "I don't like it either, but I cannot help worrying about Chloe. My own hands are tied and it seems no one else will help her."

"Did I say I wouldn't help her? I promised your father that I wouldn't pay Julian's debt, but I have friends among Lord Belledini's men and I will keep a close eye on what happens. If Julian cannot solve this crisis himself and the couple finds themselves without a home, they will be welcome at Whale's Keep. They will always have a home with us."

Letting his words sink in, I was ashamed. Of course Christophe could not break his word to my father, and of course he would find another way to help my sister. I should have trusted him. The day seemed brighter again.

"Thank you."

* * * *

To my surprise, Mildreth and the children met us in the courtyard upon our return, as if they had missed us.

"I've taken good care of the hens," Amanda said.

"Oh, thank you," I answered. "I knew you would."

"How is the new baby?" Mildreth asked. "Whose family does he favor?"

"He looks just like Erik."

"Heaven forbid," she said.

Was that a joke? Had Mildreth made a joke? With a smile, I linked my arm with hers and we walked inside together.

I was home.

Chapter 16

Full summer was upon us and I made the most of the warm days, as I knew the winters here were long, windy, and cold. My hens were flourishing, as were my bees. I grew and harvested herbs to make medicinal supplies for winter.

I wrote to Chloe every week, asking for news, but she did not answer. Christophe promised he would tell me if he learned anything about Julian's situation.

But for the most part, I was so busy that I lost track of time and then one morning, as I walked out of the courtyard gates with Amanda, going to feed the hens and gather eggs, I began to feel nauseated. Two steps later, I dropped to my knees, retching.

"Aunt Nicole!" Amanda cried. She looked back toward the gates. "Jerome! Jerome, come quick."

The commander of the gate guards came running toward us, but I was counting weeks in my head. My courses were late.

Amanda was distressed and Jerome knelt beside me.

"My lady?"

I was not distressed. "It's all right," I assured. "I am well."

* * * *

I waited another month and my courses did not come. Finally, I could contain the news no longer and in bed one night, I took Christophe's hand and laid it on my stomach.

Then I nodded.

He sat up. "Yes?"

I smiled. "Yes."

* * * *

No letter from Chloe arrived and my worry for her grew worse.

One night, in early autumn, I awoke drenched in sweat and lost in panic. Christophe was away for the night on shore, as the harvest month was upon us. In my mind, I could hear Chloe calling to me. It was like she was screaming for help from a great distance.

I did not know what to do and I didn't sleep for the rest of that night.

The next day, Christophe came home in the afternoon. I could see he was troubled.

"What is wrong?" I asked. "Is there trouble with harvest?"

"No, the harvests are going well in the villages I've visited."

I could see he had something to say and didn't wish to say it. "Then what?"

"I heard news from Captain Fáuvel. He learned from a friend that Lord Belledini discovered Julian had gambled away the vineyard."

I felt cold. "What did he do?"

Christophe hesitated. "He paid the one thousand silvers himself to cover the debt. He did not throw Julian and Chloe from the cottage, but he did rewrite his will and the vineyard has been left to another brother. Julian will have no inheritance."

I sank down into a chair. Though Chloe had not been made homeless, she and Julian would have nothing other than Chloe's yearly stipend. I wrote to Chloe, begging her to write back and give me news. I vowed to help her in any way that I could. I told her of Christophe's offer for them to come and live with us on the island.

She did not respond.

My fears didn't reach a breaking point until a letter from my mother arrived:

> *My beloved girl,*
> *I am in hopes that you can help put my mind at ease. I have*
> *not heard from Chloe since she left the lodge in mid-summer.*
> *I know she made it safely home because Corporal Devon*
> *returned the following day after escorting her. And yet, no letter*
> *from your sister has come. Worried, I wrote to Lady Belledini,*
> *asking after Chloe.*
> *She responded to tell me that Chloe has not been seen since*

her return. She assured me that Chloe and Julian are still living
at the cottage, but Chloe does not venture outdoors and Julian
allows no visitors.

I hope this report is an exaggeration on her part, and that
your sister has been writing to you. If so, please let me know
how she fares. I anxiously await word from you.

Sending love,
Your mother

This letter left me frightened. Chloe was not writing to my mother or to me, and she had not left her cottage since mid-summer. Something was wrong, something more than financial troubles.

Christophe had been home for two days, although I knew he had yet to visit the northernmost villages to check the harvests, and he would most likely be leaving again soon. I needed to stop him.

Clutching the letter, I went in search of him, and I found him in the courtyard of the keep, down near the gates, speaking with Jerome. As I walked toward him, he saw me and broke off his discussion, coming to meet me halfway.

"Do you need me?" he asked.

"Yes, I've received a letter from my mother. I believe Chloe is in great difficulty. Something is very wrong. I need you to take me to Belledini lands as soon as possible, tomorrow if you can arrange it."

Taken aback, Christophe reached out for the letter. He read it. "Nicole...I can see your concern, but there are a number of reasons why Chloe might have taken to not leaving her house. You know their financial situation. She may be with child again or she may have decided to live quietly."

"No! I know my sister. If that were the case, why is she not writing to my mother or me? Something is wrong and I need to see her. I believe she needs help."

His expression closed up. "You know I can't leave during the harvest and even if I could, you are carrying our child. I'll not risk you or the child on a journey. Let me see what I can learn."

"You'll learn hearsay and rumors! I need to see Chloe myself. Please, Christophe. I'm asking you. Please."

He shook his head. "No."

With that single word, my vision of our life together altered. I had thought us a team. I knew if he ever asked me for anything, I would do it. I thought the same of him, that if I truly asked him for his help, he would grant it.

But he had made the final decision for us both, and he'd said no.

The following morning, I saw him off as he left to head for the shore. He kissed me and his eyes begged my forgiveness. "I promise that I'll see what I can learn."

"I know you will."

I kissed him back and he set off for the stairwell, for the long climb down.

* * * *

I spent the day in preparations.

The following morning, Amanda accompanied me to care for our hens and then I walked her up to the keep for her lessons. I knew that Mildreth would be busy with the children for several hours.

Going up to the room I shared with Christophe, I took a bag that I had carefully packed and I went back downstairs, walking through the courtyard, through the gates of the keep, through the village, and down the long stone steps. Emerging from the final gatehouse, I found twelve of our guards at the landing.

They all started in surprise at the sight of me.

"My lady?" one of them asked.

"I need four of you to row me to shore," I said.

No one responded and then the same man asked, "Does his lordship know?"

"I need to be taken to shore, right now. Prepare a boat."

This situation may be unprecedented, but I was their lady and they would follow my orders.

"Once you return," I added, "please have word sent to Lady Mildreth that I am well, but that I have gone to see my sister." I knew this was risky, but I could not simply vanish from the keep and leave Mildreth panicked over what had become of me.

"Yes, my lady."

Four of the guards rowed me the mile to shore.

Once we reached shore, several guards there jogged into the waves to help pull the boat in, and I saw a man with a familiar face striding toward me. It was the young lieutenant who had brought Christophe the news of the attack on Chastain.

He came straight to me and reached down to hand me up out of the boat. "My lady. What are you doing here?" He sounded anything but pleased. "Captain Fáuvel and his lordship have gone north."

I stood straight. My fur-lined hood was down. "Good morning, Lieutenant…?"

"Lieutenant Solange," he finished, sounding no less comfortable.

"I'm aware that his lordship has gone north, but I've received an urgent message regarding my sister, the lady Chloe Belledini. I must go to her at once."

His jaw tightened. In truth, he was rather handsome, with red-brown hair and a close-trimmed beard a shade darker. "His lordship left me no instructions about a journey to Belledini lands."

This man was going to be more difficult to manage than the guards at the landing. He probably feared Christophe a good deal more than he would ever fear disobeying me.

"No," I said. "He left no orders because he did not know. The message only arrived today." This was a foolish ploy on my part. It should have been clear to me that with the captain gone, Lieutenant Solange been left in charge here.

"I had no messages rowed over to the island today, my lady," he answered.

Anxiety washed through me, but I had not come this far to fail and I changed tactics. "Lieutenant, my sister is in great difficulty and she needs my assistance. I am going to her. I'll saddle a horse myself if I must. But I am the lady of Whale's Keep and I am standing at the barracks of my own family guards. So you will please organize a contingent of ten men to escort me to Belledini lands."

His expression shifted to frustration and I knew what I was asking of him. But I'd meant what I said about saddling a horse and going myself, and he seemed to realize this was no hollow threat.

Perhaps to make me think twice, he said, "You won't make Belledini lands in one day. You'll need to spend the night somewhere."

"I trust the man you place in charge of my escort will be able to secure me safe accommodations."

In resignation, he sighed and said, "I'll choose nine men and take you myself. Would you rather ride in a wagon or on a horse?"

"A horse. I want to set a quick pace."

* * * *

Lieutenant Solange proved both a skilled and resourceful escort. Apparently, he knew exactly where we were going and asked my approval several times to take shortcuts off the road and through the forest.

I agreed every time, clinging to my horse and letting it follow his.

The further we travelled, the more I thought on how Christophe would react when he learned what I had done. Would he be more angry or more frightened? I hated the thought of him in a panic, but he'd given me no choice. I'd asked for his help and he had refused.

Just past dusk, the lieutenant brought our small party into a bustling town and he led us toward an inn.

"Whose lands are we on now?" I asked.

He glanced back at me. "You don't know? We're on Montagna lands. We need to cross your father's territory to reach the Belledinis'."

There was a full town on my father's lands? I hadn't known that.

Pulling up in front of the inn, the lieutenant dismounted, lifted me down, and took my traveling bag from the saddle. Then he handed a small pouch to one of his men.

"Go to the stables, settle the horses, and see if you can hire space to sleep in the loft. I'll stay here with our lady."

"Yes, sir."

As the guard took my horse and the lieutenant's, I realized it would cost money to stable the animals and house the men—and to pay for rooms. I had no money. Where would I get money? I'd never needed any. But it seemed the lieutenant carried coins.

"I will see that you are reimbursed for travel costs," I said.

He didn't respond and I knew he probably had larger concerns than the cost of a room or stabling horses. He'd led me here without orders from Christophe. This thought brought a wave of guilt—as I had placed him in this position—but I pushed it down.

I had to help Chloe.

Taking me inside the inn, he arranged for one room. This confused me at first, but he brought me upstairs and got me settled. Then he picked up an extra blanket and headed for the door.

"I'll sleep on the floor, just outside this door," he said. "No one will come in."

"You're going to sleep on the floor in the hallway?" I asked.

"His lordship would have my head if anyone came in here."

Without knowing what else to say, I bid him good night. True to his word, he slept outside my door. The room was small and the cleanliness of the sheets was questionable. But I fell asleep almost instantly, feeling safe.

The next morning, we started off early after a breakfast of rolls and tea.

We'd traveled only about an hour when the lieutenant said, "It's not far now, my lady. We've crossed over into Belledini lands. We should arrive at the manor by midday."

"Oh, that is good news." Then I thought on his wording. "But I'm not going to the manor. My sister and her husband live in a cottage west of the manor, near a vineyard. Do you know where that is?"

"I don't. But we'll find it."

Again, I was grateful for his presence.

He led the way west and when the sun was high, he pulled us up at the sight of four men working in a vineyard. Clucking to his horse, he trotted over and spoke to the men. When he came back, he pointed down a path. "They say the cottage is just over there." Then he pointed up the main road to the east. "My lady, the manor is about a half hour's ride up there. Are you sure you don't wish to go to the manor first and announce your arrival?"

I understood his meaning. I was Lady de Fiore. It would have followed more normal protocol for me to inform the family of my arrival, to offer my greetings, and then go to visit my sister. But this was not a normal situation.

"No. I would like to go straight to the cottage."

"Yes, my lady."

Starting forward again, he led our party down a path between a line of maple trees and we emerged into a clear area that appeared to be a charming setting at first. A two-story cottage stood at the center of the scene, with another vineyard stretching out behind it.

But as we drew closer, the scene took on a different quality. The door of the front gate had fallen off and lay on the ground. Two patches of ground looked as if they had once served as kitchen gardens, but there were no herbs or vegetables growing in either one, only weeds. A small rose garden to the right of the house was dead, from lack of water. There were no people about, not a single servant or a groom. There were no chickens or goats.

The place appeared utterly deserted. Was Chloe even here? Could she and Julian be staying up at the manor now? But no, Lady Belledini told my mother that Chloe was living here at the cottage and had not been seen since mid-summer. And somehow, as with that night I'd felt Chloe calling to me across the distance, I knew she was here.

"My lady?" said the lieutenant, his voice thick with caution.

Grasping the front of the saddle, I took my feet from the stirrups and jumped to the ground, not caring how ungraceful I looked.

"Wait here," I ordered. "Don't move any closer."

Walking to the front door, I knocked, waiting for a servant to answer. There was no response, but a memory struck me of Chloe saying that she and Julian had been making promises to pay meat and bread bills.

"Hello?" I called. "It is the lady Nicole, here to see Lady Chloe. Please open the door."

A moment later, the door cracked and someone asked, "Nicole?"

It was Chloe's voice. She was answering her own door.

A knot tightened in the pit of my stomach.

Turning, I walked back to Lieutenant Solange, who sat on his horse, watching me with alarm. "What is happening here?" he said. "Why is this place so—?" He didn't finish the sentence.

"Take your men and go up to the manor," I ordered. "Ask the sergeant there to find you quarters and stable the horses."

He looked down at me. "There is no way in all the hells I'm leaving you here." He did not bother to add, "My lady."

Since yesterday morning, our relationship had altered, and he had become more of a friend than a solider. We were no longer a lady and her guard. We were a woman and a man having an argument.

"What is your given name?" I asked.

This took him aback. "Gerard."

Stepping closer, I put my hand on the shoulder of his horse. "Gerard, my sister is inside and I believe she is in need of my care. I could be in there for days. Your men and the horses need to be housed. Please take them and go up to the manor. I am perfectly safe here in the home of my sister, and I need time with her. Please."

He breathed in and out several times. "Is there a servant of some kind in there with her?"

I did not know, but I answered, "I'm sure there is."

"The manor is not far. You swear you'll send for me if you need anything? Anything at all?"

"I swear."

Finally, he relented. "You go inside first. Once you're safely inside, I'll take my men to the manor. But I'll be back to check on you first thing in the morning."

"Thank you."

In the end, he must have seen the truth in my words. There was no telling how many days I might be here. I would be safe in the cottage on Belledini lands, and he had to find quarters for his men and the horses.

After pulling my travel bag from my saddle, I walked to the door, which was still cracked.

"Let me in."

The door opened a little further and I slipped inside, closing it behind me. Then I found myself looking at my sister—or someone who might have been my sister. I barely recognized her. She was beyond thin, nearly starved. Her gown was soiled. Her hair hung unwashed around her face. Her right eye was bruised and blackened.

I wanted to weep. "Chloe."

"Nicole?" she whispered. "Are you here? Is this real?"

"Yes, I'm here."

Looking around, I took in the state of the place. Light came through the windows to show the remnants of what must have once been a parlor. There were no couches or chairs now, not even a rug; only a few low tables remained.

I saw no servants and no sign of Julian. A sudden fear hit me. "Where is baby Gideon?"

"Gideon? He is over here." She walked behind a table and as I followed, I saw a cradle behind the table. Relief filled me, but only until I looked down. He lay in the cradle naked but for a diaper. His eyes were closed and his breaths were shallow.

"My milk is going dry," Chloe said. "I cannot feed him."

"There must be milk in the house?" I asked desperately. "You have no goat? No cow?"

"No," she said without emotion. "They are gone. All gone."

"Is there any food in the house?"

She shook her head.

"How long has it been since you've eaten?"

She didn't answer.

Though all I wanted to do was sink to the floor and weep, I moved into action. Before leaving the keep, I'd packed a small basket of gifts for her and brought it in my travel bag. There wasn't much in the basket, but I hurriedly dug it out.

"Chloe, come here."

Kneeling by the table, I set out a few apples from our orchards, sugar biscuits, and a jar of strawberry jam. At the sight of the food, she came to life a little, picking up a biscuit, dipping it in the jam, and taking a small bite, but I could see how hungry she was. I'd brought tea leaves, a jar of good cream, a jug of wine, and a wedge of cheese, but I'd need to boil water for the tea and find a knife to slice the cheese. There was a more important matter first.

Lifting my skirt, I tore off a section of the white shift I wore beneath.

After stripping off my cloak, I used it to wrap Gideon and I sat on the floor. Dipping a tiny corner of the white cloth into the cream, I tried to get the baby to open his mouth. At first, he did not move, but then his mouth opened and he began to suck. Over and over, I dipped the cloth in the milk. I knew this was risky, as my mother had always warned me that human babies should be given cows' milk only in an emergency. Their bodies required their mother's milk at this age and they could react badly to anything else. But this was an emergency.

When I'd gotten him to consume about half the jar, I stopped and rocked him for a while. Thankfully, he kept the cream down and fell into a more normal sleep. Looking over at Chloe, I saw her struggling to finish half a biscuit, as if she'd forgotten how to eat. Now that the initial crisis with the baby was past, the reality of their situation was beginning to sink in.

"Where is Julian?" I asked.

"Gone."

"He's abandoned you?"

"Abandoned? No. He would never. He leaves sometimes. But he'll come back."

"How long has he been gone this time?"

"I'm not sure. Three days?"

I looked around at the remnants of the parlor. "Is there anyone here? A maid?"

"No, the servants are gone."

She spoke as if sleepwalking and I had no idea what to make of any of this. But anger was beginning to replace shock. My beautiful sister was a bruised ghost of her former self and my nephew was on the brink of starvation.

And Julian was not here.

As Chloe did not appear up to making sense yet, I moved back into action, exploring the lower floor of the cottage and finding the kitchen in the back. There was a stove, a teakettle, firewood, and an indoor water pump.

I built a fire in the stove and made tea. After pouring two cups of tea, I found a sharp kitchen knife and made my way back to the parlor.

"I've made tea, but we'll need to drink it straight. We should save the cream for Gideon."

She came to join me, closing her eyes in relief as she sipped the tea. I cut her several slices of the cheese.

"Try to eat a little," I said.

She tried to nibble the cheese. "Thank you." She almost sounded as if she didn't know me.

"Chloe, what has happened here? Where is your furniture? Where are your servants?"

"Gone," she said and she seemed able to say no more.

As I could get no useful information from her, I wondered if she might speak once she was more comfortable. First, I fetched a cold cloth for her eye. Then I took her upstairs to find her rooms. Much of the furnishings up here were gone too. But the beds and the wardrobes remained.

I found a clean gown and helped her to change. Then I brushed out her hair. It needed a wash, but I worried that might be too much for her. Reaching up, she touched the back of my hand.

"Nicole, are you really here?" she asked.

"Yes. I'm here." Thinking I might stir her with some news of myself, I said, "Soon, we will have another baby in the family. I am with child."

I was not close to showing yet. She looked at my flat stomach and said nothing.

The afternoon wore on and I spent my time simply caring for them. I fed Gideon twice more and changed his diaper and found a little shirt for him. By the time the afternoon was waning, he did seem improved. But I had as yet gained no answers from Chloe.

Then a thought stuck me. She had always liked wine.

Down in the nearly empty parlor, I knelt on the floor and sliced more cheese. Then I took the jug from my basket. "Chloe, come and try a little of this. I've brought a fine red wine from home."

Her eyes lit up and she came to join me. I poured a good portion into her empty teacup and she drank it. When she finished, I poured her some more.

I waited a while and then I said, "Please talk to me. Was the house in this state when Lord Belledini offered it as a home for you and Julian?"

She wasn't looking at me, but sipped more of the wine, and I could see her mind drifting back. Slowly, she shook her head.

"No," she whispered. "When we first arrived here, everything was as I imagined. The cottage is not large, but it was well furnished, and we still had my stipend and even some money left from wedding gifts. Julian spoke of improvements we could make, such as building a stable. We hired a cook and a maid. Belledini manor is not far from here, and we were invited to dinner at least twice a week. Julian loved to go then. His father was proud of him for having married into the Montagna family, and his older brothers—I hesitate to say this, but their wives are not pretty and when first they saw me, they did not bother to hide their jealousy of Julian. I think he relished that more than anything."

"But then things changed?"

"Yes. Julian began leaving for days at a time. I didn't know where he was. But he told me he was trying to earn money for us. I wanted him to stay here and do as his father expected, to learn a trade as a winemaker and merchant. Then one night, Julian came home angry. He told me he'd lost a card game. At first, I didn't realize how badly he'd lost."

I remembered some of what she'd told me at White Deer Lodge. "He'd lost your stipend?"

"Yes, and then not longer after, he bet the vineyard in a game and lost."

"And you went to Father for help."

"But Father wouldn't help and he wouldn't let Christophe help, and when I got back here, Julian was so angry. At first, I think he pretended to be angry that I'd gone, but he said he understood and thanked me for saving him. When I told him that I hadn't saved him, his anger was real. That was the first time he—"

"He beat you?" I finished, feeling ill. I'd thought Julian lazy and selfish. I'd never thought him violent.

She nodded. "Things went badly from there. His father found out he'd lost the vineyard—when it was not yet his—and a terrible scene followed. We were left with nothing except this cottage, but we don't own it. We are merely allowed to live here. I tried so hard to please Julian, but our debts were mounting and the butcher stopped delivering. Julian began selling our furniture, but he didn't use the money to pay our past bills or our servants. He used it to gamble. Whenever he won, he'd come home with food and wine, and he'd kiss me, and we would dance. I was so happy. But if he lost, he would come home angry."

"And he would beat you?" I asked.

"Yes. After a while, he stopped coming to my bed and I ached for him. His mother sent us invitations to come for dinner. I wanted to go so badly, but he said he was ashamed of what I'd become and that he would not sit at a table in his father's judgment. Soon, the servants left and the food was gone. Four or five nights ago, he came home so angry that he said terrible things. He said I was the one who had brought him so low. Then he dragged me upstairs. I thought at last he might take solace with me in our bed, but he wanted to hurt me. When I saw what he was about to do, I tried to fight him off, but he—he…" She trailed off and I didn't wish to hear what he had done.

This was over.

"Chloe, you need to pack for yourself and the baby and come with me now."

"Where?" she asked like a lost child.

"To Whale's Keep. I have one of Christophe's lieutenants and nine de fiore guards up at the main house. You said the manor is not far? We'll take the baby and whatever you wish to carry, and we'll walk up. There is still daylight. I don't think we should ask to spend the night there. We'll leave immediately. Lieutenant Solange can take us to an inn or make camp along the road if need be."

"Leave? But Julian will come back and find me gone."

"Good. Get the baby ready."

She did not move and I grew nervous.

"Nicole," she said, "I cannot leave Julian. He needs me. He would be so sad to come home and find me gone."

Had she lost her senses? And then I realized that perhaps she had. She sounded so damaged she was unable to think clearly. My first thought was to offer kindness and try to coax her, but I worried that might not work, so I let my anger flow.

"If you won't leave for yourself," I said sharply, "then think of him!" I pointed to Gideon in his cradle. "Your milk is drying up from lack of food. Do you want your child to die? Is that what you want?"

Her face turned stricken and I feared I'd gone too far. She was so fragile.

"Listen to me," I said more gently. "Come home with me for a little while. We have honey and eggs and cream and apple tarts at the keep. Just stay for a few weeks. Eat well and grow stronger so that you can feed young Gideon. We'll leave word for Julian and if he comes in search of you, Christophe will have him brought to the keep, and we can all be together as a family. Wouldn't you like that?"

Of course as soon as Christophe saw Chloe's condition, he'd give our guards orders that Julian not be allowed to set foot on the island, but in this moment, I'd have said anything to make her leave with me.

The image I painted got through. "Yes," she breathed. "Julian would come in search of me, wouldn't he?"

"Of course he would, and finding you gone will only make him miss you."

I couldn't believe I was saying these things, but my sister was broken.

She nodded. "He *would* miss me, and that might help him to be kind to me again." She looked up. "And once Julian comes, we'll all be together at the keep? Christophe truly won't mind?"

"No," I rushed to say. "He won't mind. We'll have lovely meals while we wait for Julian to come and then we'll all be together."

"Yes," she said and smiled. The sight was heartbreaking. "Come and help me pack."

I'd not expected it to take long for us to prepare to leave the cottage, but upstairs, she began putting gowns into a trunk and I had to remind her several times that we were on foot and would need to walk up to the manor. Had I known how events would play out, I'd have had the lieutenant leave my horse. No, I'd have had him wait here.

But how was I to know the state in which I'd find Chloe? I thought perhaps she'd fallen ill. I had not anticipated this.

"No, my love," I said to her. "Pack only one gown, your hairbrush, and anything you need for Gideon."

In the end, I decided to leave my bag behind. I would carry the baby and Chloe could carry her bag. Finally, we were down in the parlor and we donned our cloaks and were ready to leave. Dusk was upon us and the light was growing dim.

"You know the way to the manor?" I asked.

"Yes, I know it well."

She lifted her bag and just as I leaned down to pick up Gideon, the front door opened.

Julian stood in the doorway.

Chapter 17

Had Chloe straightened and given Julian the haughty, withering gaze of the woman I'd once known, he might have stepped aside to let us leave. He was a bully and all bullies are cowards at heart.

But as he stood there, his eyes moved first to me and then to her, taking in the sight of her cloak and her bag. Her expression took on an expression of wild guilt.

"Oh, Julian. This is not as it seems. Please don't be angry."

It was the guilt that set him off. It was her pleading tones. His own expression shifted to a mix of pleasure and cruelty. He was like a cat that longed to torture a mouse. For my part, I couldn't help my rising anger that he appeared well fed. His hair was clean and so was his clothing. He'd left his wife and child in this near-empty cottage to starve, while he himself was clearly taking meals and comforts elsewhere.

He carried no food or gifts, however, suggesting that if he'd been off playing cards, he'd lost. Chloe had told me he came home angry on the nights he'd lost, looking to punish her.

"Not as it seems?" he asked, walking in. "It seems the lady Nicole has come to rescue you from your poor excuse for a husband." He looked to me. "Is that not the case?"

I met his eyes. "Yes. Please stand aside."

He wavered and glanced back outside. "Where is your guard? Where is your paragon of a husband?"

At this, it was my turn to waver, cursing myself. I should have kept the lieutenant here. But I had not anticipated danger.

When I didn't answer, Julian smiled. "Don't tell me you're alone?" He closed the front door.

"I'm taking Chloe and the baby out of here," I said. "And if you have any care for them, you'll let me."

"Care?" he repeated. "Who else has ever had a care for her? Your family? Hardly. Your father would happily let her starve here without lifting a finger. I'm the only one caring for her at all." His eyes locked on her. "And this is how you repay me, by taking my son and sneaking off into the night?"

She dropped her bag. "Julian, please—"

He strode forward, grabbing her by the arm and dragging her from the parlor to a side room. She cried out and begged him to stop, but he flung her through the door, slammed it from the outside, and slid a bolt across the frame, locking her in. I wondered where the bolt had come from. I'd seldom seen doors that locked from the outside.

Gasping, I glanced down at Gideon in his cradle, but he was still asleep.

Julian paced toward me, his voice dripping with hatred. "I've so long dreamt of coming home and finding you here, but I never thought it would happen. You ruined my life. You know that, don't you? You must have planned it."

He sounded mad and I backed away.

"I was in training for the military," he went on, "to be an officer. I had great things waiting for me. But you had to go and tattle to your father, betraying me, betraying your sister. You forced me to marry her so that you could marry the great lord Christophe yourself, living in eternal comfort at Whale's Keep. Then I was sent away in shame, saddled with a wife, hidden from the world in this shabby cottage, forced to sell my furnishings for food money."

He must be mad if this was truly how he saw the chain of events. Could he take no responsibility for himself, for his own choices and actions? I glanced at the front door, wondering if I could outrun him. Did he have a horse outside? Could I get to the horse? I'd bring help for Chloe and Gideon straightaway.

"But I have you here now, don't I?" he said, smiling again. "Like a gift from the gods. However shall I repay you?"

I bolted, running for the door.

But he was faster than I'd expected and he caught my arm, dragging me across the room and pinning me against the wall. When one of his hands gripped my waist, real fear hit for the first time. I did not sense desire from him, or at least not the desire of a man for a woman. He wanted to hurt me and he was enjoying using both his strength and his manhood.

"You didn't seem to know it," he whispered, "but you were always pretty." His hand moved up my waist. "Very pretty."

In panic, I brought the heel of my boot down on his toe, and I tried to break away. He swung with his right hand and hit me across the mouth hard enough that I fell, and he had to catch me. With his other hand, he caught hold of the neckline of my gown and ripped it partially off my shoulder.

I screamed.

A loud crashing sounded behind me and the front door broke inward. I could not believe what I saw. Christophe stood looking in. I worried that I was the one who'd gone mad. How could he be here? He could not be here.

His gaze moved from Julian to me, taking in my torn dress and my face. Warm liquid ran freely from the corner of my mouth. Christophe's features twisted into rage and he let out a roaring sound as he charged. He never even drew his sword.

Julian's eyes widened and he dashed forward to the table where I'd been slicing the cheese. Snatching the knife off the table, he lunged at Christophe and my fear turned to terror.

"No!" I cried.

But at the last second, as they rushed each other, Christophe somehow stepped to one side. He grabbed Julian's wrist, turned his hand, and rammed the blade through the base of his throat. Christophe continued moving, dragging Julian back against the wall without letting up on the blade, but it all seemed effortless for him.

He kept pushing. Julian gurgled and struggled and then went still.

Christophe released the body and let it fall to the floor. He stepped away. He wasn't even breathing hard. Blood flowed from Julian's throat and pooled around his head. The knife was still in his throat.

I don't how long Christophe and I stood there. I could not seem to think or move.

But then Christophe turned toward me. His body was taut and his eyes were manic. "You! You placed yourself in this danger. You came all this way without telling me, without even asking me!"

This was too much. I had been through too much and now, how he could stand there and say that? "I did ask you. I begged you. You said no! You didn't understand."

"Then *make* me understand!"

How could I make him understand? I could not explain. Finally, I said the only words that made sense.

"Christophe, she is my sister."

He closed his eyes, let out a breath, and held out both arms.

I ran to him.

* * * *

The aftermath proved one of the longest nights of my life.

When I released Chloe from the room where she'd been locked, she came out slowly, as if uncertain what to do. When she saw Julian dead on the floor, with the knife still in his throat, she began screaming.

The sound was high-pitched and anguished and she did not stop. Christophe was not accustomed to screaming women and he put one hand to his ear. I started toward Julian to remove the knife, but Christophe stopped me.

"No," he said over the sound of Chloe's screams. "Leave everything exactly as it is. Where is the kitchen?"

Puzzled, I pointed down the hall outside the parlor. "There."

"Bring the child," he said. Then he swept Chloe up in his arms and walked down the hallway to the kitchen. Carrying Gideon, I followed him.

He sat Chloe in a chair. "Stop!" he ordered. "Now."

She stopped.

"Nicole, give her the child," he said.

Seeing what he was doing, I walked over and handed Gideon off to Chloe. "Here, sister. Hold your son."

She held the baby to her, but her eyes were unfocused.

"There is still much to be done this night," Christophe said to me. "I'm going up to the manor to fetch Lord Belledini and his captain, perhaps Julian's brothers if they are there. I have a horse outside and I won't be gone long."

It dawned on me then that justified or not, Christophe had killed the third son of another lord.

"Don't alter anything here," he went on. "Don't change your dress or treat the wound on your mouth or touch Julian's body."

I could see what he was doing and I was so glad for his presence, but this led me to more questions. "Not that I'm ungrateful, but how can you be here? You were riding north."

"Lieutenant Solange sent a rider after me before he left the barracks with you. When the rider told me what had happened, I turned around to race back. I rode alone and I've not stopped since yesterday morning, except when I needed to find a village or town to change horses."

The lieutenant sent him a message? Illogical as it was, the act made me feel slightly betrayed. I thought Lieutenant Solange to be on my side. My face must have given away my thoughts because Christophe stepped closer.

"Don't place blame on him! That message is the only reason his head will stay on his shoulders. I haven't decided what to do with him yet."

His words and tone both stunned me. In this matter, Christophe sounded more than angry. He sounded almost vindictive. But I knew that could not be the case. Christophe didn't have a vindictive bone in his body. Nor would he ever abuse his power over others.

"You cannot think to punish him," I said. "He was only following my orders."

"He doesn't follow your orders!" Christophe shouted. "He follows mine."

I stared at him. "Of course he follows my orders. I am the lady of Whale's Keep. Had you forgotten that?"

The anger faded from Christophe's eyes. "No, I've not forgotten."

* * * *

By the time Christophe returned, full darkness had fallen. Thankfully, the lamps inside the cottage still contained oil, and I had been able to provide illumination in both the kitchen and the parlor.

From the kitchen, I heard the entrance of the men only an instant before Christophe called out, "Nicole? Bring Lady Chloe."

Somehow, I got Chloe to stand. She still held Gideon.

"We must return to the parlor," I said. "But you cannot scream. Lord Belledini is here."

To my relief, she followed me.

We entered the parlor to find four men: Christophe, Lord Belledini, a man in a red tabard, and a man who looked a good deal like Julian— probably one of his brothers.

Lord Belledini's face was ashen as he gazed across the room at Julian's body. Then he looked over at Chloe and me—her with her black eye, me with my torn dress and bloody mouth. Pointing to my mouth, he asked, "Julian did that?"

"Yes. He attacked me. I screamed. My lord came in. He moved to defend me and Julian ran at him with a knife. Lord Christophe had no choice."

All the men were listening to me. I was certain Christophe had told the exact same story before their arrival.

Then Lord Belledini looked about the room. "Where is all the furniture?"

"Julian sold it," I answered. "For gambling money." When none of the men came to Julian's defense or even appeared surprised, I grew angry. "When I arrived today, there was no food in the house. Chloe had not eaten for days and her milk is drying up so she cannot feed the baby."

To his credit, Julian's brother looked abashed. "I didn't know."

"Did you ever think to check?"

I knew I sounded accusing, but I could not help it.

"Back to the matter at hand, my lord," said the man in the red tabard. He was speaking to Lord Belledini, but he motioned to Julian's body. "To me, this appears justified. I think any magistrate would agree."

Lord Belledini nodded. "Yes. Lord Christophe bears no blame."

Anyone attempting to prosecute Christophe would have faced a daunting task indeed, but I was gratified that the matter of Julian's death had been so easily decided.

Then a more difficult problem reared its head.

Lord Belledini said to Chloe, "Come, girl. We'll take you up to the manor. You and the child will stay with us."

Whether this was due to guilt or kindness, I could not tell.

"She will come home with Lord Christophe and me," I said.

But Chloe shrank back. "No, no, no, no, no. I will stay here. I am safe here."

Had I been in her place, I would have viewed this cottage as a cage, but she viewed it as a wall of safety from the world.

Lord Belledini walked over. "My lady," he said, more gently, "this place is not fit to inhabit, for you or the child."

"Don't make me leave," she begged. "Please. I must stay here."

My poor sister. She had suffered and she was so broken.

Lord Belledini frowned and then spoke to me. "If she insists on staying here, I can have supplies brought in tonight. Tomorrow, I can send servants and new furnishings. I will pay any debts and provide for her. I do give you my word. She and the child will be cared for."

Again, it seemed he spoke from a place of guilt, but he appeared sincere. I wanted Chloe to come home with me, but I also knew what it was to have my wishes ignored, and I laid my hand on her arm. "You won't come with me? You truly want to stay?"

"Here," she said. "I want to stay here."

* * * *

Christophe and I remained with Chloe for several days. Julian was buried in the family crypt and the cottage was stocked with food and furnishings. Lord Belledini sent a cook, a maid, and a gardener.

The day we departed was difficult for me, but Chloe was determined to remain at the cottage. I looked ahead into her future and Gideon's, seeing years of isolation. But she would not come with me and I could not stay here.

Christophe needed to return home.

I asked him to promise there would be no recriminations against Lieutenant Solange and he agreed. Three days after Julian's death, Christophe and I rode at the head of our small contingent, traveling home.

* * * *

After the long journey—when at last I walked through the courtyard of Whale's Keep and the main doors were flung open—Mildreth came running out, straight to me, grasping my hands.

"Oh, Nicole. You are safe." She touched my stomach. "And the child is safe?"

She was so distraught that I embraced her. "I am well. The child is well. I am so sorry to have worried you."

It was clear she had worried. She had suffered from worry and to my astonishment, I could see that she cared for me. Somehow, somewhere along the way, she had come to care for me. Perhaps Chloe was no longer my only sister.

"I am home too," Christophe said, but I could tell he was teasing.

In spite of everything, I smiled.

* * * *

The next day, Christophe did not go back to shore to ride out to a village. He stayed on the island with me and we walked in my meadow to visit the beehives.

"You are glad you married me and came to Whale's Keep?" he asked.

"Yes."

I was glad, more than glad. No one had ever looked at me the way he did, with such open admiration and love.

I belonged here.

I belonged with him.

The Choice

Chapter 18

The meadow around me vanished and I found myself inside my bedroom, looking into the three-tiered mirror. The memories of all three experiences I'd just lived existed in my mind at the same time.

Now, there were three reflections of the dark-haired woman as she gazed out at me from all three panels.

"Which path?" the woman asked. "You must choose."

Images and memories continued turning in my mind.

"Which of the paths will you follow?" she asked. "Telling Erik…or remaining silent…or telling your family?"

Choose? How could I choose?

Faces passed by me one by one.

My thoughts flowed back to the first choice. Erik would kill Julian and stop him from ever threatening or harming Chloe. Gideon would grow up as the heir to Whale's Keep. Christophe would have a son he loved unconditionally. Chloe would be safe and live in a place of honor as the lady of Whale's Keep.

No one who I loved suffered in this choice.

But Christophe would never know the truth. Chloe would be safe and honored but unhappy. And I would lose Christophe. He would forever be a beloved brother-in-law.

When I thought on the second choice, my heart ached. Christophe would learn of my betrayal in the worst possible way and I would come to see the depths of his true self, and he would see the depths of mine. The damage we would do to each other was irreparable.

I saw that awful wedding in the hunting hall.

And yet, Chloe would be able to take her rightful place as a daughter of White Deer Lodge. She would find her strength and her power, and Gideon would grow up in a place of honor, a potential heir to the family title and lands, as a son of White Deer Lodge. He would be so loved.

My mind flowed to the third choice, to the perfect life I had shared with Christophe. I saw our beautiful exchange of vows by my family's dining hearth and the joy that surrounded us. I saw our wedding night. I saw how proud he was to bring me home to the island. I saw myself in his eyes.

More, I thought of Mildreth. Poor, lonely Mildreth. She was not cold or hard as many people thought. It simply took more to reach her and I had reached her. We had formed a family at Whale's Keep.

But Chloe...I saw the image of her half-starved and beaten and broken. I saw how she had suffered. I saw her hiding out, afraid of the world. What of Gideon? What would become of him? He seemed to have no place in the Belledini family, and how would he fare growing up in isolation with no prospects and no future?

Could I do this to her or to him in order to gain my own happiness?

Was there any way that I could marry Christophe and stop her from marrying Julian?

"Once I choose," I asked, "will I remember what I've seen? Can I alter events via what I've seen here?"

"No. These are the possible paths and you have been given the gift to see and to choose. Once you have chosen, all the memories you have seen will be gone."

I'd remember nothing.

"Choose for yourself," she said. "This is a gift and there is nothing more I can tell you. Which of the paths will you follow? Telling Erik...or remaining silent...or telling your family?"

How could I choose?

Then I thought on the second choice. By the end of what I was shown, Christophe and I were finding a way to breach the distance between us. We would never have that perfect love. We would hurt each other. We would see each other's deepest faults.

But we would end up together and we had been creating the start of a life together.

And Chloe and Gideon would both find their true place and neither would suffer.

For a few moments, I couldn't speak.

"Silence," I whispered.

The woman hesitated as if she'd not heard me correctly. "Silence?"

"Yes. I choose silence."

She nodded, standing now only in the center panel. "The second choice."
The air before me wavered and the mirror vanished

* * * *

I was standing in Chloe's closet, feeling disoriented. Peeking out a
crack between the closet door and the wall, I saw my sister standing in
her bedroom with Julian Belledini.

Then I remembered. I'd come in here to find her dress from the banquet,
so that it might be laundered, and I'd overheard that she was carrying
Julian's child. Panic rose inside me. I couldn't betray Christophe and yet
I could not betray Chloe either. What should I do?

Why had I heard any of this? I should *not* have been in this closet.
Had Chloe's gown not been hung back up by one of the housemaids, had
Jenny not remembered that it needed to be washed, had I not heard Chloe
retching on the night of the banquet and therefore been so determined to
come find the gown, I would not have come here.

Had one small event played out differently, I would be ignorant of this
awful truth and I would not be faced with the decision of what to do with
what I had learned.

And then, I knew the answer. This was not a decision for me to make.
Were I not in this closet, I would be as blissfully ignorant as everyone else
and fate would take its own course. I could not choose between Chloe and
Christophe and therefore, I would not.

I would pretend that I'd never left the laundry room, that I'd heard nothing.
I would keep this secret to myself.

Read on for a preview of Barb Hendee's

THROUGH A DARK GLASS

Also available from Rebel Base Books

Chapter 1

I was trapped, and I knew it. Worse, it came as a shock on my seventeenth birthday, the same day my elder sister died.

Daughters of the nobility are mere tools for their families, so in truth, what transpired shouldn't have come as such a surprise, but I'd been trained and honed as a different type of tool than my sister, Helena.

She was beautiful, tall and well figured with ivory skin, green eyes, and a mass of silken red hair. She was quick-witted and skilled in the art of conversation. When she walked into a room, all heads turned. She expected everything in life to come to her just as she wished, and as a result, it usually did. Our father had always intended to profit from her by way of a great marriage to improve our family's fortune.

In contrast, I was small and slight, with light brown eyes and dark blond hair. Although I was much better read than Helena, my prowess in circles of social conversation normally amounted to nodding and appearing attentive to those more proficient than myself.

Helena was the shining star of our family.

Yet, on my seventeenth birthday, I stood over her bed, wringing my hands as she lay dying. Her once ivory face had gone sickly white, and her green eyes were closed as she struggled to breathe, each attempt resulting in a gasp followed by a rattle.

My mother stood beside me, looking down at the bed, her face unreadable.

"She may yet recover," I said by way of attempted comfort. "She has always been strong."

I shouldn't have bothered.

My mother glanced at me in contempt. Like Helena, she was tall with red hair, and she had no patience for offers of false comfort.

Only three days ago, Helena had complained of feeling warm at our midday meal. Shortly after, she'd been helped to her bed by several of the household servants, and within hours, the fever had taken hold. In a panic, my father had called upon our physician, who had done what he could—which in my opinion hadn't been much. The illness settled quickly into Helena's lungs.

Although I had been allowed inside her room, I'd not been allowed to touch her.

As Mother and I stood over her, my sister fought for one last breath. The following rattle was loud, and then all sounds vanished from the room as

Helena went still. Looking down, I didn't know what to feel. We had not been close, but she was still my sister.

As if summoned, my father walked in, dressed in a blue silk tunic and black pants. He was of medium height with broad shoulders and a thick head of light brown hair. He shaved his face twice a day.

"Well?" he asked.

"She's gone," my mother answered. "Just now."

Father frowned, but that was all. His initial panic at the prospect of losing a valuable tool like Helena had passed yesterday—for he was ever a realist.

Walking over to the bed, he didn't even look at his eldest daughter. Instead, he looked at me, and I couldn't help noting the disappointment in his eyes. "Megan," he said. "The Volodanes arrive this afternoon. You'll have to take Helena's place."

I blinked several times, not certain I'd heard him correctly.

"Take her place? What does that . . .?"

"You know what it means," he said coldly. Then he turned to my mother. "Make sure she's presentable."

I took a step backward as the awful truth set in.

The Volodanes were arriving afternoon.

And I was to take Helena's place.

* * * *

Less than hour later, I found myself seated at the dressing table in my own room, wearing a muslin dress of sunflower yellow—that had been hanging in my closet for over a year—and staring at my own reflection as my maid, Miriam, tried to do something with my hair.

Her mouth was tightly set, and she was not any happier about the situation. Miriam was pretty with dark hair, and only five years older than myself. She'd been hired by my mother when I was fifteen and Mother had deemed it necessary that I should have a "lady's maid." I'd resisted at first but not for long. Miriam had soon become devoted to me, and I welcomed her friendship.

The turn of events today had taken her by surprise.

"Your father was very clear," she said, holding handfuls of thick hair. While the color might not be enticing, at least it was abundant. "I may have to cut a few pieces in the front."

"Do what you must," I answered quietly.

Normally, I had Miriam weave my hair into a single thick braid, as no one cared too much about my appearance. All my life, I'd been told that

I would never marry, that I'd remain here in my family's manor serving as a shadow advisor to my father, for I possessed a unique . . . skill that was of use to him.

He was the head of our great family, the house of Chaumont, and he held a seat on the Council of Nobles that met four times a year in the capital city of Partheney.

The power and prestige of our name reached back over eight hundred years, and every family for five hundred leagues envied us our name, our bloodlines, and our political power. Unfortunately, noble bloodlines don't always correlate into wise financial management, and my grandfather had nearly run our reserves of wealth into the ground. He drank. He gambled. To pay debts, he'd sold off our more lucrative investments such as the family's silver mines, which decreased our income.

Though my father possessed greater wisdom, upon inheriting the family title, he'd fought to make a good show of things, to try and prove we were not paupers. This had meant quietly borrowing large sums of money, and now several of those debts were being called in.

To his great relief, Helena had proven herself everything he'd hoped for, and in recent months, he'd made an arrangement to solve all his immediate financial woes.

Another family, the Volodanes—of noble birth so low they were scorned by the better families—had made my father an unprecedented offer.

When a young woman married, a part of her worth was determined by the size of her dowry. Lord Jarrod, the head of the house of Volodane, had offered a small fortune in exchange for Helena marrying one of his three sons. For while the Volodanes might suffer snubs for their painfully low birth, in recent years, they'd become one of the wealthiest families in the nation. They had money in silver, in cattle, in wheat, and in wine. They also ruled their own territories in the north without mercy and taxed their peasants nearly dry. Now, they wanted to use this wealth to link their name to the name of a great family.

Jarrod offered to forgo a cash dowry and pay my father a great deal of money for Helena. She in turn would bring certain furnishings from Chaumont Manor to make it appear as a dowry. In this way, the secret could be kept.

My father had jumped at the bargain.

At first, my mother and Helena had not. They'd both been appalled at the thought of regal Helena tied forever to some brute who most likely had no idea how to dine at a proper table. But instead of ordering Helena to obey, our father had cajoled her, and then he'd promised that of the three brothers, she would be allowed to meet them and choose one for herself. Then he'd appealed to her sense of family honor and obligation.

In the end, he got his way . . . and this afternoon, the Volodanes would arrive so that Helena might spend time in conversation with the young men, allowing her to make her choice.

But my sister was dead.

Staring at myself in the small mirror of my dressing table, I wondered what a slap in the eye I was going to be.

Miriam continued twisting my thick hair and piled it on top my head. She left several strands in the front loose, and before I could follow what she was doing, she took up a pair of scissors and snipped those strands at about the length of my jaw. The strands instantly curled up to frame my face. The result was astonishing. I *did* look a bit more like a lady than I had a few moments before.

She put small silver earrings in my earlobes and then drew something from her pocket. I blanched. It was a diamond pendant.

"That's Helena's," I said.

She glanced away. "You mother wants you to wear it."

Without another word, I let her fasten it around my neck. This was only the beginning. Miriam wasn't even dressing me for dinner yet—but rather to help greet the Volodanes when they rode into the courtyard.

I rose from the dressing table.

"You look lovely, miss," she said. "You should go down."

I didn't feel lovely. I felt a knot growing in my stomach, and I wanted to reach out and grip her hand. In the entire manor, Miriam was the only one who cared for me, and she had no power.

So, I left my room and made my way down the stairs, past the great dining hall, and down the passage to the main front doors. The guard there opened the doors for me, and I stepped outside into the open courtyard.

My father, my mother, and six other manor guards stood waiting.

Turning, my father looked me up and down. Instead of looking at me, my mother looked at him. His eyes focused on my sunflower-yellow gown and my hair. Then he nodded once at my mother in approval. She returned to her vigil of waiting for the Volodanes.

I held back, near the doors. We didn't wait long.

I heard several of our guards down at the front gates calling to each other before I saw anything. Then I heard the grinding of the gates being opened . . . followed by the sounds of hoof beats.

Within moments, an entire retinue pounded into our courtyard, led by four men—one out front and three riding behind. This quartet was followed by at least thirty guards. I wondered where we were going to house them all.

Then my attention focused entirely on the four men at the front.

Although I had never met any of them myself, and neither had Helena, she'd been provided with a good deal of information, and before falling ill, she'd spoken of little else in the last weeks of her life.

It wasn't difficult to note Jarrod, the father, riding at the lead. As he drew closer, my trepidation began to grow. He appeared in his late forties, tall and hawkish. His head was shaved. He wore chain armor over a faded black wool shirt that had seen many washings. My eyes dropped to the sword sheathed on his hip.

My own father never wore a sword.

As Jarrod pulled his frothing horse to a stop, I turned my gaze to the three men behind him. Again, it wasn't difficult for me to name them by gauging their age.

Rolf was the eldest, in his late twenties. Like his father, he wore his head shaved and he wore chain armor, but there the resemblance stopped. There was nothing hawkish about Rolf. He was muscular and wide-shouldered with broad features and a bump at the bridge of his nose. Every inch of him exuded hardness and strength.

I shivered in the summer air.

Next came Sebastian, in his mid twenties. He was smaller than either of his brothers, with neatly cut black hair. Noticing my attention, he flashed me a smile. He was handsome, and the only one not wearing armor. Instead, he wore a sleeveless tunic over a white wool shirt. I had a feeling Sebastian cared about his appearance.

Last came Kai—wearing armor and weapons. He looked only a few years older than me. In many ways, he resembled his father, tall and slender with sharp features. But he wore his brown hair down past his shoulders. His gaze moved to the front of the manor, which was constructed of expensive light-toned stone.

As Kai took in the latticed windows, whitewashed shutters, and climbing ivy vines, his features twisted into what I could only call an expression of resentful anger. If hardness rolled off Rolf and vanity rolled off Sebastian, it was anger that rolled off Kai.

Jarrod jumped down from his horse and strode up to my father.

"Chaumont," he said shortly, not bothering with my father's title or given name.

Both men gauged each other in mild discomfort, and it occurred to me that this was their first meeting. All marriage negotiations had transpired in writing or by proxy. Under normal circumstances, a family as lowborn as the Volodanes would never be invited to Chaumont Manor—and they knew it.

My father nodded and responded in kind. "Volodane."

Then Jarrod's dark eyes swept the courtyard, stopping briefly on me before moving onward, and he frowned.

My father leaned forward, speaking softly. I watched Jarrod's expression flicker in surprise, and to his credit he said, "Oh . . . my condolences."

A few more quiet words were exchanged, and I heard my father say, "daughter, Megan." Jarrod's eyes turned to me again, this time in cold assessment. After all, he had never seen Helena and only heard the tales of her beauty. He had nothing with which to compare her. I struggled to look back and hold his gaze. After a moment, he nodded his assent.

"Good, then," my father agreed, sounding relieved. "You must be tired from your journey. We'll all meet again at dinner." He seemed equally relieved this initial meeting was over and he was now able to extract himself.

But the knot in my stomach tightened at the thought of leaving my home and going with these men, with a warrior for a father and one of his sons for my husband.

Trapped or not, I couldn't do this.

I would refuse.

* * * *

My father and mother both went to the room he used as his study, and without asking permission, I followed them in and closed the door. They were both taken aback by my boldness. This was certainly something Helena might have done, but not me.

"I can't do it," I said instantly. "And I cannot believe you would force me."

Mother's eyes narrowed in caution. I had never spoken to either of them like this. My father's face turned red in anger, but my mother held up one hand to stop his tongue.

"Megan," she began slowly. "Of course I understand your reticence. It is beneath us to even have them in the house, but this must be done, and the middle son . . . Sebastian? He looks less savage than the others. Could you not consider him?"

I stared at her. "Less savage? You would have me in his bed merely because he seems less savage than his brothers?"

She flinched at the indelicacy of my question and then drew herself to full height. "And would you have our situation exposed? Our debts known publicly? Would you have bailiffs in the manor taking our paintings and tapestries and furniture? Would you have your father disgraced from his seat on the Council of Nobles?"

Feeling myself begin to deflate, I shook my head. "Of course not."

The anger left my father's face, and he stepped toward me. "Jarrod has already agreed to my provision that Helena choose from among his sons. He doesn't care which of them marries into the house of Chaumont. He wants only the prestige of the connection and grandsons who carry our blood. You'll have the same provision as your sister. You can choose."

"And if I don't?"

His eyes hardened. "Then I will pick one myself, drag you to the magistrate, and use my power as your father to answer and sign for you."

Breathing grew difficult as I realized he meant it. He would sell me off like a brood mare rather than face public humiliation and lose his seat on the council.

In desperation, I played one last card. "But, Father, what will you do without me? In meetings with the other nobles, how will you know who's honest and who is not?"

This was something we rarely spoke of openly. I could do something no one else could, something that made me of great use to my father. Would he throw it away so easily?

His expression flickered once and then steeled again.

"Do you choose one for yourself, or do I?" he challenged.

The room was silent for a long moment.

I somehow managed to answer. "I'll choose for myself."

What else could I do?

* * * *

A scant few hours later, I found myself seated at our table in the dining hall.

Miriam put a great deal of effort into dressing me for dinner. The result was both awkward for me and a triumph for my parents.

I looked nothing like myself. Miriam had arranged my hair even more elaborately and used a small round iron on the curls around my face. Then she'd put touches of black kohl at the corners of my eyes. I wore an amber silk gown with a low, square-cut neckline that showed the tops of my breasts.

I don't know where she'd found the gown. It wasn't mine, and it was much too small to have fit Helena. I supposed my mother must have had it made at some point while anticipating its need.

However, at the sight of me, my father beamed. I couldn't meet his eyes.

Seating at dinner was equally awkward with my father at the head of the table, my mother and I seated on one side, and all four of the Volodanes seated on the other—so I had no choice but to look at one of them when I raised my eyes from my plate of roasted pheasant.

None of them had changed for dinner, and with the exception of Sebastian, they all wore armor and swords. Jarrod hadn't bothered to shave his face and sported a dark stubble. I could almost feel my mother's discomfort, but she smiled and made attempts at polite conversation.

Only Sebastian responded to her questions about weather and wild flowers in the northern provinces. Rolf spoke only to his father or mine. Occasionally, he glanced at me as if I already belonged to him.

I wasn't listening to any of them. My heart pounded too loudly in my ears. But then I did hear Rolf say something about heading back north as soon as he and I were married.

A long pause followed, and for the first time, I paid attention.

"It is not settled yet that she will marry you," my father finally responded. "Per our agreement, Megan will choose for herself."

Rolf's face clouded. "I never agreed to that. I am the eldest. She will join with me."

Jarrod turned in his chair. "You'll do as I tell you! Nothing less and nothing more!"

Mother, Father, and I all flinched at his tone and his unthinkable manner at the table. Rolf's face went red, and Sebastian leaned back in his chair, smiling. Something about him was beginning to strike me as sly. He clearly enjoyed his older brother's chastisement and discomfort.

"Now, now," he said, dryly. "We mustn't seem uncouth."

Kai ignored all this. He ignored everything but his surroundings. His eyes were light brown like mine, and they moved from the opulent tapestries on our walls to the peach roses in silver vases on the table to the porcelain plates and pewter goblets.

Then for the first time, he looked directly at me.

"I fear you'll find the furnishings at Volodane Hall somewhat lacking," he said.

His voice dripped with resentment, and I knew I'd not been wrong in my first assessment. He was angry.

His tone was not lost on my mother, who answered him with a strained smile. "Of course, we'll be sending some household things with her, and Megan will give your hall a woman's touch."

These words made me wonder what had happened to Kai's mother. I'd never asked and no one had mentioned this, but it seemed I would be the lady of their house. The very thought ensured I would not manage to eat another bite of dinner.

Kai studied my mother evenly and breathed out through his teeth. "Our hall won't be good enough for her. Nothing of us or ours will be good enough."

Then I realized the source of his anger. He resented the need for this bargain as much as we did. He knew that we—and most of the noble houses—looked down upon the Volodanes, and the last thing he probably wanted was a permanent reminder in his home of their lowly state in comparison to ours.

"Quit!" Jarrod ordered him, pounding one hand on the table.

In obedience, Kai stopped talking and withdrew back inside himself, ignoring everyone again.

Sebastian looked at me and raised one eyebrow in amusement. I glanced away.

Somehow—and I never quite knew how—we made it through the rest of dinner.

By the time my mother rose, signifying the meal was over, my heart pounded in my ears again. I felt the edge of my self-control slipping away and knew that I had to gain a few moments to myself or I might possibly do or say something I'd later regret.

"Please make my excuses," I said quietly to Mother. "I will return quickly."

She frowned briefly, but then her face smoothed in annoyed understanding, and I realized she most likely thought I needed to relieve myself.

I didn't care what she thought.

Turning, I fled the dining hall as fast as I could without running. Upon reaching the passage that led toward the kitchens, I couldn't stop myself and broke into a run, racing in my heavy silk skirts until I reached an open archway in one side of the passage, just a few doors from the entrance to our kitchens.

There, I took refuge in an old, familiar hiding place.

As a child, I'd come to this storage room whenever I didn't wish to be found. It was filled with crates, casks, and places to hide. No one ever entered except servants from the kitchens, and none of them ever noticed me secreted away behind a stack of crates.

I hadn't come here in years, but now, I breathed in relief at the respite of solitude and the illusion of safety.

Slowly, I sank to my knees.

As we were expecting a delivery of goods any day now, the storage room was nearly half-empty. I didn't even attempt to hide behind crates or casks, as I knew I'd have to return to the hall long before anyone came looking me.

A dismal prospect.

What was I going to do? I couldn't face the thought of my life married to any of those men. Until this afternoon, I'd never faced the prospect of marriage at all . . . but to one of *them*? I was not a weeper. My parents had never allowed such an indulgence, and I honestly wasn't aware I knew how to cry, but tears came to my eyes and one dripped down my cheek.

The water in my eyes made the following moment even more uncertain than it might have been.

The air in the storage room appeared to waver. Alarmed, I wiped away my tears, but the motion of the wavering air grew more rapid, and then... something solid began taking shape.

Jumping up to my feet, I gasped.

There, near the far wall across the storage room, a great three-paneled mirror now stood where there had been only empty air an instant before. The thick frames around each panel were of solid pewter, engraved in the image of climbing ivy vines. The glass of the panels was smooth and perfect, and yet I didn't see myself looking back.

Instead, I found myself staring into the eyes of a lovely dark-haired woman in a black dress. Her face was pale and narrow, and she bore no expression at all. But there she was, *inside* the right panel gazing out me.

Was I going mad? Had my parents driven me mad?

"There is nothing to fear," the woman said in a hollow voice.

I doubted that statement. I feared for my sanity, but as yet, I'd not found my voice to answer her.

"You are at a crossroad," she continued, "with three paths." As she raised her arms, material from her long black sleeves hung down. "I am bidden to give you a gift."

Here, sadness leaked into her voice, especially at the word "bidden," and my mind began to race. Was this truly happening?

"You will live out three outcomes . . . to three different choices," she said. "Lives with men . . . connected by blood. Then you will have the knowledge to know . . . to choose."

I shook my head. "Wait! What are you saying?"

Lowering both hands to her sides, she said, "The first choice."

Before I could speak again, the storage room vanished. Wild fear coursed through me as the world went black for the span of a breath, and then suddenly I found myself back in my family's dining hall, only everything was different.

Chairs had been set up in rows, and guests were seated in them. I wore a gown of pale ivory and held my father's arm as he walked me past the guests toward the far end of the hall.

Flowers in tall vases graced that same end, and a local magistrate stood there with a book in his hands.

Beside the magistrate stood Rolf, wearing his armor and his sword.

Turning, he looked at me in grim determination.

He was waiting.

About the Author

Barb Hendee has published twenty-one highly popular fantasy novels, including the *New York Times* bestselling Noble Dead Saga, co-authored with JC Hendee, and the newer Mist-Torn Witches series, which she penned alone. All twenty-one books are still in print. She maintains a devoted following, has had books on the extended *New York Times* list and the *USA Today* Top 150 Books, and is constantly writing and developing new ideas.

A
CHOICE
of CROWNS

A
DARK
GLASS
NOVEL

BARB HENDEE

NEW YORK TIMES BESTSELLING AUTHOR

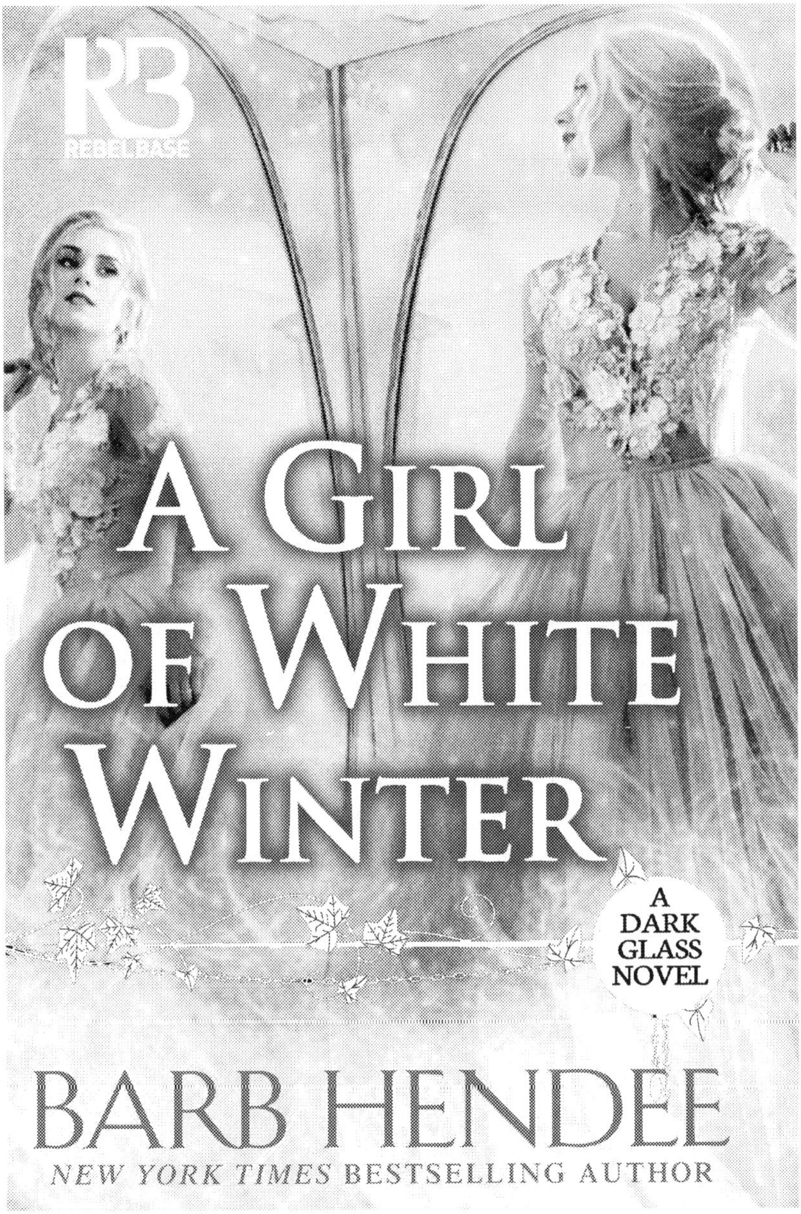
RB
REBELBASE
A GIRL OF WHITE WINTER
A DARK GLASS NOVEL
BARB HENDEE
NEW YORK TIMES BESTSELLING AUTHOR

THROUGH a DARK GLASS

A DARK GLASS NOVEL

BARB HENDEE

NEW YORK TIMES BESTSELLING AUTHOR

Printed in the United States
by Baker & Taylor Publisher Services